# CHARLOTTE
# STONE
## AND THE CHILDREN
## OF THE NYMET

# CHARLOTTE STONE

## AND THE CHILDREN OF THE NYMET

*If The Memory Dies, A Forest Falls*

TASHA O'NEILL

Matador
9 Priory Business Park,
Wistow Road, Kibworth Beauchamp,
Leicestershire LE8 0RX
Tel: (+44) 116 279 2299
Email: books@troubador.co.uk
Web: www.troubador.co.uk/matador

ISBN 978 1784620 325

British Library Cataloguing in Publication Data.
A catalogue record for this book is available from the British Library.

Printed and bound by CPI Group (UK) Ltd, Croydon, CR0 4YY
Typeset by Troubador Publishing Ltd, Leicester, UK

**Matador** is an imprint of Troubador Publishing Ltd

*This book is dedicated with love and gratitude to Mum and Dad.*
*Thank you for all your commitment, support and belief.*

*Thank you also to my other Beta readers Kevin and Sally.*

*That ancient tree, don't let it fall,*
*until old age is knelling;*
*so many things it can recall,*
*what tales it could be telling.*
**Hans Christian Andersen**

*Q*uite spontaneously and in a matter of seconds, a rose bush bloomed, withered and died in the snows of an English winter. This was the only sign that anything was amiss, and it went unnoticed by all but one – unless you included the Echo. Deep below the surface, worms turned and wriggled away from the desiccated body that had, till now, lain dormant and harmless – held fast by the Golden Root.

The Echo had known what it was to be human once; but that was now a faint memory. However, it still felt 'the bond' to its kind and instinctively reached out to the mortal thoughts that drifted in the air far above.

Earth pressed down hard yet it felt the stagnant blood in its veins start to flow again, cold limbs warming back into life as the root slowly loosened its grip. In the mouldering dirt below the Great Tree it waited for each part of this body to awaken. Synapses started to fire in the brain while the heart jerked into motion.

The foreign lips twisted into a grimace as the Echo reviewed once again the moment of terror in these eyes. The terror of the original owner as they had drifted off into the abyss, light dying, ripped unceremoniously from the fragile threads of the life-giving Wyrdweb. The Echo liked to relive the firework display of raw light as the silver cord was severed and a new shadow was born, condemned to drift forever in the darkness of the Dreamtime.

A familiar pain started in the stolen body but he ignored the sensation. Well used to the process now, he knew the pain would soon fade. To kill time, he tested a few names and languages over his new tongue, trying to decide what this body's new identity should be.

He had no idea how the Great Tree had loosened its grip but there would be time for that later. Plenty of time. All that mattered was he was no longer trapped in this crack in the Dreamtime. The whole Triverse spread out before him; oh such freedoms to savour – and scores to settle. For now though the Shriven could wait.

Transition complete, he simply extended long nails; and began to dig.

# The Family Stone

## PINAR, CADIZ

*R*emote mountains in the heart of Andalusia may not be a normal classroom for a thirteen-year-old girl, but Charlotte Stone was no normal thirteen-year-old girl. Being the daughter of explorers meant curiosity was in her genes (an argument she would often use whenever she wanted to do something her parents were against), and it was curiosity that had led her here.

In fact, it was more than that, because Charlotte had a gift. She was very good at finding things – and unlocking their deepest secrets simply by touch. Her parents' research student Neva often joked she was more reliable than carbon dating.

Charlotte sat in the dark, cool cave halfway up a mountain in the Sierra Del Pinar, grateful to be out of the relentless Spanish sun. She looked at the large, lozenge-shaped stone, rolling it around in her hands as she tucked a stray lock of red hair behind her ear. Her strange visions had started when her family had discovered this cave. A withering rose, the symbol, a fireball and perhaps most disturbing of all, the blood-curdling scream in the darkness. Charlotte had hoped this stone might provide some answers.

It was smooth to the touch and seemingly undamaged with no obvious markings, yet she had no idea what it was. Charlotte would normally be able to at least identify the basics: location of origin, date and use. But this unusual object was totally silent to her – and it felt wrong. A shadow fell over the mouth of the cave.

'You going to sit there with that thing all day, sweetheart?' Ella Stone smiled at her daughter. 'Pop it away now and let's go.'

Charlotte placed the stone and its cloth wrappings warily into a padded box.

⚓

Strings of fairy lights twinkled on the bandstand that evening as both locals and foreigners alike enjoyed the balmy warmth in the numerous café bars of the main square in Pinar. The Stone family and their crew had been in town for just over a month and it was their last night. Richard and Ella were taking the opportunity to relax before their gruelling journey across the Sahara sands, and were currently taking in the fiesta atmosphere from a table at their regular haunt, Casa Vargas.

'Unusual find by Charlotte today, love, any ideas?' Richard said, swigging an ice cold Moritz.

'I have some theories...'

'No idea then.' He winked at his wife but Ella didn't rise to the bait.

'There's certainly something intriguing about it. Neva is still studying it now. Never stops working that girl.'

'Perhaps it's the elusive Benu egg?' Richard was wide-eyed and made a mock gasp. Ella jovially punched her husband's arm.

'Don't be daft. Anyway, you know she is the best research student we have ever had. OK, perhaps some of her ideas are a bit... wacky, but I'll bet she'll have some exceptional reports for us by the time we get back.'

Ella took a sip of wine as she tried to phrase her next thoughts. 'I did see something weird today, as we were removing that stone.'

'You sure it wasn't a mirage, or lack of sleep? We have been overdoing it a bit out here what with the time restrictions and all.'

'No, I know I'm not going mad,' Ella said more harshly than she meant. Perhaps the heat was getting to her.

'I didn't mean it like that, love. Go on, tell me what you saw.'

'You've got to promise you won't mock.'

'Promise.'

'There was this plant, like a cyclamen I think, just above the cave where we found that thing. While you were busy digging it out... well...' Richard was staring intently, urging her to go on.

'... well... it sort of bloomed and withered right in front of my eyes.' Richard raised his eyebrows.

'I'm not joking, darling. And that's not all... once we had the artefact boxed up and halfway down the mountain, this plant... it returned to normal, like nothing had happened.' There was silence.

'I believe you, love,' Richard finally said, before adding, 'not sure what to make of it though.' He took another swig of his beer.

'Where are the twins?' Ella changed the subject.

'You really have to ask?' Richard laughed. 'Edessa will be trying to find some way to get on the stage and Charlotte will be with Jairo doing what she does best – interrogation.'

'Debating,' Ella corrected with a smile. 'I guess we can relax then.' She sighed.

In the bandstand of the little town square a guitarist ordered them all into silence with a few bars of a flamenco folk song while a singer solemnly walked onto the stage. Richard and Ella looked at each other and a silent agreement was made to discuss the strange incident later. For now, they simply held hands and enjoyed the show.

'*Mishto... hom me... di... dikava tute.*' Charlotte stumbled over the words while her new Gitanos friends exploded with laughter. Charlotte blushed; Romani was proving to be her Achilles heel and she wasn't used to failing at things. Jairo shook his head and waved his hands dramatically.

'You are like timid rabbit, you will never learn this way. You have to be without fear, own the words. *Mishto hom me dikava tute,*' he chanted in a sing-song voice, conducting as he went. 'It means you are glad to meet, so fill your voice with gladness.' Charlotte smiled in spite of her frustration.

'*Mishto hom me dikava tute*,' the others chorused before bursting into a fresh bout of laughter.

'You must not be so hard on yourself, *miri kushti*,' Jairo smiled as he boldly swept an unruly strand of hair out of her eyes.

'Bet Edessa isn't struggling like this,' Charlotte smiled, trying not to feel so defeated.

Charlotte's twin, Edessa was at the other end of the square loitering around the colourful vardos parked behind the bandstand. She marvelled at the polka-dot dresses as the dancers twisted and reeled through their final warm-up dance. Edessa loved to dance and flamenco was fast becoming her favourite – but it was the singers that fascinated her the most.

Edessa, like Charlotte, had a gift. Whereas Charlotte could read information locked in solid objects, Edessa could read information locked in people. Though she didn't understand the words, she could still feel the stories and emotions in the Gypsy songs.

'Flamenco is not just sound, not mindless entertainment, little one,' said one of the older singers who had taken Edessa under her wing. 'The song is always there, woven through all of creation, like a thread in a tapestry. We do not create the song, we simply carry it within us for a short while.'

Satisfied that Edessa understood, the woman smiled before continuing. 'A true singer weaves the energy of that song into their own voice. They remind us of our place in the web of life, our interconnectedness. Gypsies call it *Duende* – that indefinable ability to communicate through emotions.'

The woman sang a string of notes and Edessa could feel the emotion pouring out of her, giving the simple tune a life of its own. Edessa could feel it vibrating her whole body, awaking shadowy memories that didn't belong to her. Taking a deep breath, Edessa echoed the tune back and the memories flowed away.

The woman was clearly shocked.

'There are few outsiders who can do that.' She nodded approvingly. 'It seems you might just have a little Gitanos blood in you, *me chavi*.'

Edessa beamed with pride. 'I've been listening.'

The old Roma woman sat in the archway of her courtyard garden, smoking a pipe and watching the girl with the red hair and curious green eyes as she tried to learn their language. She had a feeling about this one. She was without the grace of the other, but she had the soul of an adventurer. Though not Gitanos, her family was another kind of nomad and she had a touch of destiny about her. Was it her own? the woman wondered.

'Madame Cortes,' Jairo said, bowing respectfully, the rest of the group following his lead.

'You, child,' Madame Cortes waved at Charlotte. 'I have words for you, but not here in this… *Jaleo*.' She emphasised the last word to make her disapproval of their raucous behaviour clear. 'Come, come.'

Jairo pushed Charlotte to her feet and she followed the woman through the archway. The cloistered courtyard was much quieter than the main square and the air was full of the sweet smell of jasmine, which left her feeling quite giddy.

'Sit,' the woman ordered, 'and listen, I won't waste words on *gadje*.'

Charlotte sat bolt upright at that word: 'non Roma'. It was the first one Jairo had taught her. If Madame Cortes was indeed suggesting she considered Charlotte as one of her own, it was a huge honour so Charlotte listened intently.

'Let me see your hand, child.'

'Are you a fortune teller?' Charlotte asked, extending her hand. 'Fortunes take care of themselves, have no need of me. I am *Drabarni*.' The woman scrutinised the lines on Charlotte's hands. 'Is healer and seer,' she said in answer to Charlotte's unspoken question.

Madame Cortes seemed to go into some sort of trance and in the long silence Charlotte could hear the music of crickets and other night bugs. She got so caught up in the melody and the feel of the warm night breezes on her sun-crisped skin that she jumped when Madame Cortes finally spoke.

'You have been dreaming of a tree I sense. Well, it has been dreaming of you too; for a very long time, *miri kushti chavi*.' She smiled cryptically.

'You have important work to do and many knots...' The woman paused, her forehead wrinkled with concentration. 'No... is not the right word, many... roots... to untie.'

Charlotte held her breath in anticipation. She desperately wanted to ask questions but suspected she would learn more by keeping silent and letting the woman talk.

'Your hand shows you were born to travel, you are akin to us in some ways. How many countries have you visited already?' Madame Cortes continued.

Charlotte had to think for a moment. 'Ten.'

Madame Cortes smiled and nodded. 'Very soon you will be going on a journey to a land not on any map, through a gateway that has long been shut. But it will start normally enough, with you voyaging to meet ancient family in the East... they won't be going with you, however.' She nodded towards the town square where Charlotte's parents sat and Edessa danced.

Charlotte's stomach flipped at those words. She couldn't shake the feeling that Madame Cortes meant trouble was coming, but going anywhere without Edessa was out of the question.

'Surely I can choose to...'

Madame Cortes would not entertain any interruptions and she had already moved on.

'Your lifeline is broken too, see here…' The woman indicated the crease sweeping around the base of Charlotte's left thumb. '… See how it overlaps. You live both a normal life and a hidden one; this is how it is for all of your bloodline, but with you this duality must end. For the good of all worlds you must heal the severed root… it begins and ends with the tree. You must protect it at *any* cost.'

Charlotte felt shivers down her spine; it was like Madame Cortes was reading her thoughts. Charlotte instinctively knew the tree was important though she still had no idea where the stone came into it all. However, there was something that bothered her more.

'What about the scream? Have you any idea what it all means?' Charlotte's voice was small in the night air.

'Ah yes, the scream from the Dreamtime,' Madame Cortes nodded solemnly. 'The space between worlds and home of the Fey. It has become a dark and dangerous place indeed since the Withering began; especially for the likes of you. You have great power indeed if you can sense it.' Madame Cortes pulled Charlotte closer and stared at her with the darkest eyes she had ever seen. The Gypsy woman held Charlotte's gaze for an uncomfortable amount of time and just as Charlotte thought that was her cue to leave, the old woman added: 'You will need to overcome your innermost fears to recognise your greatest ally, but you can trust the diamond heart. *Shala?*'

'Yes, I understand,' Charlotte said quietly, though she wasn't sure she did.

'Sleep soon, *me chavi.*' Madame Cortes' voice was gentler now. 'Perhaps dreams will bring the answers.'

# LOUVRE, PARIS

Paris was calming after the excitement of Spain and Charlotte loved walking the streets of Montmartre where their guardian,

Morag, lived when she wasn't in London. Morag De Beau was a naturally stern-looking Scottish woman in her late sixties with thick brown hair and a fondness for tweed. She was an old family friend and wife of the late Renoir De Beau who had been Richard and Ella Stone's university history professor. They had been his favourite students and a friendship was forged for life.

When alive, Renoir had relished teaching Charlotte pretty much all he knew while Morag, on the other hand, nurtured Edessa's creativity. The twins were like the grandchildren the couple had never had. Since Renoir had passed away, Morag spent most of her free time with the Stones and was virtually one of the family, acting as guardian for the twins when their parents were away. While she had business in Paris, they were all staying in the tiny apartment above a bakery on the Rue des Saules.

It wouldn't be long before it was back to the relatively boring Pimlico flat and a classroom routine (there had even been disturbing suggestions of the twins actually attending a school), so they were determined to make the most of their final days of freedom. Edessa and Morag adored spending hours floating around the various art galleries Paris had to offer, while Charlotte was most at home in the airy halls of the Louvre amongst the Egyptian antiquities.

The various artefacts on display were like old friends to Charlotte and she knew each one intimately. She smiled as she walked leisurely through the collection, mentally correcting a number of the information cards as she went. On the back wall a new stela caught Charlotte's attention and naturally she made a beeline to it.

'Hello, you're new,' she muttered excitedly to herself, checking there were no guards around.

Charlotte ignored the *Ne pas Toucher* sign and placed her hands on the cold stone tablet, breathing deeply. It had been marked up as 18th dynasty – that was wrong, this was much older. She got a feeling of 5th dynasty and the birth of Hieroglyphics.

The image showed an acacia tree under which stood two identical people, one on each side of the tree in traditional, symmetrical Egyptian poses. She had no idea why, but the image gave Charlotte goosebumps, especially when she noticed the lozenge-shaped object at the bottom of the stela. It radiated light, each beam tipped with an ankh symbol, while a third figure buried it deep in the ground. Charlotte scrolled quickly through the glyphs that accompanied the image for any clues of its meaning, but there was nothing – just like the stone in the cave.

As she closed her eyes Charlotte could feel the power of chisel against granite, biting out deep flecks of sparkling rock; this was an official proclamation and the stela had been manufactured in haste. It was also deliberately vague, its meaning to be understood only by a select few. Soon Charlotte found herself in a blur of Nile sounds and the heat of an ancient sun. She would get nothing more.

'Charlotte,' someone hissed.

Charlotte snapped back to the stark light of the Louvre to find Morag looking over her square glasses with a serious look on her face. Morag always knew exactly where to find her: amongst the Egyptian collection as usual. She was nothing if not predictable, like father like daughter.

'Charlotte, you need to come with me please.' Morag beckoned her to hurry.

'What's happened?' Charlotte could feel her stomach tighten; she could tell something was wrong as soon as she saw Morag's face.

'You have to come quickly,' Morag replied.

'I'm not going anywhere till you tell me why,' Charlotte insisted. If Morag had bad news she wanted to be in familiar surroundings.

'This really isn't the place for this.'

Charlotte crossed her arms resolutely. 'It's the perfect place, and I'm not moving from this spot till you tell me what's going on.'

'Fine,' Morag sighed, taking a deep breath before she continued. 'You might want to sit down for this.'

Under a colossus of Rameses II, Morag divulged the full contents of the email she had just received.

'Lost? Presumed... dead?' Charlotte repeated the words. There had to be a mistake. She had seen her parents alive and well less than forty-eight hours ago, waving excitedly as they boarded a plane for Ghadames. No, she refused to believe it; they knew how to take care of themselves.

'There's more.'

Charlotte was not normally prone to panic but the room felt as if all the oxygen was being sucked out of it and she was having trouble breathing as her skin became clammy and crawled with dread. Edessa! Something had happened to Edessa.

'Your sister...' Morag struggled to find the words and avoided eye contact, '... well, she's... we don't know how it happened...'

'She's unconscious,' Charlotte whispered.

'She's in a coma, Charlotte.'

There was no other way to say it.

Morag put her arm around the girl. Normally so full of fire and determination she had never seen her so fragile and deflated; and in the blink of an eye. Morag had been dreading this moment. She knew Charlotte would take the news of her sister the hardest and she felt powerless as the young girl sat there, silent as a statue. Morag imagined she could see the light dim slightly in Charlotte's eyes, and her heart broke at the sight.

'Let's go home, sweetheart,' Morag finally whispered.

'No, I need to see her. Take me to the hospital... please,' Charlotte murmured, determined not to cry.

# Rosemary Heights

Charlotte didn't say a word all the way from London to Norwich. She would have made it all the way to Wykenhall if it hadn't been for the chatty conductor.

'So, you off to the seaside, little lady?'

Charlotte just scowled, something which she now had down to a fine art. Morag gave her a warning glare.

'I guess so,' Charlotte muttered mutinously, staring resolutely out the window. The conductor mumbled something about the youth of today before walking off down the aisle.

It wasn't long ago that Charlotte had had a normal life. Well, maybe not normal compared to most thirteen-year-olds, trekking around remote places in the dust and bones of ancient civilisations, but she had a family and a life she loved. She'd even been known to smile then, Morag had once barked after losing patience with her for the umpteenth time. Morag herself had been more laid back and fun then too, Charlotte recalled.

She would visit the Stone household almost every evening, cooing over Edessa's artwork and enthralling them all after dinner with a rendition of some Scottish fairy tale. That had been part of 'family Stone normal' though, and that had long since disappeared.

Outside, the view was looking decidedly cold and wet and Charlotte's heart sank. She was not fond of the drab English countryside and it was clear Morag considered her an inconvenience, to be dumped on some stranger in the back of beyond. Anger bubbled inside her.

'It's best you're with family,' was all Morag would say on the subject but Morag was family and Charlotte felt betrayed.

Charlotte's things had already been packed and sent ahead to East Anglia and her head was still spinning from the swiftness of it all. *Brackenheath-on-Sea.* She didn't know exactly where it was but she already knew she wouldn't like it. She rolled the word round in her mouth and it felt weird, tasting of sour milk, twigs and damp grass.

Madame Cortes' prediction was not lost on Charlotte – 'A journey to the East' – but it didn't mean she had to be happy about it. A jumble of noise over the tannoy brought her back to reality and the train began to slow.

Though the platform was surprisingly busy, Wykenhall station did nothing to reassure Charlotte. It was little more than a hut. Sickly green paint peeled off the walls and the wooden benches lining the platform were crumbling into dust. Outside, the road wasn't even tarmac, just a narrow dirt track. Squat oak trees enclosed the place, their gnarly trunks stained with dark goo that filled the ugly splits in their bark.

While Morag tried to locate their host Charlotte just stared through the branches into the blue sky above. A breeze sent a shower of waterdrops down on her and as she brushed them out of her eyes she thought she saw something on the track. A watery shimmer appeared for a split moment to her left before disappearing into the air, reminding her of the mirages of the Moroccan deserts.

As the breeze picked up, dust and twigs tumbled down the track in its grasp. Charlotte swore she could hear chanting, like the navigation song of the Bedouins – perhaps her parents were singing their way back home right now. It was a crazy notion and she dismissed it immediately. Charlotte strained to make out the voices but they were indistinct. She couldn't tell if they were male or female but she could just about make out the sounds as they echoed around her. '*Saaaaaaar, Reeeeeeeei, Gaaar...*'

The sudden blast of a car horn startled her as a yellow VW Beetle came charging down the road and the chanting was gone.

*So this is the mysterious Aunt Clarissa I've never heard of,* Charlotte thought to herself as a thin, silver-haired woman dressed in purple gracefully extricated herself from the car.

'So sorry I'm late, dears, traffic is awful again.'

Charlotte raised an eyebrow, looking up and down the road that was empty of any other 'traffic'.

Clarissa and Morag exchanged greetings like long lost friends then, without warning, Clarissa rounded on Charlotte. She stared intently for a good couple of minutes, which unnerved Charlotte. It wasn't so much the staring – Charlotte would have enjoyed a good staring match – it was the strange, almost sinister look in the old woman's eyes and the sense that she had seen her somewhere before.

*Impossible*, Charlotte thought but Madame Cortes' words 'ancient family' echoed in her ears.

Aunt Clarissa was not so much looking at her but through her, as if she was in some sort of trance. Even the sky had darkened as if in sympathy with her solemn mood. Charlotte was just about to say something just to break the silence when Aunt Clarissa suddenly announced cheerfully, 'You must be Charlotte. You have your mother's eyes.'

The clouds rolled away and a beam of sunlight suddenly burst through the branches above them making Charlotte jump. *What is wrong with you?* she thought, trying to maintain her air of indifference.

'Well, I'm sure you must both be parched after your trip so why don't we head home for a nice cup of tea…' Aunt Clarissa beamed, pushing the front seat forward so that Charlotte could get in the back. '… And yes, of course you can have something "a bit more interesting", my dear,' she added, winking at Charlotte.

'How old are you?' Charlotte asked as they drove off, face pressed against the car window.

Morag reddened. 'You, child, have the manners of a goat. What has happened to you?'

'Well, let me see…' Charlotte's voice was loaded with sarcasm and she desperately wanted to find something clever to say but the statement simply hung in the air while memories threatened to engulf her. She said nothing more in case her voice betrayed her.

'Eighty-six, dear.'

Distracted from goading Morag and grateful for the break in the silence, Charlotte swivelled round in surprise. 'But that's ancient!' Her eyes narrowed suspiciously. 'You don't look that old.'

'Well, thank you, dear,' Clarissa stifled a laugh. 'Coming from you I suspect that is a compliment!'

'How are we related exactly?' Charlotte changed the subject.

'Technically I'm your great aunt on your mother's side… it is good to finally have you home, though it's a shame it had to be under these circumstances.' Clarissa gave her a sympathetic smile in the rear view mirror.

The landscape was alien to Charlotte; flat and boring with too much sky. Chocolate-box cottages trailed with the bare branches of rose and wisteria passed her by, alternating with freshly ploughed brown fields as the car sped onwards along the bumpy and ridiculously windy country roads. Most were barely wider than the car with bushy hedgerows obscuring from view anything that might be hurtling, equally as fast, in the opposite direction.

*A madman must have made them,* Charlotte concluded as she was tossed around in the back of the car, *and a crazy old bat is driving on them; what a way to die.*

The first sight Charlotte had of the family house, Rosemary Heights, was a glimpse of the turret room above the tree-tops of the small wood that cascaded down the shallow valley of Brackenheath-on-Sea. Aunt Clarissa pointed out with enthusiasm that it was to be her room. At the top of the cliff, the grand house dominated the skyline, towering over the little village.

As they drove through the main street they passed the only local amenities – a tiny shop, a park and weathered old pub. In that moment the true horror of her situation dawned. She would find no solace in grand libraries and museums here.

Rosemary Heights was impressive and old, but it was out of keeping with the modern buildings that now surrounded it. If it wasn't for the soft green lawn, rosemary bushes and the climbing ivy that gave it a more gentle feel, it would have been very sinister indeed.

Sea mist melted the pointed turret tops, and moss-encrusted stone gateposts, topped with gargoyles, guarded the entrance. Charlotte could smell the rosemary that gave the place its name. Large bushes of it full of delicate blue flowers were growing along the neat gravel drive adding a dash of colour to the sleeping landscape. The drive wound its way through a huge undulating front lawn up to the main door at the side of the house and to the most spectacular stained-glass window Charlotte had ever seen.

A life-sized, serene female dressed in simple robes of various greens holding a bouquet of rosemary coloured from white to dark blue flanked the heavy wooden door. Below the window was a man-made pool, which caught the flowing waters of a natural spring.

'It's a depiction of St Lucci,' said Aunt Clarissa, noticing Charlotte's thrall as they got out of the car. 'She's a local saint and this place used to be her sanctuary at one point in its long history.'

Remembering that she didn't actually want to be here, Charlotte just shrugged and turned to get her bags out of the boot. Behind her the two women smiled at each other knowingly; she hated it when adults did that and they probably thought she hadn't seen them!

Aunt Clarissa retrieved a heavy-looking iron key from her pocket and opened the front door to reveal a stone-floored porch beyond which was a large circular lobby, its walls partly covered in light wood panelling. On either side of the glass porch doors were two huge geodes of dark purple crystal that were slightly taller than Charlotte.

They sparkled in the sunlight and the cream carpet and walls of the lobby beyond were covered with jewel colours that flickered and shifted like the patterns inside a kaleidoscope. When Charlotte looked up she saw the cause of this light display was another stunning piece of stained glass in the domed skylight overhead.

The place felt wonderfully calm and even had that smoky sweet smell of churches. No other children lived here, that was clear, but that didn't bother Charlotte as she removed her shoes reverently; she was quite happy to have this beautiful place all to herself.

Stepping past the crystal geodes Charlotte suddenly felt her legs buckle beneath her and she almost fainted, just managing to steady herself at the last minute on the glass doors. A brilliant light pricked the back of her eyes and after a moment of silence a single note pulsed through her body from the soles of her feet to the hairs on her head. A sense of being home overwhelmed her.

Charlotte couldn't be sure how long she had been stood there, but the gentle brush of a cat's tail and plaintive meow brought her back to her surroundings. *This is not my home,* she thought angrily before marching into the hall. In the middle of the hall a fluffy grey cat sat staring at her, head cocked as if it was assessing this new addition to the household.

'That's Quintillian,' Aunt Clarissa said behind her as if nothing had happened, and the cat meowed again at hearing its name, before running off into the depths of the house.

*Pets; that could be fun,* Charlotte thought. She had never been allowed pets before, well, if you didn't count the hamster that Morag had ended up looking after and eventually donating to a local school.

'Do you have any other animals?' Charlotte asked.

'Why yes, dear,' Clarissa beamed. 'There's Quintillian's brother Cicero; he's a skittish little thing so you probably won't see him for a while. Then there's Maude and Maurice the chickens and Obadiah the goat.' Charlotte nodded politely but said nothing. It was not exactly a typical home menagerie.

Around her now were four chunky wood doors leading to rooms she would explore later. Her attention was drawn instead to the magnificent sweeping staircase to her right that led up to a balcony overlooking the lobby. Somewhere up there was her own turret room. Without even a backward glance at the adults she picked up her suitcase and headed up the stairs taking them two at a time. As first impressions went, she had to admit that this place was amazing – but she still wasn't planning on staying long.

Charlotte instantly disliked her suite of rooms, impressive as they were. Not only was it very girly with the light pink walls, Charlotte had never had so much space to herself. Here she had her own bathroom and sitting room complete with an open fireplace. There was even a veranda and lots of beautiful antique furniture, including a mahogany desk inlaid with green leather and a number of bookshelves, perfect for her collection of scientific journals, artefacts and history books. It should have been heaven, but it felt too big and empty without her sister.

The massive windows allowed light to pour in and gave her panoramic views of the sea and surrounding heathland. Other people might like such a view but to Charlotte it seemed like the landscape was intruding and she felt vulnerable and exposed.

The Stone residence by comparison had been a small flat close to the Thames in Pimlico, which they had inherited from some distant relative on her father's side.

Edessa and Charlotte had shared a room as the tiny third bedroom was needed for their parents' study but it had been no hardship sharing with her twin. Even though the room was barely large enough for the double bunk they shared, it hadn't felt overcrowded, just snug and cosy like the rest of the flat. Charlotte had always been neat and tidy but her sister took after her parents and the flat was full to bursting with an organised mess of ballet pumps, art brushes, archaeology books, tools, journals and trays of various bits of rather boring ancient relics like bones and broken pottery.

An all too familiar sensation knotted in Charlotte's chest as she thought about her family so before it reached her eyes she busied herself again with exploring her new surroundings where at least there were no painful reminders. Just as she was about to make her way back down stairs, something caught her eye.

On the far wall of the sitting room was a painting of an oak tree, its sturdy trunk topped with a rounded canopy thick with green leaves. The artist had added a golden glow as if to frame the tree and a wild rose wound itself around the base of the trunk. Charlotte was rooted to the spot, her skin icy cold – it was the tree of her vision down to the last leaf. She swore she could even see them moving in the wind the way they did before fire consumed them.

'Maybe I could visit for weekends,' Charlotte muttered to herself, unable to take her eyes off the strange painting while shoving her whole suitcase into the sturdy antique wardrobe and shutting the door.

Charlotte could hear the adults talking and shuffling around in the kitchen as she came down the stairs and she stopped to perch quietly on a stair.

'Did you see that, Clarissa? She's sensitive to the energy of this place, just like her mother.' Morag's familiar Scottish brogue was hushed but clear.

'Yes well, the house has certainly accepted her. I think it's pleased to have family around after all these years.' There was the sound of a kettle whistling, which stopped abruptly. 'How much have you told her?'

'My goodness; where to start?' There was tiredness in Morag's voice, as if she hadn't slept for days. 'I am so ill-equipped to deal with this whole situation. How could I bring up a child like her?'

Aunt Clarissa said nothing.

'I am so sorry I've had to bring her to you, I feel as though I have fai…'

'Perhaps you would like to explore the garden?' Aunt Clarissa interjected beaming innocently as Charlotte hovered outside the kitchen door.

'Not especially,' Charlotte growled in response, stepping into the kitchen, annoyed that she had been rumbled.

She knew it, she hadn't even been here five minutes and already this stranger was trying to get rid of her. And there it was, predictable as ever, another of Morag's evil looks. She had got so used to them over the last couple of months that they had lost their threat.

'… A drink then?' Aunt Clarissa carried on unfazed as she walked into the pantry, returning moments later with a plate of homemade cookies and a large jug of a pale yellow liquid topped with a doily.

Morag poured the tea and filled a heavy tumbler with ice, which crackled as Aunt Clarissa poured over the liquid. Charlotte sipped her drink cautiously; it was an unusual flavour but rather good.

'Elderflower cordial, the last of the season's batch,' Aunt Clarissa chuckled. 'It'll be time for them again soon. Perhaps you could help me gather them this year, though I usually pick more than I know what to do with.'

'Clarissa grows her own food and sells her homemade biscuits and preserves,' Morag added, seeing the opportunity to get a conversation going.

'And that earns you enough money to afford all this?' Charlotte sneered. She had perfected the art of goading Morag, whose face was getting redder by the minute, but this woman wasn't even flustered yet.

'Not exactly…' Aunt Clarissa looked at Morag '… I also hold meditation classes, and then there's…'

'So, you're a hippy; or maybe even a witch!' Charlotte smirked triumphantly.

Morag had had enough. 'That is it, Charlotte Stone, you are an ungrateful little toad with no manners, none at all. All we are trying to do is our best for you and you just throw it back in our faces.'

Charlotte could see that Morag was close to tears as Clarissa put a comforting hand on her shoulder and this made her even angrier. She slammed the glass down on the table.

'Do you think for one minute that I wanted to come here, to be passed round from person to person like a smelly pair of old boots no one wants!' she screamed at the two women; she couldn't stop, she had been bottling it up for too long. 'I didn't ask for this you know, I just want my old life back, I want my sister back, and I want my parents back. Is that too much to ask?'

Charlotte turned to run; it didn't matter where, just so long as they didn't see the tears streaming down her face.

# The Search

*I*t had been hours since Charlotte had run out of the kitchen at Rosemary Heights and she wasn't feeling any better. She was pretty sure she wouldn't be welcome back at the house after her latest outburst which meant she was officially homeless, except for the empty, boarded-up flat in Pimlico.

Her old key was in her pocket and she toyed with it thoughtfully – it was of no use to her now of course. Ever since the house had been emptied, there had been all manner of padlocks and metal grilles installed. She had nowhere to go and this notion gave her a strange sense of freedom.

Her stomach rumbled but she ignored it, focusing instead on what she was going to do next – wandering aimlessly around Brackenheath-on-Sea wasn't going to help. Ahead of her was a pair of rusted iron gates set in an overgrown hedge and from the faded sign she read:

BRAC  E  TH   SE PARK

As she followed the weed-cracked path, a strange silence descended and the air seemed to buzz with anticipation. She recognised the feeling, it was the same way she felt when she was about to make an important find – like the stone in the cave. But what on earth was she likely to find here?

Charlotte walked to the end of the avenue of sycamore trees and the full forlorn landscape of Brackenheath-on-Sea Park unfolded in front of her. To her right was a bare patch of dirt, which Charlotte figured must be the remains of a formal garden. Ahead of her was a smelly, snot-green stretch of water set in undulating brown lawns after which was a rundown pavilion filled with broken glass and wood. It should have been another reason to want to leave but Charlotte kind of liked the place. It looked just like she felt, unloved and forgotten, and she found it comforting.

Wandering past the boating lake, complete with rubbish and submerged shopping trolleys, she headed over to the half-moon pavilion. It was obviously a brilliant stage in its day and it still had great acoustics.

'*Saaaar, Reeeeei, Gaaaaaaaaaaaar,*' Charlotte toned absentmindedly as she perched on the edge of the raised platform of the stage. They were the first sounds that came to mind, the ones she heard in the train station, and a plan formed. She would get a train to London, find her sister and... well, that was as far as she had got, but it was a start.

Charlotte needed to get her bearings. She could see the turret tops of Rosemary Heights through the trees – that was definitely not the direction she wanted to go. To her left she could hear the river, which flowed past a giant willow, beyond which were open fields with a ramshackle cottage in the distance.

Turning to see what was behind the pavilion, Charlotte gasped. Set on a small hill, the gnarly old oak was clearly visible through a thin veil of silver birches. It was just a skeleton of a tree at this time of year but there was no mistaking it was the tree from her dreams – and the painting at Rosemary Heights. As she drew closer she could see the naked briar of a wild rose snaking its way around the trunk and the twiggy upper branches swaying in the wind. She found herself swaying along with them.

'Are you alright, Miss?' A man stood a short distance away with a bemused look on his face.

'What? Oh! Yes, er... I'm fine.' Charlotte rubbed her eyes as she realised where she was.

'You were away with the Fey there,' he added with a beaming smile now he was sure he had her attention.

He was a strange-looking individual, older than her parents but younger than Clarissa she guessed but his attire was oddly Victorian. He was already very tall and thin but his grey pinstripe trousers and waistcoat along with the top hat he was wearing made him look even taller. Charlotte had no idea where he had come from but wondered if there was a wedding somewhere nearby.

'Forgive me, where are my manners, I am Etienne.' The man tipped his hat and gave her a formal bow before looking at her expectantly.

'Er, Charlotte,' replied Charlotte.

'Wonderful to meet you.' Etienne shook her hand vigorously. 'You must be new here; locals take the Evergreen Oak very much for granted, most don't even know it is here. No appreciation for history.' He beamed again.

Charlotte hadn't figured him for a local but he was clearly knowledgeable and, not for the first time, she wished she had Edessa's ability to read people.

'I didn't realise it was special, I just stumbled across it a moment ago,' she replied.

'Well, you've been standing there... actually more swaying there, admiring it for over an hour.'

Charlotte wrinkled her forehead. 'No, I've only been here a minute, if that.'

'I assure you, Miss, you have been there much longer.' The man pulled out a pocket watch to prove his point. 'I wouldn't worry, it does that to people it likes. Where were you headed?'

Charlotte vaguely remembered her plan to catch a train to London, but now she wasn't so sure, the tree had changed things.

'I was heading to the train station...' she said, noncommittally, '... but I...'

'My my, you had better hurry then, my dear, the last train departs in ten minutes.'

'I don't really know the way so I think I'll just go another day.'

It was a lame excuse and she knew he was just trying to be

helpful but her feet were like lead and she was becoming more and more reluctant to leave.

'Nonsense, it would be a privilege to escort you, I'm going there myself anyway,' Etienne insisted.

He offered her his arm and Charlotte smiled at such old-fashioned manners. She shrugged off her misgivings and allowed him to guide her. While something within her desperately wanted to stay with the tree, her logical side needed facts; something she was sure Etienne could provide.

'Why is it called the Evergreen Oak when it's clearly not?' she asked, looking back one last time.

'That is an interesting story; and a good question.' He threw her another of his charming smiles. 'Some centuries ago people around here were starving due to a particularly lengthy and cruel winter and the crops failed. One smart soul remembered this was a fairy tree and asked the Fey Nation for their help. The following morning, the Evergreen Oak was full to bursting with green leaves and, more importantly, acorns which magically replenished themselves every day. It was a miracle and the only thing that kept the locals and their livestock from death.'

It was an interesting story but it didn't shed any light on her dreams at all.

The air had cooled now the sun was below the horizon and the train station was empty as Charlotte and Etienne stepped into the foyer.

'A one-way ticket to London please,' she said to the holes in the glass window.

An old man who looked about ninety sat behind the counter reading a battered old paperback that looked as old as him. His movements showed that no one would rush him. Peering over his spectacles, he stared at her, a look of suspicion blooming on his face.

'Yer a bit young to be travlin' on yer own aint cher?'

'She is not alone, my good man,' Etienne stepped forward before Charlotte had the chance to reply and dipped his hat to the man, 'and make that two tickets if you would.'

The old man looked Etienne up and down but didn't budge. He simply bent closer to the glass and gave Charlotte a pleading look.

'Why not go home? I'm sure yer folks are gonna be worryn' sick over yer.'

'That is exactly what she intends to do,' Etienne spoke for her again, his voice strained though he still wore one of his charming smiles, 'as soon as she has a ticket, dear fellow.'

'You sure you want to go, Miss?' The man ignored Etienne again.

Charlotte nodded and the vendor gave Charlotte her ticket without another word.

As the train sped through the descending darkness Charlotte fished her iPod out of her shirt pocket. Switching it on, the angry staccato of flamenco music blared into her ears; it certainly suited her mood but it also reminded her of the very last night she had spent with her family before disaster struck.

Blocking out the real world she relived the joy of that balmy Andalusian night. In her mind's eye she could see Edessa desperately trying to keep up with the beautiful Gypsy women, their skirts flaring and faces contorted with concentration and passion as their feet duelled skilfully with the guitarist, while their parents watched from their table at Casa Vargas.

Her parents! The thought of them brought her down to earth with a bump. 'Missing presumed dead'. That's what the report had said. The morning after the fiesta they had departed on a plane to Ghadames where they planned to travel across the Sahara into Egypt. That was the last time she had seen her parents, her mother smiling and waving as she left, blowing them kisses.

'There we are, one hot chocolate,' Etienne said, as Charlotte removed her headphones and wiped her eyes furiously on her sleeve.

He had insisted on accompanying her and she felt it would be rude to refuse, considering. Besides she wanted him to tell her more about Brackenheath, Clarissa and perhaps, most importantly, the mysterious oak tree on the hill.

'I've interrupted you, haven't I?' Etienne gave her a pantomime sad face.

'No it's fine.' Charlotte attempted a smile.

'Alright then, well, as we are going to be travel buddies, how about telling me what brought you to our little village of Brackenheath?'

Charlotte's emotions threatened to engulf her again and she had to take a deep breath to steady her voice before she spoke.

'I've come from London to stay with my aunt,' was all she could manage.

'Ah the infamous Clarissa Aherne I assume; life will never be dull in that household.'

Charlotte was beginning to suspect Etienne knew more about her than he was letting on but before she could challenge him, he was already talking again.

'Judging by your presence in the park, I am guessing you were looking for some private time for reflection. Brackenheath is not measuring up to your expectations I suspect.'

Charlotte shrugged. She didn't really have any expectations; life had changed at such a dizzying pace recently it was all she could do to keep up.

'I shan't pry my dear,' Etienne continued, patting her hand reassuringly, 'and if you do return, the park is certainly the perfect place to be alone. Most people think it's haunted.' He laughed as if the idea was preposterous. 'Personally I think the Fey drove the humans off,' he added with a whisper.

Charlotte raised her eyebrows at Etienne's last comments. He clearly didn't think believing in imaginary creatures was as crackers as thinking the place might be haunted. She was intrigued.

'What exactly are "Fey"?' Charlotte asked him.

'Oh, my dear girl, where have you been all your life? The Fey Nation lives all around us; they are sometimes known as the "Little People" or the "Lords and Ladies".'

'You mean fairies?' Charlotte couldn't hide the sarcasm in her voice anymore; she just didn't believe in such things.

'Not just fairies anymore: dwarves, drakes, trolls, sprites, selkies… the list is endless. They all come under the banner, and protection, of the Fey Nation. I guess it's even more important they to stick together now.'

'And why would they want rid of humans?' she humoured him.

Etienne shifted in his seat uncomfortably. 'Relations between Human and Fey have been less than amicable for a while, ever since the "Tinkerbell Scandal" in fact. They made a formal complaint after that, citing all human fairy stories as insulting and derogatory. As for the local Fey – they blame us for a great many things, not least the state of Brackenheath Park, so they retreated to the Dreamtime.'

*Dreamtime.* Charlotte's skin tingled at the word as she heard Madame Cortes' warning in her head.

'It is the space between the worlds, the "in-between",' Etienne continued. 'The fey left mundane Earth in order to dwell there… but it appears they may be coming back.'

'What makes you say that?'

It was some time before Etienne spoke and the way he stared at her reminded Charlotte of Aunt Clarissa – except unlike her, his eyes were filled with a strange mix of curiosity and fear.

'You must have heard the tree singing, did you not feel the darkness pouring through? No living creature could survive in that. My guess is the Dreamtime is collapsing and they had no choice.'

Charlotte had begun to shake her head but as Etienne spoke flashes of memory from her afternoon in Brackenheath Park flickered into life. She remembered the subtle buzzing she had felt and dismissed, the shimmer she had thought just a trick of the light, the low hum that had kept her rooted to the spot. Etienne and Charlotte stared at each other. Whatever he thought he saw, Etienne was obviously pleased.

'I knew it was you,' he beamed.

The train grated to a stop and in the melee of the crowd departing the train, the guards were unconcerned by the strange pair of a scruffy redheaded tomboy and a man in a grey top hat.

Etienne, of course, refused to leave her alone in the marbled concourse of bustling Liverpool Street.

'Someone of your age should not be travelling the streets of London alone,' he had insisted, something Charlotte found amusing considering she had travelled through more dangerous places without incident, but she knew he was just being kind. They made their way to an Underground map.

'Things have changed somewhat since I was last here,' Etienne said, scratching his head as he tried to make sense of the knot of coloured lines. 'I'm sure there weren't this many lines. Where did you say you were heading?'

'Belleswater.'

'Ah well, seems we have a way to go in that case.' Etienne offered Charlotte his arm as he pointed to a blue dot. 'Sure you don't want to take a stroll in the night air?' His face fell when Charlotte shook her head.

It was obvious that Etienne did not enjoy being so far underground so Charlotte got little else out of him for the rest of the journey other than Clarissa had lived on her own for years and that the house had been in the family for centuries. He was clearly relieved when they had returned to the fresh air of the city streets.

'I trust you will be alright from here?' he said, looking a little pale.

'Yes, thank you, Etienne,' Charlotte grinned.

'Excellent, in that case I really must be going, I am already late.'

'I'm sorry, you shouldn't…'

'Nonsense, I won't hear it. What sort of gentleman would I be to leave a lady stranded?' Etienne, with his usual chivalry, tipped his hat and bowed to Charlotte before adding, 'We will meet again, Miss Stone.'

His tone sent chills down her spine; it sounded almost like a threat and she had to force back an urge to run. Charlotte immediately felt stupid. Etienne had shown her nothing but kindness but she was still pleased to see the warm lights of Belleswater Hospital.

The welcoming calm of the Crankshaw Wing engulfed her. It smelt clinical like any hospital, but there was an underlying hint of vanilla with soothing pipe music and soft carpet underfoot. This was the one place she felt safe and at peace at the moment.

Visiting time was coming to an end and the hospital was settling in for the night so she ducked into a store room to avoid the burly nurse Collins who was making her last round of the evening. Charlotte had met her before and she was not someone to mess with so only when she was absolutely sure that the coast was clear did she sneak out into the corridor. Soft strip lighting lined the ceiling, plenty enough for her to find her way around, and soon she was outside room 11 – Edessa's room.

She still couldn't get used to seeing her sister like this. It was unnatural seeing her so inactive, quite apart from all the machines she was hooked up to. Charlotte went over to the bed, pulled up a chair and got as comfortable as she could for the long night ahead.

She reached for her sister's hand and felt the faint pulse in her wrist. Though she needed a ventilator to breathe, the doctors had said it was a good sign that her heart was still working on its own. All Charlotte could think of at the moment was that the one person she could talk to about anything and needed most of all right now was unable to help her. She had always thought she was the strong one, but now she felt weak and alone.

It had been hard enough to face the loss of her parents but

the double whammy of her sister's coma had been too much to bear – almost. For the first time since that dreadful night she let herself really cry. She cried and cried till she thought her heart would burst and still she couldn't stop. Eventually she cried herself into a mercifully dreamless sleep.

A fierce wind whistled in the pitch-blackness around Edessa Stone but she felt and heard nothing. She couldn't recall how she'd got here (wherever 'here' was) and though she couldn't feel them, she knew tears flowed down her cheeks as she desperately tried to keep her fear in check. The last thing she remembered was being with Morag at the Opéra Bastille in Paris and now she was alone in the darkness. She had no way of marking time in this place but it seemed as if she had been here for an eternity.

If only Lottie were with her, she'd know what to do; she was practical like that. Edessa was sure her mind was playing tricks on her because she thought she had just heard her sister calling out to her only moments ago. That must be just wishful thinking though – there was no sound in this terrifying place. There was the vision, however.

Edessa knew it off by heart now. It started with the gnarly oak, perched high on the hill, with roses wrapped around it. Snow lay on the ground yet the rose was still in full bloom. In her mind's eye, Edessa saw its petals fall to the ground as the plant began to wither in front of her eyes before the hand, long broken nails thick with dirt, burst out of the ground. As fire engulfed the scene she felt the blood-curdling scream reverberate in her skull, its sound lingering in the dark long after the vision had faded.

Edessa could feel the light of the fireball building and she steeled herself for another onslaught of disturbing images; but something was different this time. She convinced herself the light was not in her imagination this time. For a start, it was cold and silver; a tiny pinprick in the distance like a lone star in the night sky – and it was calling to her.

*I wish you could hear me, Eddie,* it whispered in her sister's voice.

Charlotte was out there somewhere looking for her, she just knew it. Edessa could feel her sister again and this gave her renewed courage as she focused with all her might on the new silver light, straining to hear Charlotte's voice again. But it never came. The silence was deafening and most alarming of all, the silver light was flickering and beginning to fade.

*Don't go out, don't go out,* Edessa repeated over and over, willing it to grow brighter. Somehow she knew her life depended on it. To her surprise it seemed to do as she asked.

As the light drew closer, Edessa noticed for the first time the ominous shadows floating in the air around her. Evil-looking creatures with deformed limbs and lifeless eyes flashed razor-sharp teeth at her in an evil smile of anticipation, making their intentions clear. She could feel their longing, their desire for her to become one of them – and that they had been human once. She shuddered inside.

One creature was showing particular interest in her and was the only one not disturbed by the light. Its eyes were pupilless and as dark as obsidian while its pale white face was lined with marble-like streaks. It reached a long taloned finger to her chest. Edessa could almost taste its curiosity and felt something (almost physical and definitely disturbing) flickering across the edges of her consciousness.

Before she had a chance to think, a cord burst from the starlight and lunged at her, attaching itself to her chest where the creature was pointing. Her first instinct was to scream, but in moments energy flowed through her and... she could feel her body again. She still couldn't move but the cord was pulling her away from the hungry shadows as they recoiled from the light.

Images bloomed in front of her: a hospital room with all manner of machines, Charlotte sitting in a hospital chair and… Edessa gasped as she saw herself lying in the bed. Tubes protruded from her nose, arms and mouth; she barely had time to take it all in as the silver cord pulled her into her body.

In an instant, the sounds of the hospital, the traffic noise outside and her sister's heavy breathing filled her senses. It was as if someone had turned up the volume full blast on a TV and Edessa realised just how used to the silence she had become.

*Lottie, Lottie? Can you hear me?* Edessa's inside voice whispered but her sister didn't stir.

Edessa wondered how she had managed to hear her sister in the silence; she was so convinced she had heard her thoughts so why wasn't it working the other way round? A vague memory bubbled and a word repeated over and over: *Duende.*

Edessa remembered the Gypsy woman's lesson on projecting her emotions through the song of creation. As the lessons of that night came back to her, Edessa imagined she could hear a low, constant humming underneath the noise of the traffic and she latched onto it. Taking a deep breath, Edessa focused with all her might and in her head she sang as loudly as she could.

*Charlotte.*

The marble-faced creature, who was still hovering nearby, nodded and smiled before disappearing back into the blackness.

Charlotte sat bolt upright and rigid, not daring to breathe, not daring to move…

Rain was falling so heavily against the window that it almost drowned out the sound and Charlotte thought she was still half asleep though her eyes were open.

*Eddie? Is that you?* Charlotte whispered half-heartedly. Talking to the air, she must be mad; it was scientifically impossible for her sister to be talking to her in her head, but she desperately wanted it to be true. She missed her sister so much.

*I'm here, Lottie, I can hear you. I can feel you. Please, let this work.*

Edessa's voice was more determined than before and growing louder. So loud in fact that Charlotte worried that someone would hear – till she remembered it was all in her head.

*I… I can… hear you, Eddie.* Charlotte imagined she heard a sigh of relief.

*Thank goodness, you have no idea how much I've missed you.*

*I think I might. How is this possible?* Charlotte replied tentatively.

*Beats me, I've been floating in the dark for I don't know how long then all of a sudden, there you were.* If Charlotte had had her sister's skill she would have felt the wave of fear and relief.

*What do you remember?*

*Paris, Monet… then pitch-blackness… oh, and the vision…* The sentence trailed off.

*Me too.* Charlotte tingled all over as she remembered her encounter with the Brackenheath Oak but there was another matter she had to deal with first.

*Eddie…* Charlotte began. She was no use at giving bad news. *… something has happened… to Mum and Dad…* She paused to let her sister absorb what she was telling her. The silence stretched into minutes.

*I stopped feeling them when I was in the dark…* Edessa finally answered, *… but I thought it was just this place.*

*Can you remember the last thing you felt?* Charlotte persisted.

*Discomfort, like being too hot, then… maybe falling?*

*Heat is simple enough… but where on earth could they have fallen to in a desert?*

*Do you think they…*

*Don't know,* Charlotte replied abruptly. *They know how to look after themselves.*

Edessa could feel Charlotte's emotions in turmoil and knew not to push the subject any further. She changed the subject. *You had something else to tell me?*

That was enough to prompt her sister to tell her all about the strange encounter with the tree in the rundown park in Brackenheath.

*Do you think it's the one we have been seeing since Spain?* Charlotte asked.

*How could it be any other?* Edessa replied.

*I don't know, but I'm not going back. I don't want to live with that strange hippy woman. Besides, I've got to focus on finding Mum and Dad.*

*Be sensible, Charlotte,* Edessa pleaded. *That "hippy woman" is family and how exactly do you intend to search the entire Sahara desert by yourself. Anyhow, there must be a reason you found the tree… or that it found you.*

*You think it could be linked?* Charlotte had come to the same conclusion but it was good to have her sister confirm her thoughts.

*I honestly don't know, but it ties in with what Madame Cortes told you and it's as good a place to start as any. I think it deserves further research.*

Charlotte thought about what her sister had said for a while. She was certainly good at research.

*I don't want to leave you.*

*Well, you can hardly live in the hospital, and we can always talk like this now.*

*How do you know?* Charlotte was not convinced. The scientist in her still needed proof.

Edessa didn't know – but she did *feel*. For some reason the face of the marbled creature smiling at her in the silver gloom came to mind.

*Things are different now.*

Those four simple words summed it all up and with that they both fell into a comfortable silence.

Neva removed her glasses and rubbed the bridge of her nose. She had been working for ten hours solid and was making slow progress. The sun had set ages ago and security would be coming soon to lock up for the night. Outside was now blowing a gale and rain lashed down, so it looked like she would be getting wet on her walk back to the dorms.

The carbon dating of the cloth wrappings she'd requested that morning had finally come back and she smiled to herself – Charlotte had been right again, they were of little interest. However, the stone had remained a puzzle. She studied the pictures taken of the object in situ once more in case they could offer any inspiration but they gave her nothing. She returned to her notebook.

*O ushalin zhala sar o kam mangela*

She had written the translation underneath: '*The shadow moves as the sun commands*'. It was Romani and they had found it on a wooden marker post near the site. It had been easy enough to translate with Madame Cortes' help. She assumed it was some sort of spell for protection but against what? And what of the stone itself? A C scan had determined it was hollow with a second object inside, *like a Russian doll,* Neva mused, intrigued by the results.

Neva stroked the smooth surface of the lozenge-shaped object but it gave away none of its secrets. Unusually there were no markings and no way to open it but then, perhaps that was the point.

She wished Richard and Ella were there, they'd have some theories. Neva was sure there was something they hadn't had a chance to share with her, she could tell from their faces when the object had been discovered. They were always like excited school children with new discoveries but this had been different, it was as if they had seen it before. She was probably wasting her time; she didn't even know if she still had a job after what had happened but she couldn't help being drawn back to the project.

An idea struck her and, mixing a mild acid solution, she carefully brushed an even coat on a small section of the artefact. Nothing. The solution caused no obvious damage so she risked trying another section but this came up blank as well. She threw the brush down in frustration. However, just as she decided to pack up for the night she saw it.

Gradually, lines started to appear and, as they darkened, began to form strange symbols. Neva's arms prickled with goosebumps as she hurriedly coated the rest of the vessel she couldn't believe what she was seeing. The symbols seemed to be letters of some sort but in the form of tree roots, branches and leaves. Neva was alarmed to see the writing begin to fade so she hurried to jot it down before it disappeared. She was so engrossed she didn't hear anyone come into the room.

'Hello, Neva.'

Neva cursed under her breath as she nearly dropped the fragile artefact. She turned towards the source of the voice.

'Who the hell are you?'

The man tipped his top hat and bowed.

'I'm the money,' he grinned.

As the first rays of sunshine filtered through the blinds of room 11, Charlotte squirmed in her chair. She was in that space between sleep and wakefulness and vivid images swirled through her mind. Images of her parents falling through the air, of a rosebush blooming in snowfall before withering and dying in moments and a golden flash of fire that left her blinded. In the edges of her vision a marble-faced figure moved and strange chanting filled the air, just like the sort she had heard when she arrived in Wykenhall.

As Charlotte came to, she swore she could hear the chanting filling her sister's room and not just her own head, but as she opened her eyes the sound disappeared. Her body was sore from a night in the hard plastic chair and demanded her attention, so as she focused on stretching the stiffness out of her limbs, the disturbing images of the night soon floated away.

The hospital was also waking and Charlotte heard the clattering of pans from the kitchens as breakfast was prepared for staff and patients – but not for her sister. In the corridor outside there was the soft footfall of the morning nurse going about her rounds and Charlotte knew she would have to leave soon or face discovery.

Having stretched out the kinks in her neck, arms and legs, Charlotte listened by the door to work out if the corridor was empty. Just as she thought the coast was clear, the handle turned and she was nearly knocked to the floor by the person entering. There were three of them and she didn't need to look up to know who the purple dress belonged to.

'Thank you, Nurse Collins, I think we can take it from here,' Clarissa said calmly.

Nurse Collins looked as if she had a few choice words she wanted to share with Charlotte but luckily she relented and left her to what she obviously hoped would be a long and severe lecture from her relatives. That was clearly exactly what Morag had in mind but as she stepped forward, her face a picture of fury, Clarissa intervened again.

'There is no need for recriminations, Morag, the important thing is she is safe.'

Morag's face softened and she nodded gently in agreement before throwing her arms around Charlotte who could see her makeup was streaked with tears. She had obviously been very worried and, feeling guilty, Charlotte hugged her back.

*Go with them.*

The hair on Charlotte's neck prickled as Edessa spoke. She looked at the adults but they showed no sign of having heard. Charlotte shut her eyes and concentrated.

*There's no time to explain so listen to me, Lottie, something bad is coming, I can feel it, and you need to protect the oak till we work out what it is.*

'What is it, Charlotte? What's wrong?' Aunt Clarissa's voice sounded worried but Charlotte could sense something else, something like expectation, lurking underneath it.

*Find me by the tree, Lottie. I'll be waiting.*

Charlotte opened her eyes. 'Nothing.' She smiled. 'I'm ready to go now, Aunt Clarissa.'

'Wonderful… and call me Clarissa, the "aunt" makes me feel like an old maid!'

Charlotte smiled to herself. Edessa had always been a good judge of character so maybe living with this crackpot wouldn't be so bad after all.

# Face in the Flames

As the festival fire burned in the central grove of the Tree Weaver village, on the edges of the last great forest of Syluria, a small group sat some distance away exchanging worried glances. Their harmless game had started to take a dangerous turn.

'It doesn't look like he is breathing,' Mor'seka mumbled, 'and he's cold as river water.'

'Stop fussing, Mor'seka, you think I don't know what I'm doing?'

Anya tried to hide her own panic as she played with her newly acquired dreadlock. Fashioned to mimic the roots of the Great Tree, she hoped it would be the first of many – so long as she didn't accidentally kill her brother before her priestess training was finished.

'This is how it's supposed to go. Stop being such a Galoofin. What I want to know is did he manage to break through the Dreamtime? What do you think Albion is like? I wonder if the legends are true?'

Mor'seka was no fool. He knew Anya was concerned for her brother but she was also genuinely more interested in her little experiment. Not for the first time, he worried about her sanity.

'A worm? You're actually comparing me to a skittish, flatulent worm?' Mor'seka retorted as he tried to rub some warmth into Tar'sel's freezing limbs. 'It's no good, I'm going to get some help.'

'Don't.' Anya grabbed his arm. 'Any second now the nut is going to...' She was interrupted by a loud pop and a hazelnut shooting into the sky.

She stared intently at Tar'sel for a moment. 'It worked.' She beamed.

The full moons of Syluria bathed the Nellpa Barra in burnished silver and the river wound its way across the valley like a glossy black serpent. Ice blue stars hung in the frosted winter sky and the last crops of lotus grain rippled gently in the wind. On the hill overlooking the Tree Weaver village the sacred Nymet tree, a sturdy gnarly oak, glowed gently in the darkness.

The festival fire had long since collapsed into itself and in the dying light of the fire, the sculpted branches of the dwelling trees, with their hide and woven bark bowers, cast strange shadows which spread over the grove as if trying to tempt people to bed. In the highest treetops of the Nymet temple on the northern hill, the Draoi priestesses continued their soporific heart song in honour of the animal that had provided the feast.

The Nabinder ritual was an anxious time, when the world was vulnerable as time reset itself. The ceremony, always a sombre affair, had gone without incident, and the grove was lit by the warm glow of individual fires lit from the main festival hearth.

Young and old still feasted and drank, finishing the last morsels of the great feast and chatting in the fading light. The air was thick with the smell of applewood hearts, roasted stuffed quinnarra roots and Rheadak meat, the burnt fat from the remains infusing the night air to feed the ancestors.

Gathering around each other's hearths, they tried to outdo each other's storytelling skills but Anya, bored of the same old tales, had suggested a traditional divination game instead. Both Mor'seka and Tar'sel had been keen to join in, curious to see what Anya had been learning in her priestess training.

Tar'sel's body lurched and with incredible force of will, he drew his mind back into his body. He could feel the consciousness pouring back into the young male body sitting by a small fire. He

40

became aware of the reassuring heaviness of the trees rooted behind him, the wet grass beside him where he had knocked over his beaker and followed at last by the fact that the male body was him.

'I am Tar'sel Aderquaile, Child of the Nymet. I belong to the great forest of the Nellpa Barra, heart of Syluria – and that was *not* real!' he muttered to himself for reassurance, while the heat of the orange flames crackling in the small stone circle brought him round.

Beads of sweat decorated his ashen face, his normally spiky blond hair pasted to his head, and the points of his green ears began to tingle. He soon realised that the buzzing noise in his ears was in fact voices, voices that belonged to real, physical people, people who were talking to him.

'Tar'sel! Tar'sel? Are you OK?'

He could hear the tone of panic in his sister's voice, even though she would have denied it was there, and managed to acknowledge that he was fine. However, the image of those long, dirt-encrusted nails that had gripped him, and the pain of that ruthless mind which had plunged like a thousand daggers into his own, still lingered. He felt nauseous from the memory of the smell of decay and blood; and that scream – where had it come from?

Exhausted, he slumped gratefully against the nearest supportive trunk and waved away the suggestion that they should take him to the medicine woman. He wasn't ready for the questions that would inevitably result from such a visit. Away from the fire, the cool night air soothed him.

'At least drink then,' Anya insisted, thrusting a beaker of greenish fluid into his hand.

He downed the mixture in one; it was weird, but not unpleasant and almost immediately he felt better, more solid, more real.

'What was that?' He held the beaker up as Anya refilled it.

'A simple concoction of nettles… amongst other things.' Anya smiled, clearly relieved.

'This what they teach you in your Draoi lessons?'

'Don't be stupid, I learnt this from Mother when I was four!'

'Never mind the brew.' Mor'seka nudged his friend. 'You going to leave us in suspense all night? Did you get through the Dreamtime?'

'Give him a minute, for Goddess' sake,' Anya chided. She was very protective when she was in Draoi mode and Tar'sel was glad of it. He needed a minute to gather his thoughts.

Anya had explained the rules as Tar'sel gazed into the glowing embers. The molten flames had long since subsided and the remaining coals throbbed with orange heat which flowed through them like a river current, and it had swept him along too, into the Dreamtime.

He had never consciously entered this half-world of shadows before, only the priestesses had the skills to do so, but curiosity had got the better of him. The journey had started with the silver cord.

He recalled how golden dust drifted around him in the dark and he began to wonder if he should be doing something as he stood there. Suddenly, a punch to the chest knocked him to the ground, the force of it all swirling the dust into a frenzy. As it cleared, Tar'sel noticed a silver cord attached to his chest, and it began to gently pull him forward.

The hairs on his arms and back of his neck stood up as he remembered the sense of foreboding that had coiled in his guts. Out of the corner of his eye, wispy mist curled into strange shapes he couldn't quite make out and the silver cord led him round the deep craters that pock-marked this desolate, grey landscape. It was not at all how he had expected it to be.

Menacing images swirled in the deep black pools of the craters and Tar'sel averted his gaze as he passed. As his eyes began to adjust to the gloom, he could see that the light of the dust settled into a grid-like formation that floated at chest height.

'The Wyrdweb,' he muttered to himself. It should have been

no surprise; they were all taught from a very young age about the web that connects all things, but he had never considered it would exist out here, in fact he had never really thought about the web at all, let alone seen it. The intricacy of the pattern was like lace and he marvelled at its beauty as the silver cord led him slowly on, pulling along a single thread, looping and twisting and spinning as they went.

Ahead of him was a vortex, very much like the one he had entered, and it was obvious the silver cord was leading him there. Tar'sel took a few deep breaths; he knew how deadly panic could be, but he couldn't help but worry that he was now getting out of his depth. He hoped and prayed that Anya knew what she was doing.

At the vortex, the silver cord stopped. An image of a world bloomed around him so colourless and blank like a half-drawn picture, but it made the Dreamtime look real. He was standing on a hill with a large oak tree. Bryony curled through nearby bushes of wild rose and birch trees that swayed at the base of the hill. Despite its unfamiliar feel, Tar'sel knew where he was: the hill of the Nymet – only, this was not his Nymet.

A rustling noise behind him made him turn, alerting his hunter instinct, and he made a grab for his knife only to realise there was nothing there. He walked away from the vortex feeling the silver cord tugging at his chest; it clearly didn't want him going this way but eventually he felt it slacken.

There was a cluster of craters to his left, filled with the same black liquid he had seen in the others. Images began to fade in and out so quickly he caught only fragments: a glowing stone, a withered tree, a flame-haired girl... and the claw. Red lightning danced across the mouth of the crater before the claw erupted from the black water, the nails gripping his face, digging into his temples and dragging him down. There was a searing pain in his chest as the silver cord was stretched to breaking.

That had been the moment when Anya had used the nut to

bring him back. Tar'sel suspected that it had brought something else back as well though he had no way to prove it.

Even now, as Tar'sel sat around the fire drinking Anya's potion, the last image of the girl's face was still burnt into his mind's eye. Those pleading eyes set in an alabaster face and wild red hair as she began to fall away from him… screaming. Like everyone, he knew the story of the flame-haired girl from beyond the Dreamtime. The one who would come at a time of great tribulation. Had this been her? Was this the time? Tar'sel shuddered from an inner chill.

Tar'sel realised he had been sitting in silence for ages with Anya and Mor'seka staring at him expectantly. The tree canopy seemed to be drawing in around him and for the first time in his life he felt claustrophobic in the forest.

'Where are you going?' Mor'eska moaned.

'I need to walk, eat… to do something… normal,' Tar'sel shouted over his shoulder.

'Wait, you can't go. I need to know if it worked properly,' his sister replied.

'Forget it.'

'But…'

'*K'hul*, Anya! That was dangerous and I wasn't prepared…'

'I was always in control,' Anya protested. 'You…'

'No. I'm done.' Tar'sel strode off to the central grove.

Tay'mor, the Nymet guardian, was settling down to perform his rendition of the 'Vorla Lamp' as Tar'sel entered the central grove and a large crowd was gathering around the embers of the festival fire waiting in anticipation. The stars shone brightly in the open sky above him. It was the perfect distraction.

The stories of the sinister Vorla had always been Tar'sel's favourites and Tay'mor always told them best. More importantly they were comforting and familiar. *Just what I need right now*, he thought, as he took his place amongst the crowd, accepting the offer of a plate of spiced Rheadak meat and his favourite creamy quinnarra roots, perfectly smoked. The food warmed him, helping to clear the remnants of the terrifying vision.

The Nymet tree shone from its place on the hill, a familiar beacon that told him all was right with the world. However, Tar'sel couldn't shake the feeling that something was wrong. He wasn't sure what he had been expecting but he always thought the Dreamtime was a place of light and wonder; instead he had found only darkness and he felt polluted by it. He didn't know if it was him or the tree but it seemed to shine less brightly than normal tonight.

'The tale of the Vorla Lamp,' Tay'mor announced loudly, allowing time for the crowd to cheer before he began.

Tar'sel decided to put his concerns to the back of his mind for the time being and settled down to enjoy his meal and the entertainment.

Long ago, before the beginning of time, the land known as Syluria existed only as the tiny island of Inish, surrounded in all directions by the primordial waters of the Dreamtime.

Inish was the bleeding heart of the Sleeping Mother, which oozed molten fire as she dreamed. Little by little, over aeons of time, the island grew, but it remained barren under the fierce gaze of the triple suns.

The only other forms of life in this empty universe were the Manush de Bar, creatures of living stone that had absorbed the pulsing life-force of the Sleeping Mother; and among them were the oldest of the Manush de Bar, the Vorla. They lived, locked outside of time, in their bed of crystal caves deep within the darkness.

Even to this day, the Vorla live within the original Isle

of Inish, known now as the Mountain of Mourne, far to the north close to the Barra of Arkturus. These lovers of knowledge and learning would send their minds out into the Dreamtime, hoping to gain new experiences, yearning to connect with other sentient life, yet alas, they found only emptiness.

The Vorla, who had been observing the dreams of the Sleeping Mother, devised a plan to change the balance of power between her and the suns. They sent a terrible storm of flame shooting into the sky in order to dim the light and quench the heat of the surface, but the plan failed. However, as the molten rock hit the primordial waters, it hissed and spat and cooled, and as the largest ball of lava touched the water, it split open. A feeble black bird stumbled from the remains of the rock and, before the suns had time to burn it to ashes, it swooped into the sky and swallowed all but one of the balls of fire.

Instantly, the bird grew, its plumage turning from black to iridescent gold, red and orange tinged with blue, while its eyes shone like topaz, and its tail dripped flames. Its wings became long and graceful as it glided and danced through the air.

So pleased with its beautiful new form was the bird that it began to sing with joy. With each new sound, life blossomed on the island of Inish. Lush rainforest, plains of rippling grasses, vast forests and glistening lakes spread across the land, giving birth to all manner of creatures of earth, sea and sky; and still the Benu bird sang.

Soon this little universe was full to overflowing and the Sleeping Mother could feel the sadness in the heart of the Benu bird, for it wished to continue its song. As the Sleeping Mother exhaled, the universe expanded and a Great Tree formed in the wake of her breath. The Sleeping Mother exhaled twice more into the void, hanging two new universes from the branches of the Great Tree and so the Triverse was formed. The Benu bird swooped and soared through these new worlds, filling the air with its beautiful song of creation and disgorging a sun into each.

In time, the fire within the Benu bird was spent and it returned, exhausted and feeble, to the island of Inish. Once again the Sleeping Mother felt the sadness in its heart. The Rani, Queen of the Vorla, sent her most trusted aide Durga to the surface to attend to the Benu bird on the orders of the Sleeping Mother. So pitiful was the Benu that Durga split the Sylurian sun in two and, extracting a little light from each half, she fed the Benu bird, restoring its beauty.

However, the Benu bird was not content and wished to continue to sing. Durga knew that this could not be allowed; the Benu's song still echoed through the Triverse, even rippling into the Dreamtime, and a new melody would jar with the original song of the creation, bringing it collapsing in on itself. With the permission of the Rani, she trapped the Benu bird within a crystal jar and wrapped this in layer upon layer of stone.

In spite of its confinement, the Benu bird continued to sing and the stone glowed with its happiness. In this little world, the Benu was perpetually renewed by its own light and song.

The Vorla took the stone deep into the recesses of the crystal caves, gilding it in a beautiful cage of silver, gold and precious jewels. The stone was hung in the chamber of the Rani where it infused her and her diamond veil with its dormant life-giving light. Bathed in the light of the Vorla Lamp, these creatures of living stone lived for millennia in peace and happiness.

Tay'mor paused for a moment, taking in the faces around him as they sat listening intently while passing round mead horns and the last scraps of the feast. A gentle ripple of applause wafted through the crowd, but most knew the story wasn't quite over yet.

> Since that time, the Vorla vowed never again to interfere with the evolution of any lifeform within the Triverse, but they still stalk the Dreamtime with an eternal, unquenchable thirst for knowledge. They have even been known to drive men insane in their quest. You would do well, dear friends, to ensure you never sleep on an argument or you may find yourself suffering nightmares, as the curious Vorla discover and unravel your darkened mind.

A proper cheer went up this time, as the storyteller took a bow and people began to retire to their bowers. Tar'sel, however, was still stuck in the story.

*Vorla still stalk the Dreamtime.* The words echoed in Tar'sel's head. Could this be what he had just encountered or was he just letting his imagination run away with him? Sinister as they were, the Vorla would not deliberately harm other Sylurians, would they? After all, they *had* made a promise not to interfere. Was the scream from one of their victims?

This was perhaps the weirdest night he'd had in all his sixteen seasons; he needed to speak to someone, but who? Anya was only interested in experimenting with magic she should not be using and Mor'seka was looking for any bit of excitement he could find. There really was only one person he could trust with something this big, not just for sound advice but to be discrete.

Tar'sel could see the elders heading towards the hill and the sanctuary of the Nymet temple and his father nearby was preparing to head over and join them. It didn't seem right to interrupt but Tar'sel wouldn't see him for a few days once he has in the temple. He had hoped to speak to him before that. It could wait, couldn't it?

Tar'sel watched the orange sparks coming off the festival fire as they floated one by one into the night sky and winked out and allowed himself to drift off with them. A heavy hand on his shoulder made him jump.

'Now is the time for rest not planning adventures, young one.'

Tar'sel quickly rose to his feet. 'I was just thinking about the Vorla, Father. Are they real? Do they really send people mad?'

The leathery face of Tay'mor wrinkled into a smile, his green skin mottled with age, and the firelight dancing in his blue-grey eyes.

'Now is probably not the best time to be discussing the attributes of the Vorla but yes, they are real.'

'Have you ever seen one? Are they really evil and dangerous?'

'So many questions.' Tar'sel's father laughed. 'I doubt anyone has seen them; they are older than time and they keep to themselves. As for evil, that would do them an injustice, it's too simplistic. Do the Rheadak think us evil because we hunt them?'

'But that's survival.'

'It's nature,' Tay'mor corrected. 'Everything has its place in the Triverse and a right to exist, including the Vorla. Let's just say though, when it comes to the Vorla, I wouldn't go out of my way to find one but perhaps I'm too full of fear – they can take your negative emotions and use them against you. Besides, many of the old creatures have faded out of existence, there's not as much magic in the world as there used to be.' He sighed. 'Not since the Fey Nation retreated into the Dreamtime.'

'Shouldn't they be here, looking after the Nymet tree?'

Tar'sel stopped short of telling his father his fears. Tay'mor was the guardian of the Nymet after all; if there was anything wrong, he would surely know about it.

'Don't worry yourself, Son we have the skills we need to ensure the Nymet remains strong,' Tay'mor replied, but Tar'sel could swear he heard doubt in his father's voice.

In the distance another elder signalled to Tay'mor that his presence was required up at the temple.

'I have to leave you now, there is still work for me to do, Son. Fine dreaming,' Tay'mor said, then turned and hobbled off towards the Nymet temple.

# Corn Pads, Crystals and Dental Floss

Charlotte had been right about the slow pace of life in Brackenheath but she was surprised to find it wasn't as painful as she had thought. The nearest neighbour was a nosey old woman called Mrs Bunratty but Charlotte wasn't in need of company and she didn't miss the noise and bustle of Oxford Street or the numerous museums and shows all that much. Her new suite of rooms now housed her own personal collection, every surface covered with artefacts discovered by her own family, and even a whole wall of Edessa's artwork.

It was Edessa she pined for most and Charlotte tried to cling to her last words as she busied herself with unpacking and exploring. Knowing there may be a way to talk to her was not the same as having her near.

*I wonder how long the novelty of this place will last?* she wondered as she walked into the morning room, stopping in her tracks at the sight of Clarissa cross-legged on the floor, incense smoke weaving around her. Yep, no need to worry, there was plenty of novelty factor left.

'It's OK, you can come in, dear.'

'I didn't mean to disturb you,' Charlotte whispered.

Clarissa smiled. 'Being able to meditate isn't much good if you can only do it in complete silence surrounded by incense and candles, dear, nice as that may be. I'm of a mind that you can only truly meditate if you are able to do it on a crowded, noisy train, and there are many Taoist monks who agree with me.'

'Fancy putting that to the test some time?' Charlotte replied.

Clarissa extinguished the candle flames between her fingers.

'We can go visit Edessa any time you want, dear, you name the day.' Clarissa got to her feet gracefully and stretched. 'I have no desire to keep you from your sister, I know you must miss her terribly.'

Quintillian, the portly, long-haired grey Charlotte had met on her first day at Rosemary Heights, purred softly as he weaved around Charlotte's legs.

'But for now, I don't know about you but I'm famished; shall we do breakfast?' She picked up Quintillian who now had a look of indignation on his face. 'I know someone else who wants food!'

'He looks like he always wants food,' Charlotte laughed.

'Too true,' Clarissa nodded sagely and addressed the cat in sombre tones. 'Time to put you on a diet, old moggy.' Quintillian snorted and wriggled out of her grip. Landing clumsily on his feet, he straightened his fluffy coat for a moment before shooting off into the garden. If his owner wasn't going to feed him, he'd just need to look after himself, and a juicy mouse would make a tasty hors d'oeuvre.

Clarissa was laying the table for three in the kitchen just as there was a knock on the back door. 'How did you know?' Charlotte asked as she went to open the door; she wasn't really expecting an answer and Clarissa just smiled enigmatically. *This one is very astute,* the woman thought to herself.

'Heellooo, my lovelies, what a fabulous day. How are we all? I've bought pastries.'

A woman in Doc Martens, garish summer dress and orange shirt waved a large, oily brown bag, and the various crystal and shell bangles she wore jiggled with her every move.

'Oh, Clarissa sweetie, you must remind me to tell you all about the Earth Goddess camp I went to last weekend, it was amazing; I feel so alive!' The woman sing-songed her way through the sentence before bursting into a gush of laughter and kissed the air around Clarissa's face.

The whirlwind in front of Charlotte made Clarissa look tame and it was a struggle to keep her mouth shut. The woman's most striking feature was her hair and Charlotte couldn't help staring at the multicoloured Mohican. It looked like a parrot was perched on the woman's head.

'Charlotte, this is my oldest and dearest friend,' Clarissa announced aloud, while her face made a silent but emphatic request for Charlotte to be polite.

'Ahhh, you are the infamous Charlotte, such a pleasure to meet you. Clarissa was soo excited to hear you were coming to stay. It was Charlotte this, Charlotte that.'

Charlotte couldn't suppress laughter. That just didn't fit her picture of Clarissa at all, but she was amused to finally catch a look of shock fleet across Clarissa's face before it returned to its normal composed self.

'Nice to meet you... ?'

'Jude,' the parrot-haired woman declared like an actress greeting her adoring public. 'You can call me Auntie Jude if you like.' She chuckled, ignoring Charlotte's outstretched hand and giving her a bear hug.

*Why not,* Charlotte thought, *it's what I seem to be calling everyone else these days.*


'Pastries' consisted of almond croissants, seeded brown rolls with creamy French butter and pain au chocolat; Clarissa had even made hot chocolate and sweet, milky coffee to accompany them. They reminded Charlotte of the bakery below Morag's apartment and the many lazy Sunday mornings in the Place du Tertre cafés taking in the views of the city while Edessa bartered with the portrait artists to teach her their techniques. Charlotte found herself fighting tears again at the memories.

'What do you think then?'

Charlotte was brought out of her daydreams by the question.

'They're really good, just like the real thing,' she replied and Jude looked visibly pleased.

'I ordered them especially from the bakers in Wykenhall, they are so helpful you know.' Jude gesticulated to emphasise her point. 'I heard you are a well travelled soul and I thought it would… well, make you feel more at home if that makes sense?'

Strangely, it did.

'That's really kind of you.' Charlotte was genuinely touched.

'My Adam sends all sorts of interesting stuff home from his travels in Afghanistan – tree barks and frankincense pearls as big as your finger – he knows how his mother likes her incenses. It's always nice to get gifts, isn't it.'

'He *did*, my dear,' Clarissa said gently, touching Jude's hand.

'Oh well yes, in this dimension perhaps.' Jude waved away Clarissa's hand. 'But I know my sweet boy still looks out for his mother.'

'Of course,' Clarissa replied.

For hours Jude grilled Charlotte on her life and they swapped travel stories. Jude had been up and down the Nile twice, chanting in the king's chamber of the Great Pyramid, and had even attended a few digs as a volunteer at Karnak. She compared the light shows of Giza and Philae, showed Charlotte a piece of rock she had picked up from outside the temple of Hatshepsut and discussed the merits of various hotels and day trips she had been on.

You couldn't help but like Jude; her enthusiasm was infectious and Charlotte was thrilled to have someone who didn't look at her blankly when she talked them through her 18th dynasty pottery collection. Best of all, Jude 'ooohed' and 'aaahed' at all the right places. Clarissa, however, had long since bored of talk of deserts and archaeology and retreated to the garden to feed the chickens, Maude and Maurice. It wasn't till she came back in with fresh eggs, a pail of goat's milk from Obadiah and a basket-load of fresh vegetables that Charlotte and Jude even looked up.

'Oh my, is it that time already?' Jude gasped. 'Doesn't time fly.

Shall I start on dinner, Clarissa sweetie?' she asked, already rolling up the silk sleeves of her orange blouse.

'That sounds like a wonderful plan, dear. I still have a few things to finish off in the garden. I'm planning to make a batch of mint shaving cream this afternoon.'

'Orders picking up then?'

'Thankfully,' Clarissa nodded. 'Between you and me I'm rather sick of making nothing but jam and biscuits.' She laughed before heading back outside to make the most of the rare spring sunshine.

⚜⚘

Charlotte had left Jude to the cooking and was now watching Clarissa who, having just planted various crystals and sprinkled essential oils amongst the fruit trees, was now relocating a patch of nettles into the herb garden.

'I know I don't know anything about gardening,' she said sarcastically, 'but isn't the goal to remove weeds not replant them?'

Aunt Clarissa smiled. 'You are quite right, dear, you know nothing about gardening.'

Charlotte began to regret she had said anything as Clarissa went on to enthusiastically tell her all about friendly plants, or something like that, as well as detailing the numerous uses for nettles – which, of course, included eating them.

'Nettles, flowers, tree sap; have you never heard of Sainsbury's?' Charlotte said exasperatedly. Clarissa chuckled to herself as Charlotte stomped playfully towards the chapel ruins at the bottom of the garden.

From the chapel, Charlotte could see the river flowing past the end of Clarissa's garden, weaving under the wooden bridge flanked by two willow trees, and out into the fields of the shallow valley below. Charlotte lost sight of it as it entered the woodland of Brackenheath Park, but at that point something else caught her eye.

The tree, her tree, stood alone atop a small hill to the far end of the park and it must have been a trick of the light but… it appeared to be glowing, just like the painting in Charlotte's room.

'Does that happen often?' Charlotte called to her aunt. 'The oak tree in the valley looks golden in the sun.'

'That'll be the famous Evergreen Oak,' Aunt Clarissa said. 'Seems there is going to be a fairy ball in Fargale tonight.'

This was not the answer Charlotte had hoped for but she suspected it was the best she was going to get. She decided she would Google 'weather phenomena' later for a more satisfying explanation.

'I thought the Fey lived in the Dreamtime?' Charlotte asked her aunt.

Clarissa gave her a strange look and Charlotte realised what she had said was clearly not common knowledge. Her aunt did not challenge her though and carried on as if they were having a normal conversation about the weather.

'Sometimes they come home,' Clarissa responded matter-of-factly and returned to her gardening. 'In answer to your question, no, it doesn't happen often. In fact, the last time was when that picture in your room was painted.'

'How long ago was that?'

'You don't need me to tell you that now, do you?' Clarissa smiled one of her knowing smiles.

Charlotte gazed at the tree again. The golden haze was gone but she couldn't shake the feeling that it was happening now for a reason. Maybe the tree was trying to tell her something? Or Edessa?

Charlotte suddenly had an unnerving feeling they were being watched. A flash amongst the raspberry canes, like light on metal, followed by a fizzing sound took Charlotte by surprise. *I've had too much sun,* she thought to herself as she saw the shimmering outline of a tiny human figure for a split second before it popped out of sight.

'You don't happen to have CDs amongst those, do you?' she asked her aunt.

'No need, the birds know full well which ones they are allowed to eat.'

There was a certain logic to that, Charlotte guessed, though she wondered, not for the first time, if Clarissa was just winding her up.

'So what would happen if a human went along to one of these balls?' Charlotte asked, trying to distract herself from what she had seen.

'You would have to find it first.'

'But let's say I did? I do come from a family of explorers after all.'

Clarissa smiled as if to say she doubted it, but humoured her anyway.

'Fairies don't take kindly to human gatecrashers.'

'I could wear a disguise?'

Clarissa laughed at this. 'A false pair of wings and pointy ears do not a fairy make. They would smell you out in a heartbeat.'

Charlotte said nothing, but was still planning an expedition to the tree and busily devising ways she could pass herself off as a fairy, the flash and ghostly image forgotten.


'There's a vegetable stew bubbling away nicely on the Aga, should be ready soon,' Jude said cheerily, as Charlotte strolled into the living room. 'I'm just taking a moment to do my breathing exercises, helps me with my asthma.'

Jude reached two palm-sized clear crystals out of her oversized handbag. 'Gives it a little boost.' She smiled before settling down in front of Clarissa's meditation altar and started taking deep, noisy breaths.

Charlotte dropped into the plump sofa, propping a sari silk cushion under her head. Cicero landed lightly on her chest and pawed her nose looking for attention.

'More novelty factor,' she whispered to the cat but he was totally absorbed in directing Charlotte's hand to just the right place behind his ear to scratch.

A copy of the *Wykenhall Free Press* lay on the coffee table with the headline 'SAVE OUR PARK' and an image of the same tree on the hill – though it wasn't glowing.

Charlotte read the article about a proposal for a new housing and industrial estate to be built where Brackenheath Park currently stood. The new site would include facilities such as a cinema, restaurants and bowling alley as well as new housing and community facilities.

*Mr Julian Ransell, teacher at Wykenhall High School and resident, is in favour of the proposed development, saying it will be a boon for locals as well as improving the local economy and attracting tourism.*

The article finished with a further picture of a bony, hook-nosed man with cold eyes smirking at the camera, his dark hair greased to one side of his head. Below was the mention of a public meeting about the proposed development as well as an online petition, encouraging people to sign it. Charlotte tossed the paper onto the coffee table.

'This place could do with some livening up, Cicero,' Charlotte whispered, smiling as the cat simply yawned and curled into a ball on her chest.

There was no contest, a run-down old park or an array of fun facilities, but she couldn't help wondering if the oak would escape such development. If it was as famous as Etienne said, it would be preserved, surely? Doubt gnawed at her and there was one person she trusted over anyone. Edessa had told her she needed to protect the tree, that something bad was coming. Was this it? Charlotte's instincts told her it wasn't that simple – but it was a place to start. 'It begins and ends with the tree,' she whispered to herself.

Charlotte was dozing off when Cicero pressed himself tightly against her and mewed, staring intently into thin air. She heard the same fizzing noise she had heard in the garden and saw a shimmering outline forming at the other end of the room.

A translucent figure appeared and started to slowly make its way across the room. It was a boy about three or four years older than herself with light green skin, wild blond hair scraped roughly into a ponytail and swirling patterns on his arms and face. His nose was his most striking feature, elongated and wider than her own, while his ears were slightly pointed underneath his hair. But it was his eyes that Charlotte was drawn too most, piercing and brooding – and they were looking straight through her.

He was not like the silhouette she had seen in the garden or at the train station, she was sure. For a start he was much bigger. Could this be one of the Fey? He seemed more like a ghost.

The boy was focused on something in the corner by the television, completely oblivious of Charlotte and Jude. Soon, he began striding purposefully through the furniture, stopping about a foot from Jude's shoulder. He slowly raised a spear to the side of his head before, quick as lightning, he launched it through the air. Charlotte watched as it disappeared through the wall. The boy darted after it before fading behind the TV.

Suddenly, Jude let out a loud moan and a flash of light burst out of each of her palms. Cicero dug his claws into Charlotte's chest in alarm before shooting across the coffee table, sending Jude's bag flying.

Makeup, a tub of dental floss, crystals, corn pads and glass vials of flower remedies spilled across the pale rugs and Charlotte watched as a tin of pink blusher rolled across the wooden floor at speed before colliding with the skirting board and exploding in a puff of pink powder. Crystals bounced on the wooden floor and still more stuff poured out of the bag: a wind chime, dowsing rods, mala beads, keys, phone, a virtual avalanche of postcards and pictures, incense sticks and finally, a copy of *The Little Book of Calm*.

A bottle of tonic had smashed on landing and spilt over some of the pictures which Charlotte noticed seemed to be of a young man in army uniform, his nose sunburnt as he stood in various desert locations smiling, thumbs up at the camera. This must be Adam.

'Oooh, my pictures!' Jude howled as she hurriedly swept all her belongs into a single pile of clutter. She wiped the pictures dry but the liquid had already started to do its work and they were beginning to blister. Charlotte looked on helplessly as the older woman howled and blubbed.

'Haven't you got other pictures at home?' she offered weakly, trying to comfort Jude, but it just made her howl even more.

'My word, what is going on here?' Aunt Clarissa announced from the main door. 'Jude, dear, what's wrong?' Jude was so beside herself she couldn't speak and just offered the pictures as explanation.

'Now now, dear, we can fix these, don't fret. You sit here and I'll sort those out in a jiffy, what a terrible fuss.' Jude sniffed and blew her nose loudly. 'Let me get you a cup of tea,' Clarissa added before heading to the kitchen.

'Your aunt is unbelievably kind, you know.' Jude dabbed her eyes, smearing her heavy kohl. 'You really couldn't ask for a better guardian to look after you while your parents are finding their way home.'

The comment was like an electric current down Charlotte's spine.

'You think they might still be out there somewhere?' she said quietly.

'I think you always know when someone close to you is gone, sweetheart. What does your heart tell you?'

Charlotte didn't know what to say that wouldn't sound harsh or cruel but she wasn't so sure she believed that. She had no idea where her parents were or what had happened to them. She couldn't help thinking she was responsible. Besides, Jude didn't seem to be able to accept the death of her son. Did she think he was out there somewhere?

Jude was smiling gently at her through her tears.

'I'm not a fool, Charlotte darling. I know he is not coming back but this is my way of coping, of keeping him close.' Jude held Charlotte's hands in her own.

'What about my sister, you think she'll get better?'

'It's happened plenty of times before, don't give up on her.'

'I would never…'

'I didn't mean it like that… I just meant, it might take a while.' Jude smiled. They both sat for a while saying nothing.

Aunt Clarissa broke the silence with tea and steaming bowls of stew.

'I'm so sorry, but I think your rugs have been stained,' Jude said sheepishly, pointing to patches of powder and brown goo.

'I'm sure it'll come out, don't worry your head.' Clarissa handed her the photographs.

'Oh my, they're as good as new, I don't know how you do it.'

'Must be magic.' Clarissa winked.

# Fargale

'What on earth did you think you were doing, Luned?' Malik roared, thumping his desk with such force, puffs of soil fell from the ceiling. Luned tried not to flinch at the reminder that she was deep, deep under the Brackenheath oak, home to the Fey town of Fargale.

'I'm an Undine, my instincts are rarely wrong, Sir.'

'And you think that is sufficient evidence to stage an unauthorised covert op amongst the raspberry canes? A whim?'

'With respect, Sir, it's my job to protect Fargale…'

'From a nitwit human child?'

'She was able to see the Weblight, Sir. She also seemed to know an awful lot about the Fey Nation for a mere human child and I heard her discussing gatecrashing the spring ball with her aunt.'

'Clarissa was hardly about to tell her anything, Luned,' Malik scoffed, 'but now she's seen Sylurians floating across her living room she's even more likely to go sticking her nose into matters that don't concern her.'

'Her family is not her concern? I hardly think she'd see it that way, Sir. Besides, don't you think that maybe part of the reason the Nymet is sick is due to the punishment we dealt out on one of her own? Readings suggest things were knocked out of balance…'

'Remember who you're talking to, Luned,' Malik growled. 'It's our job to keep the Verses in their rightful places, something that is becoming increasingly difficult with the Dreamtime withering around us. It's just not natural for them to be blending into each other willy-nilly. And may I remind you, letting humans meddle in

Fey affairs never ends well, even if they are descendants of the Golden Root – I need not remind you of the "Tinkerbel Scandal". I should post you to tap root duties for this. Your actions were simply reckless, do you hear me?'

Malik rose to his feet and waddled across his office, dipping into various files that lay about the room. Eventually it was clear he had found the one he was looking for and he handed it to Luned with a malicious flourish.

'Well, as you are so curious, she is now your responsibility.' Malik waved away her objections. 'Your primary job now,' he emphasised each word with a vicious jab from a podgy finger to her shoulder, 'is to ensure she doesn't cause any trouble.'

Luned sighed as Malik indicated he was done with her. Given the choice she would probably have gone with tap root duties. Her first day in Fargale was not going well.

The town of Fargale didn't compare in looks to the dazzling city of Agrimony, capital of the Fey Nation where she was born, but it was special. Fargale was the gateway between the three Verses. Not only was the place legendary, it was neither entirely underground nor in the Dreamtime. She really didn't want to lose this post or the chance to live in the sun.

Back in her own office in the higher, flimsier branches of the oak tree, she took a deep breath of sweet dawn air and shuffled some of the case files on her desk. She had been posted to 'Operation Sugar Plum' and had a busy day ahead of her issuing eviction notices among the Lower Branch and Bole districts. She also had to investigate a report of a Neagle infestation by the river crossing as well as issue A.K.O.R.Ns to the Drakes and Pooka for environmental violations.

With the human domination of the traditional territories of the Fey in both Earth and Syluria, tensions had risen between the Fey species. The more their territories dwindled the more they were forced to live in each other's pockets, and certain Fey were not natural neighbours. Now the Dreamtime was withering too, their options were getting more and more limited, and Luned's job was getting harder.

Her afternoon would be taken up by the obligatory induction tour to the 'Hanging Gardens of Fargale', as the root system was known, where she would have to learn how to monitor the water levels and general health of the oak. She was not relishing being underground again but there was no getting out of it. At least she had the night shift to look forward to where she would be joining the 'Standstormers' unit (code name: Blue Fairy), facilitating 'dream adjustment' on the local human population. She certainly couldn't say her work wasn't varied.

The last thing Luned needed was more work but she couldn't stop thinking about the girl living on the cliff. Luned couldn't shake the feeling this human was going to have a huge, and not necessarily pleasant, impact on Fargale.

A dandiclock in the corner of the room released six puffs of downy seed – her instincts were going to have to wait. Luned picked up the files and a pocket version of the P.O.D charter before tucking a NETEL stun gun into her belt and heading for the river to interrogate a few trolls.

Water dripped in fat splodges from the formal avenue of sycamores that lined the main path through Brackenheath Park, and steam rose from the meadow beyond as the sun warmed the air. Charlotte wasn't a fan of wet weather, she took after her dad in that respect, and it seemed to rain a lot here. But she adored the freshness of the air after a storm, as well as the smell of green.

She was also grateful to be away from the adults too and being outside helped her to work through recent events with a sharp mind. Jude was a regular visitor, and while Charlotte knew she meant well trying to counsel her over recent tragedies the fact was

Charlotte just wasn't ready for sharing, not yet. Most of their conversations only ended up with Jude telling her another story about her dead son Adam anyway.

Clarissa still puzzled her too. She loved the fact she was so laid back and open, but she had an air of otherworldliness that was quite unsettling. Charlotte often expected her to appear on the living room carpet in a puff of smoke like a genie from a bottle. Clarissa was everywhere in Rosemary Heights, even in the oldest parts of the house. So was Charlotte's mother – another reason why she had to get outside.

In the valley ahead, Charlotte could see a couple of boys about her age, one with a wild shock of blond hair, the other a well-built bruiser, enthusiastically kicking a ball between themselves. *New classmates,* she guessed looking for an escape route. Not only was she not ready to disclose her pain and guilt to an elderly woman with a pink and orange Mohican but she was in no mood to try and awkwardly build friendships from thin air, football or not. Besides, she needed to focus.

Above the bank to her left, she could see another footpath meandering away from the main open space of the park through a thicket of bushes and on to a small copse, which promised a bit of privacy. There was a cluster of beech trees perched at the top of the bank and their thick roots, further exposed by the rain, cascaded down the bank in intricate knots forming a strange staircase over the soft, water-sodden soil. Tugging on a drooping branch, Charlotte hoisted herself onto the nearest stout root and began to climb. The wood was slippery underfoot and she would need to be careful not to twist an ankle but she had done far more adventurous and dangerous climbs than this before now, so she made quick progress. She heard the chatter of the boys pass beneath her just as she ducked into the first bush.

The air was cooler among the trees and the silence hung thickly in the gloom. Charlotte breathed deeply, relishing the complex mix of aromas. Above her, the sky darkened and a peal of thunder rumbled in the clouds. From the relative dryness of the wood, and still able to see over the fields and meadows of Brackenheath-on-Sea, Charlotte watched the tell-tale vertical streaks on the horizon, beautiful in the ruby sunset, that showed the rain drifting her way. It was mesmerising.

The vision was as vivid as ever, lurking in the recesses of her unconsciousness and waiting to pounce the minute she closed her eyes, replaying over and over again. At the base of a huge tree a rose bush glowed, releasing the most beautiful fragrance she had ever smelt. Then, in an instance, the rose bush withered and died before her vision went black and she heard that blood-curdling scream – the scream she was never ready for.

The blackness was like a portal to another world.

'If only,' Charlotte muttered bitterly to herself. Where would she go? Back to her old life? No, that was gone and there was only one way to get it back. What she wouldn't do to find her parents, and she tried to imagine where they might be right this very minute.

'Penny for 'em.'

Charlotte spun round, almost slipping in the wet leaves. She was half expecting to see the man with the top hat and gloves; instead there were only trees.

'Down 'ere, human.'

Charlotte was startled to see a rather furry man, only slightly taller than her knees, grinning up at her. He had a bushy beard and wild, bedraggled hair matted with all sorts of vegetation. He was wearing an old Hovis bread bag with holes poked out for his arms and head which was secured with a belt of plaited strawberry shoelaces. His huge feet had long toes that seemed to have a mind of their own, digging around in the dirt. *Perhaps it is the stress of everything that's happened recently*, she thought; what else could explain the fact that she seemed to be hallucinating.

'You going to say anything then?' the man persisted.

Hallucinations didn't talk, did they?

'Er... Hello?' she said, not quite sure what she was speaking to. It crossed her mind that Clarissa was pulling some sort of trick.

'Salutations to you, human fairy, I, am Boris.' The little man bowed with much aplomb.

'Hi, I... I'm Charlotte,' Charlotte offered feebly.

'You's wondering what I am?'

'Actually, I'm wondering if I'm going bonkers,' Charlotte replied.

The fairy chuckled. 'I'ms here alright. Is wood folk, Veshengo. We wood folk are an unassuming and noble folk and would live in peace and harmony with all the creatures of the trees. We protect that which you humans often abandon.'

'I... I'm sorry...'

'Perfectly alright. We actually prefer it that way, not your job anyways and you lot do make a lot of chatter.' The Veshengo eyed her up and down approvingly. 'I'm liking you though, Miss Charlotte.' He nodded.

Charlotte, who was still trying to take in the man's strange appearance, didn't know how to respond to such a speech so she felt it was safer to say nothing.

'You are a lady of few words, unlike the most of your sort, and you...' Boris lowered his voice to a whisper, '... you live in the house on the cliff?'

'How do you know?'

'Someone has been awaiting you, Miss Charlotte. I've been sent to collect you.'

Charlotte was taken aback. Was that a good thing or not? She felt slightly uneasy but her sense of adventure won out. The Veshengo smiled as if he knew what was going on in her head.

'Follow me, it's not far,' he announced, and before Charlotte could say anything, he shot off into the undergrowth.

'Wait!' Charlotte called dipping into the bushes and following him as best she could. 'I'm not as little as you.'

'Nice,' said Boris appearing in a branch by her ear. 'You discriminating on my size?' He looked at her with daggers.

'No, I just mean I can't follow you into all the little nooks and crannies.'

'Well, we simply can't stick to the paths, won't do, just won't do! Look... just do the best you can.' He patted her on the head like she was a defenceless baby and winked before disappearing. 'Follow my voice!' he shouted from a patch of brambles before breaking into a raucous song about nubile young sylphs.

Charlotte lost track of how long they played his strange game of cat and mouse but her cargo trousers were soon soaked through, with a few rips and stains, before Boris finally stopped.

'Here we are then.'

'Where?'

'Dunno.'

'We're lost? But you're a Veshengo.'

'Yes!' said the little man. 'That's what we're good at.'

'Well, now I've heard it all, aren't you supposed to know where you are in a wood?'

'Listen, human, you can't be findings the heart of the forest till you're good and lost... thought everyone knew that,' he sniffed. 'Anyways, that's what I brought you to see, right there.' Boris pointed at a tall, sturdy-looking tree.

'It's the Brackenheath Oak!' Charlotte whispered in awe and... was it... shimmering?

'Yous can feel it, I can tell. That shimmer, it's Weblight, from the Dreamtime. This tree is sitting in more than one place at the same time.' Boris was eyeing the tree suspiciously. Clearly this was not normal even in the fairy world.

Charlotte approached the tree slowly; she wasn't sure what she would find but she had the same strange feeling that she had experienced with the crystals at Rosemary Heights, the sensation that she belonged here, in this place. She noticed the air cool around her and it became almost electric with anticipation. Surely she was imagining it?

'Slow walkings, human,' whispered the Veshengo, 'and don't

look directly, blur your vision to truly see,' Boris encouraged her as he bounced along beside her.

She did as she was told, slowing her pace and feeling the ground with her feet. The shimmer became stronger as pin pricks of golden dust swirled in the air around the tree's vast trunk. The whole tree appeared luminescent and Charlotte had to shield her eyes. She stopped about a foot from the trunk, pausing for a moment before reaching out to touch the rough bark. She was a little disappointed that it felt just like any other oak tree.

'Hold, hold,' Boris encouraged her again as he backed further away from the tree.

He seemed nervous to be there which didn't instil Charlotte with confidence but she somehow knew she had to do this. Maybe the Veshengo could help her connect with Edessa.

'Feel its heartbeat, touch its soul. Has been waiting for you.'

Charlotte placed both hands and her left ear to the tree bole and shut her eyes to listen. She could hear, yes, and feel, the sap flowing through what must, by the size of it, be an ancient tree. Was that singing? Chanting? It was different to what she had heard before; just one voice and so many stories that seemed to stretch out forever. Charlotte turned to ask Boris what it was but the little fairy had disappeared.

The sky had cleared and the final rays of sunlight broke through the wood canopy but Charlotte could hear thunder. She should think about getting home soon but she was determined to contact her sister first.

Suddenly, from nowhere, a streak of neon blue cut through the air and through the trunk of the tree. Everything after that was a mass of confusion as the ground shook and Charlotte felt herself falling into the sticky mud, broken wood ripping through her clothes and flesh. Something cracked her on the head and the world went blank.

It was already getting dark as Luned made her way Underground. Despite being born in a subterranean spring near Agrimony, it always made her feel claustrophobic and she hoped the tour would be over quickly. A ruddy-faced dwarf greeted her with a hearty handshake and a pat to the back that nearly sent her flying.

'Another newbie, heh?' he chortled. 'I'm Davlin, welcome to the "engine room" of Fargale.'

'That's a good, traditional dwarf name. I'm Luned.' She shook the dwarf's hand.

Davlin beamed. 'You must be the Undine from Hazelpool Academy, I've heard good things about you.'

He led her into a huge cave alive with noise and activity. Intricate knots of tree roots hung in bundles from the walls and ceiling; some hung limply while others vibrated and pulsed with colour. Dozens of fairies weaved through the air like they were performing some sort of aerial ballet, plugging the root ends into each other, unplugging others, knitting certain bundles together, taking measurements before recording their findings and placing them into one of the numerous pools of coloured liquid that filled the floor.

'What you are looking at here is the most sophisticated communication centre in the whole of the Fey Nation.' The dwarf beamed proudly. 'Here we have the Willow board and over there is the Ash 'n' Elm exchange. Not just about modern communication mind; Fey seers visit regularly too. They read the roots to determine the fate of families and nations; you'll find them over there by the Norn Interface. Complicated science, that is.'

They weaved through the pools, some steaming and bubbling gently, releasing pleasant aromas, while others were being stirred to prevent them from freezing over. 'The nutripools,' Davlin offered by way of explanation and without slowing his pace.

'This is the *pièce de résistance!*' he announced excitedly, coming to an abrupt stop outside a heavy door.

Silence folded round Luned like a balm after the buzz of the cave as they entered the Tap Room. The air was heavy with the sweet smell of healthy soil, though a bitterness hung ghostly underneath. In the centre of the room the tap root pulsed with a soft green-blue glow.

'That's the sap rising,' Davlin whispered reverently. 'Though between you and me it's not been flowing as well as it should for the time of year... of course it'll be nothing for you to worry about, just seasonal change.' The dwarf checked himself, clearly worried that he had revealed too much.

Despite the tons of earth above her head and the weakness of the pulse, Luned, who had been feeling somewhat nauseous, felt better to be in the presence of water.

'It's so beautiful,' Luned murmured, mesmerised by the patterns that flowed in the sap stream.

'It can be a real show for sure,' Davlin nodded. 'When you know what you're looking at, you can decipher their meanings. These here show she's sensing a storm coming.'

At that moment the walls of the tap room vibrated, causing a light fall of soil from the ceiling.

'What was that?' Luned was suddenly very aware of the rock and stone above her. Before Davlin had a chance to answer, there was a second, more violent quake and they were both dragged into the sap stream.

Being an Undine, the ride was easier for Luned as she melted into the flow, but even she was glad it was mercifully short – the poor dwarf had not faired as well. Davlin was covered in gashes and bruises and his left arm was now at a sickeningly unnatural angle.

'What in *K'hul* just happened?' Luned gasped as they emerged into fresh air.

'F... Fargale... screaming,' Davlin gurgled in pain. A medic appeared at his side and called urgently to a colleague before they whisked him off on a stretcher.

Shell-shocked, Luned tried to make sense of the scene of

chaos around her. The air had been fried and was filled with arid smoke, ozone and the moans of the injured residents of Fargale – the lucky ones. It took a while to register what had happened. Black, cracked charcoal replaced healthy bark and soot covered everything. The central trunk was a sickening mass of split and twisted wood and there were pockets of fire everywhere. Something had ripped the heart out of Fargale, and the very same sap Luned had been part of moments ago was evaporating in the heat that still sat in the wood.

From her vantage point in the upper branches, Luned could see something large lying at the foot of the tree. In the fussiness of her head it took some time to realise she recognised the shape, that she had seen it before – it was the human girl who lived on the cliff. This would need to be added to the file.

As Charlotte came to, pain flooded her senses. She ached everywhere and could feel something – she didn't know if it was blood or water – trickling down her chin. Mist swirled across the ground and leaf mould crackled loudly in the silence as she moved. Tentatively, she stretched her neck. Not broken, that was a good start; clearly the spinal cord wasn't severed as testified by the pain but Charlotte had to suppress the urge to vomit when she caught sight of her hand.

'It's not as bad as it looks,' a voice said behind her. 'I think we can remove the wood easily enough.'

Charlotte vaguely remembered before she had been knocked out cold, a stabbing pain in her right hand. One of the tree's thick roots was frayed and a section of it was plunged into her flesh.

'It hasn't damaged the muscle too much and, more importantly, it has managed to avoid any veins or arteries.'

'That's alright then,' Charlotte said with feeble sarcasm; she was feeling very faint.

'You have been very lucky, Charlotte of Stone. Drink this.'

Charlotte finally saw the woman; she was young and slim with almost deathly pale skin. She shared Charlotte's own red hair and piercing green eyes but it was her clothes that were most striking purple silks and green robes in Roman style finished with a mantle of gold encrusted with precious jewels over which she wore a feathered robe as black as night. A black bird swooped through the trees to land on her shoulder.

'Caroc has alerted your kin, they will be here soon; now do as I tell you and drink. Do not put my hard work to waste.' There was an authority in the stranger's voice that could not be argued with.

The potion was warm and sweet and took effect immediately. To her right a disturbing sucking noise told her the woman was removing the jagged, torn root but surprisingly there was no pain. The woman chanted under her breath as she worked and with a few hand gestures a floating ball of light appeared in front of her. The ball glowed eerily in the moonlight and seemed to be awaiting her command. A moment later it sunk into the hole in Charlotte's hand, knitting together broken skin and bone.

'Just like new.' The woman smiled as she reached into the heart of the still-smouldering tree and pulled out some dark soot. 'This tree has been lightning struck, and so have you, little one.' She sprinkled the soot into Charlotte's skin. 'You are now bound to each other.'

The lady urged Charlotte to sit up and she found, to her surprise, that all the pain in her body had gone.

'I anoint you as a warrior of the order of the Nymet Draoi. You now bear the Mother's Kiss.'

For the first time Charlotte noticed the spidery burn marks on her arm that strangely resembled a tree. Where the soot had touched her skin the marks pulsed as if the lightning was still flowing through her.

'What does all this mean?' Charlotte muttered through her shock. 'What if I don't want to be a…'

'It is done, destiny has chosen you and there is no denying her touch.' The woman took Charlotte's chin and looked into her eyes with such intensity, any argument Charlotte had formed in her head was forgotten.

'We have but a very short time left, so listen well, Charlotte of Stone. It is as much a mystery to me that wood should choose fire and stone but it is so and a gateway has been opened for you. It is your role from this moment to protect this tree.' The woman waved at the oak which, in spite of the large hollow in its heart, still stood strong, shimmering even more in the dark.

'In this state, it will have many enemies,' the woman went on, 'but it must not fall or we are all doomed.'

Suddenly from the undergrowth Cicero launched himself onto Charlotte's chest and let out a plaintive howl before reverting to his usual gurgling purr as he started kneading Charlotte happily.

The woman stood and gathered her robes around her. 'I am done here. Tell Lady Aherne, The Morrigan will be seeing her soon,' she said before fading into the trees.

Lights bobbed below Charlotte. Aunt Clarissa and the local police officer, PC Taylor, came into view, worry etched on both their faces.

'I'm here,' Charlotte waved to them. 'I'm… I'm alright,' she shouted down to them, not quite able to believe it herself. Aunt Clarissa marched up the bank in half the time that many of her age would normally manage.

'Oh, Charlotte, we were all so worried about you.' She took Charlotte's face in her hands and went to kiss her forehead when she noticed the soot. She gave Charlotte a quizzical look.

'I've just met Mrs Morrigan, she healed me; and she sends you her regards.'

Clarissa blanched. It was the first time Charlotte had seen her afraid. In fact, she had never seen Clarissa even slightly panicked and she would have bet on it not being possible if she hadn't seen her now.

'*The* Morrigan,' Clarissa corrected, 'and she never gives without taking. What did she look like?'

Charlotte thought this an odd question. The woman had obviously known Clarissa.

'Well, surely you know?'

'She has different guises.' Clarissa was impatient now.

'Well, I… she was… youngish.'

'Charlotte. This is important, girl. You must tell me exactly what she looked like.' Clarissa reminded her of Madame Cortes with the steel in her eyes.

'Long red hair, pale skin, sort of… well, a crazy look in her eyes… and she had a bird on her shoulder.'

'A raven?'

Charlotte considered this for a moment, comparing the bird to those she had seen on her visits to the Tower of London.

'Could be, yes, I think it was.'

'Battle ready,' Aunt Clarissa whispered.

Charlotte just about caught those odd last words and wondered if she had misheard.

'Time to batten down the hatches, my dear, trouble's coming to Brackenheath.'

# Children of the Nymet

The tempeta had been a real bone-shaker; there hadn't been a storm like it in living memory, and Tar'sel hadn't had a single moment's sleep. The sap flow of his family tree, Ashter, had been erratic all night; she had been so scared and he had been chanting to her till day-break to try and calm her. As light rose he tuned into her song, mending any broken branches by adjusting their discordant notes. Ashter was singing happily by the time Tar'sel prepared to join the other weavers to check the land for any trees, plants or wildlife in need of care.

Tar'sel's quadrant was the forest edge bordering the Nellpa river delta. He grabbed his pack and a breakfast of stuffed oarweed before heading out across the main communal grove. It should have been market day with the usual brightly painted barrows and knitted throws on which the sellers displayed their wares but today there was simply a large crowd, no doubt assessing the damage, and a torrent of undistinguished chatter filled the air.

Mercifully, there did not appear to be any trees down so no one would be homeless tonight, but the atmosphere was tense. More than one would expect for a mere storm, however rough. The air was silent of the usual morning chores. No children practising their toning sounds, or farmers singing the fields of blue rice and lotus grain into fruition.

'Tar'sel, there you are, your father is looking for you.' Tar'sel's friend Mor'seka broke away from the crowd and strode towards him.

'But I've got to get to the delta.'

Mor'seka shook his head. 'The delta will have to wait, Tay'mor has ordered you to the Nymet.'

Tar'sel blanched. Something was seriously wrong; even as the son of the current guardian of the Nymet he would never be permitted to enter such a holy place in normal circumstances.

The position of Nymet guardian was an elected post and while it had been held by a number of the Aderquaile family line, Tar'sel never thought for a moment he could ever fill his father's shoes. Now here he was, being summoned by the Nymet Draoi and the sense of responsibility to make his father proud and protect the honour of their family name sat heavy on his shoulders.

'Tar'sel, did you hear me? You have to go, now.' Mor'seka roused him from the sense of shock that had frozen him to the spot.

'Do you have any idea what I'm walking into?' Tar'sel asked. Mor'seka was usually the first person in the Barra to know the latest news or gossip so if anyone knew what was going on it would be him.

Mor'seka shook his head. 'The elders haven't said a thing, don't want to cause panic I guess,' he shrugged. 'But there is a rumour going around that the Great Tree has been struck,' he finished solemnly.

'Thank you,' Tar'sel called as he ran as fast as he could to the Nymet. If what Mor'seka said was true it would explain why he had been summoned; his father was going to need all the weavers he could muster.

There was nothing obvious when Tar'sel arrived at the sacred grove. No charring and no smoke; perhaps it wasn't as bad as Mor'seka had heard. Then he heard it: the silence. There was no singing, no morning rites.

The Nymet sat atop a hillock to the north of the main grove. A circle of willow and hazel trees had been planted many generations ago and woven into intricate knot work creating the effect of a giant tree over fifteen metres wide and now, as it had grown over the years, over thirty metres tall. The knot work had been studded with jewels, agate slices and granite rings, designed to provide privacy while also letting in light to nurture the precious life form inside.

The sacred tree of life, the Nymet tree, was no ordinary oak. Evergreen and ancient, it held the memories of the before and after, it nourished the land and the people that belonged to it. The Nymet held the very soul of the forest. What would they do without it? What if there was no replacement? What if the Nymet tree was dead?

*Snap out of it,* he chided himself. *You are here to heal and you can't do that with such negative thoughts in your head.*

Tar'sel had never been so close; most of the community only came to the base of the hill, and he was not sure where to enter. A cold wind swept through the grasses as he made his way up the hill on a winding path.

Above him, light glowed through the gaps in the living willow and hazel screen and at the top of the hill a golden dust floated in front of him before settling on the ground. The dust swirled and danced unnaturally and Tar'sel fought to control a fear that was building in his gut. Hand on his blade, he tried to ignore the internal voice of wisdom which told him such things would be useless against spirits.

The dust formed the shape of a girl, perhaps a year or so younger than him, lying asleep or unconscious, Tar'sel could not tell which, and he bent down to take a closer look. Such strange clothing with unusual markings; he had never seen anything like it. He was drawn to her right hand that seemed to be impaled on something, he winced at the sight, but it was when he noticed the girl's face that a cold twist knotted in his chest; she was the girl of his vision. There was no colour in this dust, but she had the same nose, same eyebrows, same hair – unmistakeable. Just as he was processing what he was seeing, the dust swirled again before settling into another form.

'Lady Morrigan,' he gasped at the sight of the woman in her rich robes and jewelled mantle before turning his face away from her. It did not do well to stare at one of the Shriven.

'Tar'sel, son of the Manush de Rukh, hear me,' the woman announced. 'I have a task for you.'

Tar'sel bowed but said nothing.

'I charge you with the duty to protect this crystal child. She comes to save your world, and my sister.'

Tar'sel risked looking directly at the lady; she needed to see his eyes as he swore to this oath.

'As is your wish my lady, so will I obey.'

'Davlin of Fargale has been ordered to grant you passage through the Albion Gateway, when you are ready of course.'

'I am to journey to Albion?' Tar'sel was shocked.

Crossing the Dreamtime was not, strictly speaking, allowed and Anya, Mor'seka and himself could get into a lot of trouble for their stunt at the Nabinder festival. Yet now he was being granted full permission by a member of the Shriven to visit the mystical land of Albion. Visions of the many legends his father had told him throughout his childhood flashed across his mind.

'When necessary,' The Morrigan nodded. 'I have noticed your weaver skills are coming on well, they may be useful in time. This is a privilege extended only to you and not to be abused.'

Her eyes flashed a warning and Tar'sel wondered if she knew.

'The fate of the Triverse is in your hands.'

Tar'sel bowed again. '*Gestina*. Thank you. I won't let you down.'

Clearly pleased, the lady, and the dust, disappeared on the breeze. Suddenly, a willow weave screen was lifted aside to reveal his father, Tay'mor.

'We have been waiting, Son.' The tone was grave but not accusatory.

'I came as quickly as I could, Father,' Tar'sel said, touching his forehead and chest in the traditional greeting of his people. 'How may I serve the Sleeping Mother?'

Tay'mor motioned his son to enter before speaking.

'You will have heard rumours?' Tar'sel nodded. 'Well, they are not quite true,' his father replied. 'The Great Tree has not been lightning struck, but it was close. The Draoi were somehow able to deflect the bolt.'

The female priestesses, in their usual green robes, root-like dreadlocks and the distinctive Nymet tattoo on their foreheads, stood around the oak's trunk, hands to bark, chanting in low, soft voices. Tar'sel noticed another woman with the same mark and robes lying still on a board to the left of the entrance. She couldn't have been more than twenty; and her eyes were closed.

'She died in service to the Sleeping Mother,' Tay'mor whispered. 'No one is sure exactly what happened, it was so quick, but it is thought that she drew the lightning into herself.' Tar'sel's eyes were drawn to a charred area of earth next to the Great Tree.

'I have called you here because the others need time to bury their sister, Tar'sel, their hearts are too heavy to heal.'

'I am to work alone?' Tar'sel was full of fear. How could he be given such a burden?

'We will work together, Son, you are the only uninitiated the elders would allow to enter here.'

'Because I'm your son?'

'Partly, but also because you are the best weaver in the Barra.' Tay'mor sighed. 'There are things I must tell you and you must swear not to divulge these to anyone… not even Mor'seka.'

'I am to be initiated?' Tar'sel gasped.

'You are; and once you bear the Mother's kiss you will be bound to her song.' Tay'mor pointed to the mark on his own forehead to emphasise his point. 'But first, we have work. As guardians, it is our responsibility to ensure that the song does not die out.'

The Draoi had given no indication that they were aware of their presence but at these last words they silently filed round the tree before picking up the dead woman and leaving the temple.

Tar'sel took a deep breath to calm himself, and approached the tree. It was so wide that they would not have been able to reach round and join hands. The bark was rough and split, the bole bulged and undulated in places, and it was in leaf. He paused for a moment, unable to believe he was this close to the Great Tree let alone about to touch it, before he lay both hands on the trunk.

At once he felt something was wrong and looked again at the leaves; speckled with brown many were folded in on themselves and wrinkling at the edges. The sap flow was barely detectable; there was no doubt the Great Tree was dying and not from a bolt of lightning. This was Naswalemos, a powerful illness, and it had taken root some time ago.

'You feel it don't you, Son?' Tay'mor searched his son's face for his reaction to the illness.

Tar'sel nodded. 'What is it exactly?'

'No one knows, it crept upon her slowly, but it has been noticeable since the time of the weeping moons.'

The weeping moons was the one night of the year when the twin moons of Sorcha and Kyrene came close enough to the Earth's atmosphere that a strange phenomenon occurred; the moons would shed their own weak atmospheres of red cloud and appear to be weeping overhead. It marked the beginning of the feast of Nabinder – the feast where he had had his vision. Tar'sel tried not to let the shock show on his face; he realised he still hadn't told his father.

Turning his attention to the issue in hand for the moment, he started with the simple job of a broken branch to build his confidence. Tar'sel cleared his head as he had been taught, and allowed the silence to flood his mind. He listened intently as the note of creation began to hum through him, vibrating every atom of his being, and waited for the song of the Nymet tree to rise through it. It took so long Tar'sel worried that she would not talk to him but eventually, there it was, low and shy.

He knew better than to chase the sound and let it build at its own pace, gradually painting a sonic picture of the physical tree. He heard it almost immediately when the song had finished its first cycle; the off-key note jarred with the rest. Tar'sel hit a pure D with his own voice and began to knit it into the song, slowly, gently pulling the broken sound back into key.

As he brought the song back into balance he felt the strength return and the energy flow. The song grew louder and more powerful. He could feel the, now perfect, note pushing him away. From a distance, he could see her entire song, stretching through eons of time, her dance through the ages, her emotions, her experiences. This must be what the Draoi saw.

'That will do for now.' Tay'mor gently shook his son's shoulder. 'You need to rest.'

The sun was dipping into the sea and Tar'sel realised he had been working for a full day, even though it had felt like only an hour at most.

'How…?'

'She will do that to you, Son,' Tay'mor chuckled. 'She is so ancient, her memories so old, she has no measure of our little lives.'

'She has seen this valley when the rest of the forest was just saplings,' Tar'sel sighed.

'Best not to let her mind overtake you, Tar'sel, men have gone mad that way,' Tay'mor warned, 'but yes, she holds the memory of the forest, the blueprint of all things.'

In the silence, Tar'sel realised the Nymet song had subsided. This was the first time he had been alone with his father for months. Now was the time.

'Dad… there's something I need to tell you.'

'Me too, Son, me too.'

Tar'sel recounted his vision at the Nabinder feast as well as his encounter with the Lady Morrigan, fully expecting a telling off. Instead, Tay'mor just nodded sadly.

'That explains a lot and makes what I have to say that bit easier.'

Tay'mor took a deep breath before continuing. 'We have problems greater than the Naswalemos.'

'Greater than that!' Tar'sel blurted out, aware he had just interrupted an elder but unable to stop himself. Again Tay'mor overlooked his disobedience.

'Yes. What if I were to tell you that the forest in which we live no longer exists, and that even the Nymet does not live here in Syluria, but was born in a mystical place called Albion in the universe of Earth?'

Tar'sel was speechless, what his father was suggesting had never been proved; such theories could have him branded as a mad man, yet Tar'sel believed every word. It didn't make it any easier. He could feel every part of his life unravelling inside him. Every plant he had weaved into life, every tree he called a friend... every defining moment of his life was a lie.

'There have been whispers in the leaves that our beloved Nymet is in mortal danger in that realm and we need to find a way through to find a warrior to protect her,' Tay'mor continued.

Letting his head fall and trying to control his emotions, Tay'mor sighed before adding, 'If the memory dies, the forest falls. Without the Nymet, our home will die... and so will we. We are the children of the Nymet after all.'

'What's the point?' Tar'sel replied miserably. 'We are just shadows.'

'Everything has its place, including us.' Tay'mor squeezed his son's shoulders.

Tar'sel had a feeling he knew what was coming next.

'Son, you know most stories are vessels for truth. The flame-haired girl, the saviour of Syluria for example, is real.'

Tar'sel nodded solemnly. 'Yes, I know. And I think I know where to find her.'

# The Galleries

'Why don't you help me deliver these rather than sit there all day,' Aunt Clarissa chided, though she did it with a smile. Charlotte didn't look up from her book on British trees.

'I'm OK thanks, besides, I need to work on my plan to save the Nymet… I haven't got very far. In fact I still need to find out what a "Nymet" is – and I think all this involves my parents somehow.'

'Suit yourself but you know, not all knowledge can be found between the pages of a book. You never know what you might learn from the world around you or some chance encounter and I thought you could get to know the place; now you've decided to stay. You've only ever been to that tree.'

It was true she had only been to the park since moving to Brackenheath; she had been hoping to find her sister Edessa there. However, there had been nothing but the briefest whisper, a shadow in the corner of her eye. All the staff at Belleswater Hospital could tell her was her sister was 'comfortable' whenever she called and Charlotte had to keep reminding herself to be patient. Edessa would find her way to the oak as soon as she was able.

Charlotte surveyed the kitchen table covered in maps of North Africa, glass vials of samples from the oak and piles of books, from tree management and plant diseases to environmental law. There was also the latest copy of the local paper with its front cover story about the lightning strike and the headline 'IS THIS

THE END OF THE BRACKENHEATH OAK?'; she suspected The Morrigan was going to be annoyed about that. Maybe Clarissa was right, she should try to tackle this from a different angle.

Aunt Clarissa had been right of course, it was good to be outside on a day like this. Charlotte wound down the window and felt the rush of the wind on her face as they drove along the tiny country roads. For once she was glad of Clarissa's speedy driving as the cobwebs in her mind blew away. It was certainly gentler than being struck by lightning, if somewhat less dramatic.

Though the countryside was whizzing past, colour was returning to the landscape making it more inviting than the day she had arrived. Edessa would love this place; the light was amazing. The fields were covered in golden rape that seemed to reflect the sun and some of the trees still held blossom, from white through to bright pink. The elderflowers, however, were all but gone now.

'So, what are we going to do then?' she beamed.

'Well, first I need to visit a few of my clients then off to Wykenhall, that is where I sell most of my stock. It's also where you'll be going to school.'

Charlotte's heart fell at that last word, she wasn't looking forward to it one little bit. Hadn't she been through enough already without having the trauma of having to work at fitting in to a new school?

'I'm sorry, have I used a rude word?' Aunt Clarissa said, reading her face. 'I know it's hard but on the plus side you'll meet others of your own age rather than having to hang around with an...' Aunt Clarissa paused, looking as though she was trying to remember something, '... an "old bat" I believe is the term you use.'

Charlotte went red. *How did she know that!?*

'Why can't I continue to home school?' Charlotte started to itch. 'See, I'm allergic just to the idea.'

Clarissa's face told her she was wasting her time.

The Galleries was a beautiful, two-tiered back street complex of Victorian-styled buildings that reminded Charlotte of the boutique shops of Covent Garden. There was a round courtyard with a fountain in the middle, lit underneath the water with green lights. Its pool was surrounded by a low bench and, in the water, silver and bronze coins glittered in the sunlight that refracted through the glass ceiling.

The entrance was a creative twist of gothic-looking black iron archway, complete with the gargoyles that seemed to be popular here. At the far end was a small walled garden full of hanging baskets, and the tiny café tables of Bertichelli's Ice Cream Emporium.

'What say we meet back here in an hour for lunch, dear, and in the meantime you have an explore?'

'Then we'll do some clothes shopping, eh?' Charlotte replied.

'Only if you don't learn everything you need to know to pass your future exams in the next hour, dear,' Clarissa replied with a wicked smile before heading to the upper floor of the Galleries.

*I'm teaching her bad habits*, Charlotte thought to herself as she surveyed her surroundings.

Ahead of her was a shop with such curly, ornate writing she couldn't read the name. In the window, displayed on black velvet, was a geode of purple crystal like the ones in the porch of Rosemary Heights, except they were half the size and not nearly as impressive. 'Amethyst geode – Brazil' read the card and the price tag made Charlotte baulk. 'People are prepared to pay that for a rock?' she muttered to herself.

She was greeted by the same smoky sweet smell that filled Clarissa's home as she walked in. Everywhere there were stones and fossils of all descriptions: blue kyanite shaped like fans, 'candle wax' quartz points and huge dark obsidian crystal balls. She'd never heard of these but, among the tumbled stones, she found something familiar: pieces of malachite and lapis lazuli.

'I'll take these, please,' she said to the bohemian-looking guy behind the counter. He took the crystals from her and wafted them through the clouds of incense coming from the joss stick that was burning beside the till, before lovingly wrapping them in rose-coloured tissue paper.

'Do you know what these are used for?' he asked her. Charlotte stared at him.

'The green one is malachite and was used by the ancient Egyptians in eye makeup and the blue one is lapis, also known as Egyptian sapphire and used in jewellery and temple art,' she replied, amused by his astonishment.

'You know your stones,' he nodded, obviously impressed.

'I know my ancient Egyptian history,' she retorted.

A thought struck her.

'You wouldn't have anything on Veshengo, would you?'

The guy looked blank. 'Not a term I'm familiar with, if you could give me a bit more information...'

Charlotte wasn't about to tell him everything that had happened in the wood; even he would think she was mad. What was it Boris had said? 'How about "men of the woods"?'

'Nature spirits,' the guy grinned, 'sure, plenty of books on those and fairy folk.' He rummaged through a large bookshelf full of titles like *Releasing your Shadowself*, *Atlantis – the people and culture* and *Yogic Breathing for a Modern Age*. Charlotte made a mental note of the last one; Jude might appreciate it.

'Here we are, *The Revised Encyclopaedia of the Fey Folk, and Where to Find Them*,' he announced triumphantly. 'Knew it was in there somewhere. Best book on the subject. If you don't find what you need in this, you won't find it anywhere!'

'Will there be anything in there about The Morrigan?' she asked as an afterthought.

'Some.' The man nodded before tilting his head to look her up and down. 'You've met her, haven't you?' he said with a grin.

Charlotte was so taken aback she didn't have the chance to deny it.

'Tricky character, she is. You want to be careful of her,' he said, handing Charlotte her purchases.

Charlotte didn't normally do pink, yet here she was with a rose-coloured paper bag full of crystals and a book on fairies. Her inner scientist was mortified, but it couldn't deny her encounter with Boris and The Morrigan. She consoled herself with the thought that The Morrigan probably didn't do pink either.

Charlotte wandered aimlessly again, weaving in and out of the arches and up the winding stairwells. There were all manner of interesting stores and Charlotte appreciated the range but she was in no mood to shop. She just wanted to get home and dive into her new book so she decided to perch herself on the nearest bench.

'Sign the petition! Save the Brackenheath Oak from destruction. Thank you, Madam!' called a blond-haired boy in a checked shirt about her age. He was set up in a corner by the double staircase leading to the main car park, a small table with a clipboard and a guitar case in front of him.

'Make sure to add the date of the public debate into your diaries, ladies and gentlemen. And now, for your delight, another little local history ditty penned by yours truly.'

He was a real showman and while not many stood to watch, everyone that went past gave him a nod and smile, as well as a few coins in the case.

*'Evergreen Oak, tell me, do you dream*
*of silver moon and golden stream?*

*Flowering Oak, what secrets lie*
*beneath your roots, hidden from the sky?*

*Oak and Rowan, the song is sung*
*Soon the flame-haired girl will come'*

It was a strange song and Charlotte made a mental note to research it later. She found the singer just as curious; with his soft curls and easy smile that took in everyone around him. He reminded her of Edessa when he sang, with that same far-off look as he became lost in music. This was why she had not wanted to come out; she was confronted by ghosts of her family at every turn.

While he was deep in conversation, Charlotte dropped a coin into the guitar case on the floor and went to make a quick get away.

'Hey you, wait.' The boy turned away from the crowd and beamed in her direction. 'I've not seen you before, you're not the new girl from London, are you?'

Charlotte hadn't expected anyone to know who she was. 'What makes you say that?' was all she could manage.

The boy gave another warm and cheeky grin. 'This is a small town, everyone knows everyone else's business here. If you were an axe murderer with a unicorn fetish we'd probably know.' His smile was welcoming and you couldn't help but like him.

'I'm Olly.'

'Charlotte,' she replied, juggling her bag so as to shake his hand.

'Been shopping, eh? I see you're into the mystic and mysterious?'

'Erm, not so much, no.' Charlotte was now rather self-conscious and embarrassed of the pink bag. 'Just a book on folklore – research,' she lied. 'Actually, I was wondering about that last song of yours, is it a local myth?' Charlotte deflected Olly's attention away from her. He was clearly pleased she had asked and keen to discuss the subject.

'It's a nod to a number of local legends surrounding the Brackenheath Oak. The time it grew acorns in the winter, the rumour that something evil is buried safely bound by its roots and finally, the prophesy that it will be saved by a red-haired girl in a time of danger.' He was really getting into his subject now.

'Dad reckons it is the last remaining tree of a local system of

Nymets, that's a sacred grove to you and me; you might have heard about it, it was struck by lightning the other night.'

Charlotte mumbled about having a vague idea.

'They're looking at building on that whole area so this lightning strike will no doubt be a golden opportunity for them to...'

'Morning, Mr Batterbee, not protesting again are you?' Charlotte recognised the police officer as the one who had found her in the park.

'Bringing sunshine to people's lives, that's all I'm doing, PC Taylor.'

'Just make sure you keep it light, Son. Like the new song by the way.' The officer smiled amicably.

'I'd better go,' Charlotte said.

'You go easy and try to avoid any more excitement, eh?' The policeman gave her a knowing wink.

'Good to meet you, see you at school, Charlotte,' Olly smiled before entering into debate with PC Taylor.

Charlotte waved before leaving them to it and making her way down to the ground floor.

She hadn't got far before tripping over a piece of paper lying on the floor. It was a handwritten note that read 'Homeless, please help'. Sat beside one of the plastic ficuses that adorned the Galleries sat a strange, wrinkled old man who looked familiar. It wasn't till she noticed the Hovis bag that she realised who it was.

'Boris!'

The bedraggled creature squealed in surprise.

'Hello again, human fairy.'

'What are you doing here?'

'This is where I's live. I'm a victim of circumstance see. I've no plant to call my own and all fairy folks are in need of a plant of their own, see. There's not many as can see me, they just sees my sign.' He pointed to the crumpled-up paper Charlotte was holding.

Charlotte looked around to make sure there was no one to overhear her talking to herself.

89

'Sorry about that, I didn't do it on purpose. I thought you lived in the woods?'

'I should do. It's a funny story really. Some sort of mix up in the paperwork at the Fargale Offices and I gets given this here plastic monstrosity.'

'Can't you appeal?'

'Can't!' His tone had turned rather sour. 'I's havin' to wait for them at the offices to sort out the problem but in the meantime I's stuck with this...' He kicked the plastic ficus plant so that the fake leaves rustled, '... this thing; and I's can't makes a livin' from somefin' as is dead.' He shook his little fist at her enthusiastically.

It certainly looked real, Charlotte could see how a mistake could have been made.

'You're not still spouting that rubbish are you, Boris!'

Charlotte jumped at Aunt Clarissa's voice in her ear. She looked at her in wonder; she had always thought adults couldn't see fairies.

'Don't believe a word of it,' Aunt Clarissa continued. 'His plant is dead. We spent ages trying to nurse it back to health before we realised Boris wasn't doing his job properly; he's why they had to introduce plastic plants in the first place.' She glowered at the little Fey who was now cowering behind the plant pot. 'And it's not for Fargale to do your job for you, they have enough work of their own.'

'I's only wanting a little company, Shriven, I's not doing any harm.'

'Not yet maybe...'

Clarissa turned to Charlotte, ignoring Boris' high-pitched protests.

'If he thinks he's going to ruin my garden he has another think coming,' she said in an authoritive tone. 'Now then, what do you say we have an ice cream before we get your uniform? The mint choc chip is the best,' she said before heading towards Bertichelli's.

In the walled garden at the end of the mall Charlotte and Clarissa were being watched.

'You were right to monitor this one, Luned,' Malik whispered. There have been strange readings at the Guardian Oak since she arrived, and cavorting with Boris does not put my mind at ease; not one little bit.'

'As I've told you, Sir, my instincts are rarely wrong. You should also know, there have been reported sightings of The Morrigan in the wake of the lightning strike. At first I thought it was the aftermath of the lightning but I can confirm the silence has definitely been broken.'

Malik's face paled at the name. 'That can only mean trouble. Do we know why she is here?'

'No Sir, but it would appear to be something to do with the girl.'

'Keep a close eye on her, Luned, and inform Dijin and the Seelie Courts; I can feel it in my wings, she's going to be trouble.'

'Roger that, Malik,' said the spiky-haired water sprite.

'Oh and Luned, let's try not to be seen this time, yes?'

Luned affected a pained smile before racing through the air in a streak of blue.

Charlotte was still too stunned to say anything on the car drive home. It wasn't till they were back in the kitchen of Rosemary Heights that she dared comment on what had happened. *Play it cool*, she thought.

'I didn't think adults could see fairies,' she eventually blurted out with all the finesse of a rhinoceros.

'They don't, dear,' Clarissa said, once again completely unfazed.

'But you di… you called him Boris.'

'Well of course I did, dear, that's his name.'

Charlotte suspected that Aunt Clarissa was deliberately playing dumb. She was normally so sharp and there was that wicked twinkle in her eyes again. She was so infuriating when she was like this.

'YOU saw him and YOU shouldn't have,' Charlotte said firmly.

'*Not* seeing fairies doesn't mean *can't*, dear. Adults don't see Fey folk because they think they are too grown up, which seems rather silly to me, but it doesn't mean they can't see them if they would just open their eyes,' Clarissa explained before continuing in a sterner tone of voice. 'In any case, being able to see Boris is not exactly a good thing in my book!'

'Is he really a Veshengo?' The words were out of her mouth before she could think.

'And where did you hear that word?' Clarissa looked at her with surprise.

Charlotte was not ready to share her adventures just yet and was kicking herself for saying anything, but she was pretty sure Clarissa would know. 'Boris told me.' It wasn't a lie but Charlotte was sure Clarissa wasn't buying it. She seemed to be playing along however.

'Yes. Boris is a Veshengo; well, he was.' Clarissa got up to put a pot of water on the stove. 'He was banished by The Morrigan and has lived amongst humans ever since. He will die soon judging by the state of him.'

'That's awful, what on earth did he do that deserved such a punishment?' Charlotte was incensed by such cruelty.

'Who said it was on Earth?' Clarissa muttered as she busied herself with preparing tea.

'What did he do, Aunt?'

'Enough questions for today, Charlotte. I've already told you too much,' Clarissa said gently before striking a match and coaxing flames out of the kindling. 'All I will say is this: do not trust the Fey and especially The Morrigan, Charlotte. Some can be friendly enough but most would have your humanity away if they could.'

Charlotte headed for the stairs. 'Thanks for the advice. I'm going for a bath if that's OK.'

Clarissa just nodded as Charlotte left the room. A cold shiver ran down her spine. The Fey had obviously taken an interest in Charlotte, which was not good for her. *You'd better have your wits about you, girl,* she thought as she began to weave magic into the fire.

# Wykenhall High

The day Charlotte was due to start at Wykenhall High had finally arrived, and Clarissa's VW Beetle came to an abrupt stop outside the main gates leading to an old mansion house.

'Wykenhall High,' Aunt Clarissa announced cheerfully. 'I'll be here to pick you up at about three-thirty, dear. Enjoy your day.' Once again Aunt Clarissa read her mind – or perhaps the horror on her face. 'At least try, dear. It really is a wonderful school with good people.'

'If you like it so much then you go.'

'You have to go to school, Charlotte.'

'I'm sure I'm coming down with something, perhaps I should just stay at home today.' Charlotte feigned a cough but Clarissa wasn't buying it.

'It's not just about facts and figures, Charlotte dear, you need to be surrounded by people your own age. You can't closet yourself away for ever you know.'

'I could give it a blooming good shot.' Charlotte tried to add a little venom to her voice but couldn't help the small smile that curled into the dimple in her cheek. She was finding it harder and harder to be angry these days, especially around the likes of Jude and Clarissa.

'Go!' Clarissa smiled before waving Charlotte away and bombing off down the road.

It was raining yet again, which seemed fitting. Perhaps it was the fact that there was nothing between you and the sky that made one notice it more, but it felt wetter and colder here than anywhere else she had lived. The rain and cold seeped right in to the bone.

The tarmac drive that led up to the double doors of the main building was flanked either side by a grass area with picnic benches, landscaped gardens, even a small fountain surrounded by lime and ash trees. Beyond the recreation ground were a number of enclosed courts for tennis, netball and the like and a hard surface marked out for running with a sandpit in the middle as well as some larger playing fields.

This place was seriously moneyed and, not for the first time, Charlotte wondered where Aunt Clarissa's funds came from.

In the distance Charlotte could see a building she assumed must be the sports hall and swimming pool, as indicated by the signpost ahead of her. She followed the pointer which said 'Reception'.

'My name's Charlotte Stone, I think you are expecting me.'

'Good Morning, Charlotte, please take a seat and the head teacher will see you shortly,' replied a young, slim, brunette receptionist, brandishing a beatific smile. She sat in a subtle cloud of sweet perfume, her makeup and nails perfect, navy suit pristinely pressed and finished by a flush of colour in her neckerchief. The receptionist pressed a button on her intercom, exchanged a few words with someone on the other end, then continued with her typing.

The entrance hall was a grand room with gothic, lead-stripped windows and walls full of old oil paintings in gilt frames. The only concession to modern design was the bank of desks occupied by admin staff and a pair of sofas arranged around a glass table with a vase of fresh flowers and some school prospectuses. It reminded her, in a lot of ways, of the various grand hotels her family had stayed in during their treks across Europe. Charlotte felt that all too familiar knot of grief in her chest and pushed it away. Crying on her first day at school would not do.

Her new clothes were still stiff and the shirt collar dug into her neck but, mercifully, she didn't have to wear a skirt. She would, however, be expected to wear a tie once she knew what house she was in. Charlotte was not used to such formalities.

She busied herself admiring the high ceilings framed with elaborate stucco and covered in frescoes depicting various scenes. Sun-soaked cornfields, lush green hills and a shepherd and his love sat under a gnarly, flowering oak. Looking closer, Charlotte noticed the tree was covered in roses and acorns – this had to be the Brackenheath Oak. She instinctively reached out to touch the wall before something stopped her. Peeking out from behind the tree, he wasn't wearing his customary Hovis bag but… Charlotte was convinced it was Boris.

'Beautiful, aren't they.'

The voice at her shoulder made her jump, clearly the plush carpet of the reception room muffled the sound of any footfall and Charlotte hadn't heard the man approach.

'Didn't mean to make you jump there. Mr Thomlinson, head teacher.' The man offered his hand.

Mr Thomlinson was a stocky man, in his fifties Charlotte guessed, with receding silver hair and a ruddy face. His brown eyes were sharp and shone with humour, but Charlotte got the definite impression he was not to be messed with.

'Great to have you join us, Charlotte. You'll find we are a friendly bunch. Shall we?' Mr Thomlinson indicated she follow him to his office and offered her a seat. The head teacher's office had the same ornate decoration of the reception with myriad framed certificates lining the walls. There were several teak bookcases and a large glass fish tank in the corner of the room, the pump humming faintly as it oxygenated the water. A mural of what Charlotte assumed was the school motto covered the wall behind his desk. '*Adunatam in Sapientia*' – 'Unified in Wisdom,' Charlotte muttered to herself.

'I'm impressed, you speak Latin?' Mr Thomlinson was beaming.

'No, I just sort of... worked it out,' Charlotte blushed.

'I understand you have quite a talent for history and it says here you're fluent in French and have a good grasp of Arabic... and Hieratic too!' Mr Thomlinson raised an eyebrow and sifted through some paperwork on his desk. 'You'll be required to do Latin and two modern languages here,' he chuckled, 'so I'll be expecting good things from you, Charlotte.'

Charlotte, who had been distracted by the shoal of silver and electric blue fish zigzagging in the tank to her left, just smiled weakly in response. Mr Thomlinson was still engrossed in her files and Charlotte wondered where he had got them from. Education, till now, had been such an informal affair for her and... Edessa. Charlotte shifted uncomfortably in her seat at the thought of her sister.

'Now then,' Mr Thomlinson continued, 'your aunt tells me you have had quite a challenging time over the last few months.' He leaned over and looked her in the eye. 'I just want you to know from the off, we are all here to support you in any way we can, OK?' He gave her a reassuring smile.

'Thanks,' Charlotte said, feeling like she ought to say something. She wanted to be angry with him, and Clarissa for divulging such personal secrets, but he seemed so genuine and Charlotte realised she trusted him.

How about a tour of our facilities?' Mr Thomlinson grinned. 'I think you are going to be very impressed.'

The facilities were indeed everything she could have hoped for and made up for the lack of her beloved museums and libraries. Charlotte would have everything she could possibly want at her fingertips and didn't need to try too hard to be enthusiastic. Clarissa had, once again, been right. Charlotte could get used to this formal schooling thing.

'Right then, I think that's it, Miss Stone; time to meet your class.'

*There's always a downside*, Charlotte thought to herself.

Mr Thomlinson had helpfully marked her form room on the little map she had received in her welcome pack. She was to be in Banyan House and the tie would be orange, which reminded her of Jude. The tour had taken most of the morning so they headed back to the history classroom.

'Class, let me introduce Miss Charlotte Stone who has joined us from London,' Mr Thomlinson announced to the room. 'Please make her feel welcome and give her any help she needs.'

Charlotte, who had just wanted to sink into a seat at the back of the class, cringed at the attention as twenty sets of eyes stared directly at her. A skinny girl with ice blue eyes and braces walked up to the teacher's desk and smiled at her shyly.

'I'm Sissy, your buddy.' They exchanged an awkward handshake before Sissy led Charlotte to an empty desk towards the back of the class.

When they sat down, Charlotte took a sneaky look at her reluctant friend. Sissy was a good two inches shorter than herself, white hair fixed in a bun, with a few stray wisps that seemed to float around her face with a mind of their own.

'Welcome to Wykenhall High,' a girl behind her simpered, disturbing her assessment of Sissy. 'I'm Isla Hickling and this is Toni and Sonia.' She waved to two other beaming faces. 'It's always a pleasure to welcome new faces to our town, you must tell us all about yourself and your adventures; we hear you're quite an explorer.'

'Seems everyone knows everything about me,' Charlotte replied, looking around for a familiar face. 'Is Olly in this class?'

'Over there next to Charlie.' Isla nodded curtly to the row ahead of Charlotte where Olly was sat next to a scruffy-looking boy with swarthy skin and dark hair. Isla's face darkened before returning to its default setting of a well-practised smile.

'I've had a wonderful idea, Isla,' the one called Toni squealed before Charlotte could declare her innocence. 'You should hold one of your wonderful soirées in honour of Charlotte.' Isla obviously prided herself on her hospitality and entered into the planning with relish.

'I was just going to suggest that, Toni.' She turned back to Charlotte handing her a business card. 'Here's my contact details, we'll have to set a date,' she giggled as she tapped furiously on her smartphone without waiting for Charlotte's reply. 'What's your mobile number?'

'I, I don't have one,' Charlotte shrugged apologetically.

All three girls gasped in unison.

'I've never needed one.'

'Well... I suppose, hand-delivered invitations *are* nicer.' She smiled at her own ingenuity.

Isla obviously saw herself as a problem solver, though Charlotte wasn't convinced she'd be much help with her own unique situation.

'Is she always like this?' Charlotte whispered to Sissy who was covering a smile in her hands. 'She means well,' she replied, 'and she leaves me alone... which is a bonus.'

'OK, class, enough introductions, time for some work,' announced Mr Thomlinson. 'You will no doubt have read the news about the proposal to turn Brackenheath Park into another housing and industrial estate.'

'Lloyd's free-range days are numbered eh, Charlie?' a spotty-faced boy in the front row sneered. 'What's your grandad going to do when there are no trees to sing to or fields to run around in all day?'

The boy next to Olly was red in the face, his hands in fists, but he didn't say a word.

'OK, settle down now.' Mr Thomlinson gave Giles a warning glance. 'Regardless of our personal thoughts about this, I thought this would be the perfect occasion to explore a little local history.'

Olly and Charlotte exchanged looks; this was going to be easy.

'Bet I know what you're going to do for your project,' Charlotte smiled as Olly started making furious notes.

'There is so much to choose from, I might just leave the tree to you. It seems to like you best – it's never glowed for me.' He winked.

'How do you know about that?'

'I've told you before, you do anything in this town and people will know. I wouldn't worry about it though, no one but me will believe that. You should speak to my dad, he swears he has had strange experiences there too. You could compare.'

Charlotte was exhausted by the end of the day. She had been introduced personally to every one of her classmates and her head was swimming with names, not all of which had fastened themselves to the relevant faces. Isla had taken it on herself to become Charlotte's buddy and was a demanding hostess who wanted to know all about her. In truth, Charlotte felt like a bit of a circus freak, and she wished she had escaped with Sissy, who had long since disappeared.

She was currently by the second library, trying to get her bearings for the main gate. It was the first time she had been alone all day.

A woman dressed in a smart suit, red hair twisted into a tight bun, walked purposely towards her. In spite of the modern clothing it was definitely The Morrigan.

'And what are you doing here?' said The Morrigan. 'In case I didn't make myself clear, I set you a rather urgent task. There is no time for such trivialities as school,' she continued. The tone of disdain was clear in her voice.

'Suits me fine, perhaps you could tell Clarissa because she doesn't agree.'

The Morrigan's eyes flashed dangerously but she smiled sweetly.

'I would have thought she would have jumped at the opportunity to restore the family name. Perhaps she is happy as a mortal after all.'

'What is that supposed to mean?'

'Time is running out, Charlotte of Stone.' The Morrigan ignored her question. 'I suggest you get moving. If I have to step in believe me, the humans of Brackenheath won't like it.'

A girly squeal behind them prevented Charlotte from retorting.

'There you are, we've been looking everywhere for you.'

Charlotte cringed as Isla and her entourage appeared from round the corner and The Morrigan disappeared.

'We're heading to the sports hall to watch the archery try-outs, Govinder will be there. He's really good.' Isla beamed at Charlotte like she was a charity case. 'We could go through your options too if you like? There's a lot to choose from, it's important to take the time to consider them all carefully.'

Charlotte declined Isla's offer, thankful that Clarissa was collecting her early today. She said her goodbyes and made her way to the main gates.

'Hey, Charlotte,' an Indian boy in a slim-line wheelchair came powering across the tarmac courtyard before doing a wheelie on the gravel drive. Charlotte looked at him nonplussed.

'It's Govinder. Govinder Singh. Just wondered if anyone had invited you to the sports hall? It's a good place to catch up on the latest gossip,' he smiled.

'Sorry, I've been put on display so many times today, I've lost track of names and faces, I'm afraid,' Charlotte apologised.

'It's OK, I'm not what you were expecting either, I'll bet.'

Charlotte was thinking of a tactful reply when she was distracted by shouting coming from the driveway. A small group had gathered by the time Charlotte and Govinder arrived to see Sissy being pushed about by two boys, one of which she recognised as the spotty-faced boy from her class.

'The school bully, Giles Nudds… and Wilbur Trull, his muscle,' Govinder announced.

'Are they really so lame as to pick on a girl?' Charlotte was incensed. 'I mean, if anyone, you'd think they'd…'

Charlotte shot a glance at Govinder's chair and the unfinished sentence hung in the air. Charlotte waited for a well-deserved rebuke but Govinder just smiled an evil smile.

'I'd run them over; in fact I have.' He patted his chair. 'They know not to mess with me and my wheels.'

He gazed thoughtfully up the gravel drive where Giles was now guffawing as Wilbur threw Sissy's bag into a tree. 'Sissy is a prime target, however,' he said.

'I can't stand by and watch this.'

'She won't thank you, you know.'

'That's daft… why ever not?' Charlotte added, a little less sure of herself.

Govinder shrugged. 'Some obstacles we need to overcome by ourselves.' A fresh round of laughter was accompanied by sobbing and a crowd was growing.

'That's it, I'm taking them out,' Charlotte fumed, curling her fists into balls.

'Don't say I didn't warn you,' Govinder replied as he wheeled towards the sports hall.

'Oi, slime for brains, want to show how tough you really are?' It took Giles a while to realise Charlotte was talking to him; clearly he was not used to being challenged.

'Well, if it isn't the orphan,' Giles sneered. 'I don't fight with riff raff.'

'Wrong on both counts, moron.'

Charlotte was beginning to see red and that wouldn't do. *You can't fight when you are angry or you'll make mistakes*, she remembered her old karate teacher's words and took a few steadying breaths.

Giles was casually leaning against a tree eyeing her up and down. 'Come to defend your new girlfriend?'

The crowd sniggered, giving him confidence. 'Wilbur, I think the new girl needs a lesson in how things work around here.'

'I was talking to you, Nudds.'

'And I told you, I don't fight riff raff.'

'Fine, I'll fight your lackey then I'm coming for you, spud boy.'

Wilbur was on the floor nursing bruised kidneys in three moves with Giles pinned up against the tree shortly after.

Charlotte felt something biting into her skin. Giles was wearing a gold chain on his wrist and it was old. Before she could stop it images of a boy drowning flooded her head and her grip loosened.

'You're afraid of water,' Charlotte gasped.

'How do you know that?' Giles looked at her with a mixture of hate and fear.

'I'm sorry, I didn't mean to…'

'Big mistake, orphan,' Giles hissed.

'Whatever, I don't put much store in the words of bullies.' Charlotte remembered she was trying to teach him a lesson and she twisted his shoulder again making him wince. 'You want to watch you don't annoy me too much or I'll get my aunt to hex you, you cowardly toad.'

'You live in the spooky old house on the cliff with that crazy old bat who makes pickles, don't you?' Giles blanched.

'She's not crazy, she's a witch and she could turn you into an actual toad… won't take much, you're practically there already.'

'I… don't believe you. Witches don't exist.' He was getting less sure of himself now.

'You'd better believe it, faceache.' Charlotte was in her stride now. 'Witches, fairies, magic trees… and unicorns I suspect!'

Giles slipped her grip, clearly keen to put as much distance between himself and Charlotte as possible.

'You're a freak, Charlotte Stone!' he shouted over his shoulder to a chorus of laughter.

'Eye of newt, tongue of dog… bladder of a cowardly toad. Mind you don't wet yourself!' she shouted back.

Sissy's bag fell to the ground and Charlotte handed it to her.

'You're a menace, Charlotte Stone, stay away from me in future.' Sissy glared.

'I was trying to help you.'

'I don't need your sort of help,' Sissy spat. 'Now I'm going to be their number one target, you think about that? Are you going to be there to save me every time?'

Sissy readjusted her uniform. 'I just want to be left alone.' She snatched her bag from Charlotte's hands before storming off.

'Well, well, quite an eventful first day we are having,' said a voice behind her. Charlotte recognised the man from his picture in the *Wykenhall Free Press*. Mr Ransell towered over her, arms crossed, all grey suit and scowls.

'Perhaps in your old school fighting was permitted, but here it is not acceptable. Being new does not exempt you from detention.' Mr Ransell handed her a note with a room number and date scrawled in flowery handwriting. '3.45 and don't be late. I suspect that will be the first of many,' he added before picking Wilbur off the ground and marching him and Giles towards the manor house.

Beep beeeep!

Aunt Clarissa waved cheerfully from her VW Beetle and wound down the window as she pulled into the kerb.

'Have a good day at school, Charlotte?' she asked.

Charlotte scuffed her boot on the pavement awkwardly, avoiding her aunt's gaze. 'Er…'

'Did you make any friends today?'

Charlotte considered the question for a moment, 'What exactly do you mean by "friends"?'

# Mr Ransell

*I*t was definitely a safe assessment that Charlotte's first day had not gone according to plan and she wondered if she was really cut out for the whole school experience. 'Snap out of it, Charlotte. This is not going to beat you.' She chanted her new affirmation with growing levels of aggression. 'I'm going to be fine, it's a tiny blip, nothing to panic about… think of the language lab, the two libraries…'

Clarissa had been her usual calm self on the drive home, explaining to Charlotte how she really shouldn't threaten her classmates with transmogrification. 'I'm quite sure I'm not even able to do it anymore,' she had added, which weakened her moral position in Charlotte's opinion.

'It was just a spur of the moment thing, Clarissa. I thought he was being sarcastic so I was just playing along. How did I know he really thinks you're a witch.'

'Speaking without thinking often has consequences, Charlotte, and you would do well to remember that.'

The rest of the journey had been spent in silence and that had been the end of the matter. Charlotte couldn't help thinking that if she had still been living with Morag, she would probably have been sent to bed without dinner and grounded for weeks. The two women were very different, and living with Clarissa definitely had its advantages. Edessa, as usual, had been right.

Charlotte still hadn't confessed to her detention by breakfast; Clarissa probably knew anyway but she didn't want to push her luck. Probably best to stick to one transgression a day.

'I thought I might stay behind after classes today, explore the facilities a bit more.' Charlotte felt bad about lying.

'Well, well, the girl who didn't want to go to school now can't stay away?' Clarissa teased. 'I have a meeting anyway so that works out well. Shall I collect you about four?'

'Better make it five.' Charlotte busied herself with her school bag so she didn't have to meet her aunt's eye.

⚓

The headlines of the school paper, *The Wyked Chronicle*, nearly knocked her resolve to stay at Wykenhall High. It seemed her bust up with Giles had made the front page.

'You'd think they'd never seen a playground fight before,' she grumbled to Isla and Sonia over lunch.

'Well, to be fair, it is quite a rarity and, if I may be so bold, Charlotte, it is not the sort of behaviour I'd expect from one of my girls. People look up to us you know.' Isla gave her a disapproving look.

*One of her girls!* Charlotte couldn't believe she was hearing this. What did Isla think she was, a poodle?

As the bell rang for home time, Charlotte reluctantly made her way to room 122B and detention. A handful of other students were already there when she arrived so she made her way towards the back of the class in an attempt to blend in. No such luck, however, as Mr Ransell announced her presence almost as soon as she entered.

'Ah ha, our newest celebrity, Miss Stone,' he said with a tone loaded with sarcasm. 'I read all about your exploits in our school paper just this morning. I'm afraid they didn't get all their facts right though.'

He waved the newspaper about, for emphasis. 'Says here you have broken the school record for quickest detention for a new student,' he tutted, shaking his head gravely.

'Oooh… close but no cigar! That dubious record still remains with Giles Nudds… doesn't it, Mr Nudds?' Mr Ransell looked over his glasses at the boy sat behind Charlotte.

'Are you always this obnoxious?' Charlotte muttered under her breath.

'I'm sorry, did you have something to say, Miss Stone? Only, I'm not used to students answering back.' Mr Ransell fixed her with a cold stare, daring her to speak. 'We may not be permitted to use the cane anymore alas, but I can still make your life very… interesting.' His dangerous smile did not make it as far as his eyes.

*Oh I doubt you can top recent events*, Charlotte thought, deciding it was probably best she kept that to herself.

Time dragged in the gloomy classroom, especially after fifty-two lines of *I will not practise my Ninja skills on school property*. She needed to give her aching hand a rest so she watched the raindrops race each other down the window. She was starting to place bets with herself over which would win when…

WHACK!

'Miss Stone, I don't think you fully appreciate the concept of de-tent-ion.' The voice oozed sarcasm. 'The one hundred lines ARE NOT OPTIONAL, and the sooner you do them the sooner I CAN GO HOME!'

A defiant smile flickered across Charlotte's mouth before she had a chance to stop it and Mr Ransell sneered.

'Perhaps if the gut-wrenchingly stunning beauty of the school grounds is too much for you, Miss Stone, you should attend to your lines inspired by nature.' He finished the sentence with a flourish of his hands. 'Move your desk outside.'

Those last four words certainly did the trick alright; Charlotte wasn't smiling anymore.

'But sir, it's pouring.'

'Then take an umbrella, we don't want your lines to run, do we? It would be a terrible shame if you had to start all over again!'

Charlotte had thought he was just joking but she was soon sat outside on one of the picnic tables near the running track. She could swear the rain had got heavier too. Try as she might, she couldn't keep her paper dry and the wind nearly took it on a number of occasions.

'This is ridiculous!' She threw the pen across the field. 'I hate rain.'

'Well, that's charming.'

Charlotte started, looking around her for the voice. 'Boris?' she whispered.

'Certainly not,' replied the disembodied voice, which seemed to be coming from her pen, now floating through the rain on what looked like a bubble of water.

'I am Luned, your fairylore caseworker.'

'A pen?'

'Are all humans as stupid as you?' the pen barked before falling to the table.

The water bubble hung in the air for a moment before elongating and twisting into a humanoid form. Within a matter of minutes, a sinewy elfin creature stood scowling at her, sapphire eyes sparkling dangerously and pointy ears twitching under a mop of spiky ice-blonde hair. Luned wore a silken aqua-green catsuit that hugged her figure.

'So what is your problem with falling water?' Luned demanded.

'It's wet, I'm drenched, cold and my lines are ruined.'

'So why didn't you just stand between the raindrops, *dinilo*?' the fairy said, like it was the most obvious thing in the world.

Charlotte wasn't sure what the final word meant, but she was pretty sure it wasn't complimentary.

'I suppose that's some kind of fairy logic!' Charlotte retorted but Luned was ignoring her and now dancing around the table, waving her arms gracefully. When she had finished, the downpour parted and, while it seemed to be even more torrential, in a small circle around the bench it was as dry as a bone.

'I'm not a fairy, I'm an Undine; but enough banter, it's time to get down to business.' Luned gently tapped the pen at which it jumped up and started scribbling of its own accord.

'Are you going to tell me what a "fairylore case worker" is?' Charlotte was beginning to really dislike fairies.

'All you need to know is I've been tasked with keeping an eye on you.'

'I feel so reassured.'

'I wish I could say the same,' the Undine retorted. 'I am supposed to ensure you don't cause any trouble; and I've not been impressed so far.'

'I didn't ask to be able to see fairies, or be marked by The Morrigan.'

Luned gave Charlotte a sympathetic smile, which seemed out of character but genuine nevertheless.

'No, I don't suppose you did. You would have to be a real *dinilo* to desire that,' the Undine agreed. 'But know this: it's not my job to look after you, Charlotte; my role is purely to protect the oak and maintain the balance of the Wyrdweb... even if that means from you.'

A shiver went down Charlotte's spine. She suddenly had a strong instinct that Luned was not someone to mess with, the air around her tiny frame buzzed with power. *Better to have her as an ally than an enemy*, though Charlotte had no idea what she had done to earn such mistrust.

'Can you at least tell me what the Wyrdweb is?'

Luned hesitated a moment before replying. 'It is the energy that connects all things. It holds the universe together and exists in its purest form in the Dreamtime... the space between the worlds. I am telling you this Charlotte because it is important you understand; every time someone interferes with the Wyrdweb or breaches the Dreamtime it sends ripples through all creation that can have dire consequences.'

'I'll be sure to remember that if it ever applies to me.'

'Oh it certainly does.' Luned paused for a moment to check

the skies; the rain was beginning to ease. 'The Fey Nation are well aware of your family; trouble makers, every one… and the acorn never falls far from the oak. I must go very soon but first, I was sent to give you a warning. That which belongs to Syluria must stay there, do not go disrupting the order of things. And do not put your faith in the Veshengo, they are creatures of chaos, it is their nature.'

Luned hopped off the table and walked to the edge of the circle and the now thinning rain. A rainbow bloomed in the sky.

'Remember my words, Charlotte. We will be watching you,' she added, before disappearing into the rain. Charlotte barely had time to gather up her pen and paper, complete with a hundred perfectly written lines, before the rain came crashing in on her.

Aunt Clarissa's distinct yellow Beetle was waiting for her outside the school gate by the time Mr Ransell had let them go and Charlotte hoped she hadn't been waiting long. Automatically her defences went up and she prepared for a verbal battle; she knew how adults liked to lecture.

'Look, I'm sorry I'm late and if you've been waiting ages but really, it wasn't my fault and things ran over and I couldn't call you…' Charlotte launched into her speech and spoke as quickly as she could in order to get as much of her side of the story out before the inevitable lecture.

Clarissa sat patiently as Charlotte continued to plead her case as the innocent victim of circumstance and as she did so Charlotte began to run out of steam. The adult's silence unnerved her.

'What an impressive display of verbal dexterity,' Clarissa finally said in a matter of fact way and looked as if she was indeed impressed. 'How was your detention?'

'I thought you might have guessed,' Charlotte said, crestfallen. 'I didn't want to disappoint you but really, I didn't deserve it.'

'I couldn't comment on that, my dear, but I'm sure you've already been punished enough for any mistake you've made.'

'But I really didn't do anything wrong,' Charlotte retorted.

'Don't be afraid to own your mistakes. How else do we learn, dear?'

Charlotte wanted to be cross with Clarissa for not believing her, but she was no ordinary adult, and this was no ordinary lecture.

'Things happen for a reason,' Clarissa continued. 'I'm sure your detention today, for example, was a very interesting and useful experience,' she concluded cryptically, looking at her with one of those trademark stares that told Charlotte the old woman knew more than she was letting on.

Then, completely changing the subject she announced, 'I have found you a martial arts teacher. What do you think of that?'

# Syluria

'Hmmm, it seems you do have a temperature,' Clarissa finally agreed as she pulled the thermometer from Charlotte's mouth. It read 100 degrees Fahrenheit. 'I am going to have a few choice words for that scoundrel Julian Ransell when I see him today. Fancy making you sit out in the rain.'

'There is a plus side of course, I get to stay home,' Charlotte croaked.

'I thought you were enjoying the adventure,' Clarissa smiled. 'I need to go out today, I'm afraid, but I could ask Jude to come and watch you?'

'I'll be fine on my own,' Charlotte reassured her.

'Very well, but I want you to drink this before I go,' Clarissa insisted, handing Charlotte a steaming brew fresh from the stove. Charlotte wrinkled her nose at the smell.

'What is it?'

'Nettle and willow bark tea.'

'Well, tree bark is new.' Charlotte took a cautious sip. 'Ewww, it's vile.'

'You're not drinking it for the taste. It will help clear the germs from your system.'

After much persuasion, and several more cups of the noxious brew, Clarissa was finally satisfied that Charlotte was well enough to be on her own and left to do her rounds at the Wykenhall shops. Charlotte had never been a good patient and in spite of Quintillian's soothing purrs as he sprawled at her feet, she was soon bored of lying on the sofa flicking through daytime TV. The tea seemed to be doing its job and she soon felt much better. Fresh air would do her good she reasoned so, dressing quickly and grabbing her rucksack, she headed for Brackenheath Park.

Charlotte automatically made a beeline for the oak on the hill.

'The Nymet,' she whispered absentmindedly. The oak looked perfectly normal in the light of day, except of course for the cracked bark and charred blackness in its, now hollow, centre. The main side branch now bent over and upside down, its tip touching one of the thick roots that curled across the soil before disappearing below ground. It looked just like a doorway.

Perched on its little hill the bulk of the oak could clearly be seen above the main tree line and she couldn't understand why Boris had led her such a merry dance through the undergrowth; it was hardly hidden in this thin sprawl of trees let alone some imaginary forest. Charlotte wondered for a moment if she had dreamt the last encounter, but the pile of soot in its heart and the tree-like pattern burnt into her skin told her otherwise.

Sunlight flooded the branches of the oak, dappling the ground below, which was dry as a bone despite yesterday's rain. New shoots and old branches were beginning to bud but the fresh green leaves were curling and sickly with brown spots, and a strange luminous slime crept along the trunk and branches. Charlotte poked it cautiously with a stick. Spores oozed into the breeze, floating gently around the oak. *Well, that explains the 'mysterious' glow,* Charlotte scoffed to herself; this stuff no doubt looked gold in the right light. She couldn't help feeling a little disappointed though. Of course, it didn't explain away the strange Veshengo creature.

Charlotte sat on a patch of soft grass and pulled out her water bottle, a pack of cheese salad sandwiches and *The Revised Encyclopaedia of the Fey Folk, and Where to Find Them.* The book was a large, ornately decorated hardback and it still smelt of incense. She perched it on her knees, back against the oak, and settled down to read.

Normally on a day like this Tar'sel would be making his way down to the Nellpa delta before sunrise for a relaxing day of sunbathing and fishing the shallows; but not today.

The first of the year's hog violets had been sighted and the spring festival of Patragi had been formally announced the previous evening. Celebrations had already started in the village and the women were festooning the central grove with bunting made from various spring flowers and grasses but the official feast would be held that evening.

Patragi was traditionally the time for initiation rites and Tar'sel had two to complete. Currently perched on a rocky outcrop, he was enjoying the pleasantly warm morning breezes while stretching out his aching limbs after the first of these. His Draoi rite would entitle him to enter the Nymet temple on his own.

It had been a long and uncomfortable night walled into the nearby cave known as 'The Womb of the Sleeping Mother' and had been filled with terrifying sounds and visions. Without fire, food or even a sleeping fur, he had been required to stay alert throughout the night, and would be expected to recount his visions to the priestesses later.

He hadn't been surprised his visions featured the red-haired girl again. He knew she didn't belong to this world yet he had seen her standing in a thunderstorm on the edge of the Nymet summit, red lightning dancing around her as she sung it into life. Behind her a large black bird flew through the branches of the Nymet temple before swooping towards him as impenetrable darkness fell. In the black, the now familiar scream rang out. Tar'sel wondered what the priestesses would make of it all.

His head was fuzzy from the lack of sleep but he couldn't rest yet – there was still a day of hunting ahead. The golden fire of the morning sun exploded over the horizon, flooding the distant river and open plains with light; light that gave him a much needed boost of energy, though he didn't know how long it would last.

'Welcome back,' said Tay'mor to his left. He had been waiting for Tar'sel to come round properly and now handed him a beaker and some stuffed oarweed. Tar'sel took the breakfast gratefully, recognising the brew as the same mixture Anya had given him at Nabinder.

'The priestesses are waiting for you,' continued Tay'mor gently, 'and I will need your decision on the hunt as soon as you are done.'

Tar'sel simply nodded but this was enough for Tay'mor and he walked off towards the village. Tar'sel wasn't ready to speak, he was still stuck in-between the worlds, images of the Dreamtime swimming in his head, but the food was beginning to work and the roots of the forest called to him, pulling him back to the Barra.

He turned his attention to the hunt. There were two choices – one in the wet and one on the dry. He had hoped to go for the thrill and prestige of hunting Talezo fish, a rare opportunity he probably wouldn't get again for many years to come. He knew he was expected to show more stamina than most as an initiate of the Draoi but realistically, it was more likely he would get himself drowned.

The other choice was hunting Rheadak. Not exactly safe but something they were all well practised at. Normally it would earn him less kudos, affecting his ranking within the village, but since he was to join the Nymet Draoi he was outside the rules of normal village bonds now. Anya had been so pleased for him, telling him to enjoy the freedom, but instead he only felt isolated.

⟊⟨⟆

The sun was on the descent and the sandwiches long gone by the time Charlotte had finished. She was now an expert on Dryads, Hinky-punks, Jenny Greenteeth and even Undines, but there hadn't been a single word on Veshengo. Charlotte threw the book down in frustration. A warm breeze stirred the dust and leaves at her feet.

*Looottieeee,* whispered the wind through the brittle leaves of the Nymet, making the hairs stand up on the back of Charlotte's neck.

114

'Edessa?'

The wind said nothing.

'Edessa? Are you there?' Charlotte tried again but again the voice remained silent.

It was just another whisper, an echo of someone who wasn't there.

She was just about to pack up and go home when a tremor knocked her to the ground.

'You've got to be kidding!' she muttered. What was it with her and this tree.

Another tremor hit and the bare earth below her began to sink and give way. A wind whipped up leaves and dust around her and soil and stones danced like water on a hot plate before finally settling. Charlotte assessed the damage. No twisted ankles, impalements or electric shocks; so far things were looking good. Charlotte looked up at the Nymet but it was sturdy and secure. Out of the corner of her eye though, she saw something strange. Red light crackled on the ground, turning the soil grey before dancing across the roses that trailed the oak. The light withered the roses before dissipating into the ground.

Charlotte was not the sort of girl who was afraid of her own shadow and had found herself in many an eerie spot in her family adventures but adrenaline coursed through her as her curiosity battled the fear that pleaded for her to run.

A rustling behind her made her scream.

'Boris!' Relief flooded through her. She was so pleased to see his mischievous smile but she couldn't help being worried at how grey and gaunt he now looked.

'Crack in the Dreamtime,' Boris said matter-of-factly, waving away her concern.

'What?'

'That's what you be seeing,' Boris explained. 'I expect someone's been telling you of the Wyrdweb. Something has been here and messing where it ought not be a messing. Whatever it is being, it is no friend to anyone in this forest.'

Charlotte fished a set of glass vials and tweezers from her bag and started taking samples of the soil, roses and tree bark. She hoped they might give her some clues as to what was going on with the Nymet; this was clearly more than just a simple lightning strike and she was determined to get some answers.

'What do you mean "forest", Boris?' she said as she started to work.

'You can't be seeing everything as is there, Missy. But yous be seeing soon. You have the mark now.' Boris burst into a violent coughing fit that bent him double, and it took him some time to recover. His face was pale and full of fear when he spoke again.

'Someones no a liking me speaking to you... or you being here...' he shuddered.

Charlotte was now unrolling a tool set and mixing a paste.

'What is that?' Boris asked.

'Plaster of Paris, I'm making a mould.' Charlotte motioned to a strange indentation in the soil and started spreading the mixture across the ground.

'And is this beings the sort of thing most humans carry around with them?' Boris asked with genuine interest, poking at the mixture in awe.

Charlotte was reminded again of the strangeness of her family. 'No, my family is a bit odd, I guess. Now stop poking it, it needs to dry.'

'So what be we doing now?' said Boris, trying to distract her so he could poke at it a bit more.

'We wait. It should be ready in a few hours.'

'Perhaps I can be assistings with that.' Boris gave her a mischievous smile before blowing on the plaster. In moments it had set rock solid.

'I didn't know you could do that.'

'There bes a lot yous not knowing, human, I's a magical creature not from this realm,' Boris shrugged. 'And yous won't be finding us in that book; we's not supposed to be here...' he pointed at the encyclopaedia, '... and I's shouldn't be able to do that.'

'Is that why you were banished?' Charlotte asked before thinking, cursing her big mouth, but Boris just nodded.

'I stole fire from the Shriven,' he whispered, not wanting to meet her eyes.

'Seems a bit harsh to banish you for something so small; so what if you can make… instant concrete.'

'I's… can't be here… must be going.' Boris burst into another coughing fit. 'The Verses are moving, can'ts you sees it, Missy?' he spluttered, pointing at the Nymet tree.

As Charlotte followed his finger she could see the same golden dust as before blooming around the base of the tree.

'Is can't be staying,' Boris squealed. 'If I jump the Dreamtime I'ms a gonner.' He tugged at Charlotte's arm. 'You shouldn't bes staying either, Missy,' he said before running off down the hill.

'It's just spores, Boris. Nothing magical; though admittedly a little strange.'

'Yous humans think you have the answers to everything but the Nymet is nots all it seems.'

'I've heard that before,' Charlotte muttered, as she quickly peeled up the mould and turned to follow Boris – but something caught her eye, rooting her to the spot. A ghostly figure stood in the gold mist that accumulated in the doorway of branches; it was a figure she knew only too well.

'It's time,' Edessa whispered with a smile before fading in front of Charlotte's eyes.

Charlotte let her rucksack drop to the ground as she walked towards the trunk of the tree. Her sister would never lead her into danger and whatever she was about to walk into, it had to be important. Closing her eyes she placed her hands on the bark of the tree, feeling the hum of its song. She instinctively knew what to do and for a split second hundreds of trees blossomed around her before the coldness of the Dreamtime washed over her.

It was mid-afternoon before the priestesses were finished with Tar'sel, interrogating him ruthlessly on his vision yet giving him no clue of its meaning. He could see the long dark canoes of the fishing party cutting through the choppy waters beyond the sandbanks as he walked out to the plains. A twinge of envy gripped him but Tar'sel knew Tay'mor couldn't keep them waiting just for him.

Handing him a spear, Tay'mor squeezed Tar'sel's shoulder for encouragement before moving on to the rest of the group. He would be joining them in the hunt, not to help but observe for the judgement later. As he looked around, Tar'sel was surprised to see Mor'seka bounding towards him.

'I thought you'd be out on the wet.' It was not like Mor'seka to pass up the opportunity for new experiences. Mor'seka scowled.

'Given the chance I would be, but lady luck was not on my side today. Anyway, how goes it in the land of the spirits?'

Mor'seka was mocking him.

'Busy. I'd be sitting this out if I could.'

'Surely the saviour of the nation isn't flagging already?'

'Bite me, Mor'seka.'

'Not very friendly,' Mor'seka laughed. 'Well, if you will excuse me, oh Mighty One, I'll be heading up this hunt. If I can't have excitement I will have glory,' Mor'seka announced dramatically before charging off to organise the rest of the hunters.

As the group moved into the open plain, heading for the river delta, Tar'sel hung back to gather a handful of cooling ledome moss. Chewing the minty sponge soon cleared his head and as he stored the remainder in his medicine pouch, he wondered how much Mor'seka really knew. His father had warned him that to become a guardian, a walker between worlds, would mean having to distance himself from the rest of the clan – would he have to give up his friendship with Mor'seka too? He was so engrossed in his thoughts, he practically stumbled over the Rheadak stranded in the boggy marshes.

'Get back,' Mor'seka hissed from the cover of the plain grass, his eyes flashing with anger. 'Are you trying to get killed?'

Tar'sel hit the ground just in time as a sharp tongue, studded with poison sacs whistled by his ear.

The baby Rheadak, already twelve feet tall and big enough to feed half the village through the winter, had unwittingly stumbled into the boggy marshlands along the estuary of the Nellpa. The whip-like tongue tipped with poison sacs lashed the ground ferociously, spraying liquid mud and cutting its own feet while the flightless wings flapped uselessly as the creature tried to free itself from the mud. In its efforts to break free it had become more and more stuck and its forlorn cries filled the air.

Tar'sel had to admit Mor'seka was a natural leader as he ordered the others into position around the flailing bird, keeping them all out of range of the deadly tongue.

A double hoot told Tar'sel he needed to move further to the rear where a plumpish boy about a year younger than him and a sinewy girl from the next grove were banging their spears against rocks to further confuse and distract the Rheadak as Mor'seka crept closer, spear at the ready.

Tar'sel joined in, making a final assessment of the hunting party. He had been sure there had only been five of them, yet he could definitely see a sixth person moving through the undergrowth. Stealth was clearly not their strong point – that would lose them marks – and… were they trying to go for the kill? Mor'seka would not tolerate that.

The figure emerged from the grasses close to the riverbank and Tar'sel gasped. Not only was it not one of the people, he didn't even recognise it as Sylurian. He had never seen skin so white – not even in the Fey.

Mor'seka seemed oblivious to the stranger as he readied his spear, aiming for the Rheadak's heart. The figure continued to wander across the marsh – straight into the line of Mor'seka's throw.

'Mor'seka, NO!' Tar'sel screamed, but it was too late. His friend had already unleashed his spear, and it whistled through the air with deadly precision. It flew straight through the figure and landed with a heavy thud in the Rheadak's chest. The bird let out an ear-piercing scream before it collapsed and fell silent. The figure had disappeared.

'What is wrong with you? Did the Sleeping Mother fry your brain last night? You could have got someone killed.' Mor'seka splashed angrily through the marsh water.

'That's actually what I was trying to prevent.'

'What? Who, your invisible friend? You're supposed to be an adult now. You need to grow up.'

Mor'seka turned back towards the dead Rheadak to finish the ritual as the rest of the villagers waited to assist with the long process of preparing the bird for the feast. Tar'sel was soon alone in the marshes.

'What the heck just happened? I thought I was dead.'

'You!' Tar'sel jumped out of his skin as the figure floated by his shoulder. At such close proximity he recognised her in an instant.

'You can't die, you're… not really here. Take a look at yourself, I can see sunlight right through you.'

'I… I'm bloody see-through?' Charlotte waved her arms frantically, swishing them through water, reeds and Tar'sel himself. 'Am I… a ghost?'

'For Odin's sake, calm down.'

'Odin? Who are you people? Have I somehow jumped back in time?'

'Not back, no. More like… across.' Tar'sel was over the shock of Charlotte's sudden appearance. 'The Triverse is made up of Syluria, Earth and the Unseen World of the Shriven. While each Verse is a fruit hanging from their own separate branch of the Great Tree, they are also connected by it and the Dreamtime is the sap flow. That's how the Draoi explain it to us anyway.'

Charlotte didn't say a word. She could feel the hairs on the back of her neck buzzing. This was certainly a world not marked on any map she knew of.

'We're called the Manush de Rukh by the way; it means "people of wood", but people usually call us the Tree Weavers.'

'I thought the people of the wood were called Veshengo.' Charlotte found her voice again.

Tar'sel laughed. 'Are you serious? Can a Veshengo do this?' He spat a ledome pip onto the ground and scooped a handful of soil around it. Making symbols with his hands over the centre of the pile of dirt, Tar'sel chanted over and over till a tiny green shoot appeared. Changing pitch, he coaxed more shoots out of the earth and, as they thickened and unfurled leaves, he began to loosely knit the stems together creating intricate, golden and green sonic patterns on the skin of the new stems. As he did so the swirling patterns on his arms and neck pulsed with energy – as did the lightning burns on Charlotte's own arm.

'That's a neat skill.'

'It's simple enough. The trick is to tune into the plant's individual song and, with a few harmonies, you can guide its growth any way you want. It has many practical applications; making houses, growing crops, healing. The Nymet Draoi teach us weaving from birth... have you heard of the Nymet?'

There was that word again. It gave her goosebumps for some reason.

'I certainly seem to be hearing that word a lot recently.'

The boy seemed happy that she knew what he was talking about and she didn't have the heart to correct him.

'My people tell legends about you, you know. "The flame-haired girl from the mystical land of Albion." Not many Sylurians have been there but those that come back say it is a strange world covered with gold and where stars dance across the sky at night. I've heard people fly on dragons and ride on the back of whales that glide on top of the oceans.' The boy looked at her expectantly for confirmation that the stories were true.

'Hmm, well perhaps you can visit some time and I could show you around,' Charlotte said, not able to think of anything more diplomatic to say.

He seemed disappointed.

'I don't know what I was expecting but I guess someone more... regal.' Tar'sel eyed her up and down.

'Sorry to be a disappointment.'

'I didn't mean it like that.'

'So, don't you think you should tell me my story then? I'm liking the flame-haired bit. Beats "carrot top",' Charlotte asked.

'I don't know much to be honest; they vary. Some say you're a human and others say you're a seven-foot-tall, blood-drinking monster. Some even think you're a Vorla... which is impossible...'

'A what now?' Charlotte replied, concerned at the implication that she was somehow worse than a blood-drinking monster.

'Their official title is Manush de Bar – the people of rock. They are the oldest of all beings, born in the dark coldness of the Mountain of Mourne, formed from the dreams of the Sleeping Mother herself. Cunning as sharks they are, ruthless in their pursuit of knowledge and have been known to drive men insane...'

'I have to say I'm not liking this story.'

'Probably shouldn't have mentioned them.' The boy stood up suddenly. 'You should go now, it's not safe for you to be here again – not everyone sees you as a saviour.'

Again? Charlotte wondered what he meant but there was no time to ask, she could feel herself fading and there were more important things to discuss.

'Has there been anyone else like me pass through here?' she asked the green-skinned boy.

'I don't think I'd even need Mor'seka for that sort of gossip,' he laughed. 'I don't think a human of Albion has been seen in living memory. No, that would certainly be big news indeed and hard to miss. Why do you ask?'

'No reason.' Charlotte tried to hide her disappointment. 'What's your name?'

'Tar'sel.'

'I'm Charlotte, I have a feeling I will be seeing you again, Tar'sel,' Charlotte said before disappearing.

The twin suns were setting as Charlotte faded out of Syluria. Tar'sel sat up near the base of the Nymet hill as the fishermen came in with their catch. Silver scales flashed in the first light of Syluria's smallest moon and remaining sunlight as the party trekked up across the plain to the central grove of the Tree Weaver village.

In the temple above him the Draoi priestesses had begun to chant pure, clear tones in celebration of the festival feast and in the valley below, the villagers answered them.

*Saaaaaaar, Reeeeeei, Gaaaaaaaaaaar*
*Saaaaaaar, Reeeeeei, Gaaaaaaaaaaar*

Tar'sel expected to be hungry and curious to try the new delicacy, but he simply climbed higher to watch the last rays of the dying sun, whispering a prayer of gratitude and expressing his desire that it should return on the morrow.

A rough wet tongue and the smell of well-chewed pigs' ears brought Charlotte round and she came face-to-face with a chocolate brown Labrador.

'Yes, practically on death's door I see.' Mr Ransell pulled the dog away. 'You'd better enjoy the place while you can, they are going to be cutting this monstrosity down soon.'

'Who? What?' Charlotte was still groggy.

'The local council. I advised them about its recent calamity, as is my civic duty, and they have deemed it unsafe. I should think it will be down before the summer.' Mr Ransell grimaced at Charlotte and she had never felt more like punching him. Interfering old git.

'We'll see about that,' Charlotte retorted.

'Oh I do like a challenge,' Mr Ransell said before turning and heading down the hill.

'By the way, consider this a notification for your second detention. I will expect to see you in class tomorrow, 7.30 sharp, Miss Stone, or that will magic into a double detention. I have a feeling I shall be seeing a lot of you this year,' he chuckled before disappearing amongst the trees.


Clarissa was laying the table for dinner as Charlotte got back to the house and her stomach lurched as she realised she had been rumbled.

'So much for being ill, mmm?' Clarissa said as Charlotte pulled off her boots.

'I had to get some fresh air,' Charlotte replied. 'Aren't you going to ask me where I've been?'

Clarissa turned and looked her up and down. 'I don't need to, Syluria is all over you.'

# Belleswater Hospital

*I*t was raining once again as Neva walked to the Petrie research block. Summer was waking up slowly this year and she was beginning to miss the warmth of her home country. She was grateful, however, for the continued funding of her research. Mr Aherne seemed more than happy for her to take as long as she needed and was more than generous with her expenses. Still, she often had a niggling doubt in the back of her head: why was he so interested?

Etienne was waiting for her in the lab. 'Good morning, Miss Oblaha, my fellow time traveller.' Etienne smiled a cheeky smile before removing his hat and executing a deep, sweeping bow. Though she still didn't know how to take him, he was so flamboyant and charming that Neva couldn't help but smile in return.

'Good morning, Mr Aherne,' she replied. 'I'm afraid I've nothing new to report but I do have some more ideas and tests to run.'

'Wonderful, wonderful, my dear, I have every confidence in you and have no doubt you are doing the best you can.' He played with a few petri dishes and adjusted a magnifying glass as Neva dumped her coat and turned on the kettle.

'Would you like to join me for a coffee, Mr Aherne?' she asked as he stared intently at a piece of pottery collected from the Nile delta.

'Hmm? What's that?' Etienne dropped the pottery back into the box. 'Ahh no… no I won't, but thank you and please, call me Etienne, dear girl.'

Neva flinched automatically as the pottery piece cracked against the box, chipping off a minute fragment of blue glaze.

'Anything I can do to help around here, Neva?'

'No…! No I've got everything in hand,' she replied, her voice strained.

'The Stones always said you were the best, dear, and I don't doubt they are right.' Etienne shook his head appreciatively. 'Perhaps I could just see the item in question while I'm here though.'

'It's… in tests at the moment.' Neva had the strangest feeling that she didn't want him touching the stone, and it had nothing to do with his apparent clumsiness. He looked visibly disappointed and she instantly regretted her white lie.

'I see, I see… perhaps you can call me as soon as it becomes free then, I simply must see it "in the flesh" as it were.' his smile a little too sickly. 'It really is quite important.'

'Of course, as soon as it's free,' Neva promised. 'Can I ask a question?'

'Ask away, my dear girl.'

'It's not that I'm not grateful but, why are you supporting this project, Mr Ah… Etienne?'

'You are a curious thing,' he chuckled. 'Well, I have family connections to the Stones. When I heard the project was in trouble and they disappeared, being a bit of an amateur Egyptologist, I decided I could help out.'

'But this isn't an Egyptian artefact.'

'Ah but do we know that for sure? One of the interesting things about archaeology is, we can find things in the most unusual of places.'

Neva couldn't argue with that, and the stone was certainly an enigma.

'Well, if there really is nothing I can do then, my dear, I shall be off. Things to do, places to be, people to visit.'

'OK, right. It was good to see you.' Neva trusted herself with a simple smile.

'It's been a pleasure,' Etienne winked before kissing her hand, 'and don't forget to call.'

Neva breathed a silent sigh of relief as he made to leave. She nearly flinched as he rounded on her once more.

'Just one more question, my dear, was there a key?'

Neva's throat was so dry she could only shake her head.

The sun was shining and he had a spring in his step so Etienne decided he would walk to Belleswater Hospital rather than take the bus. He remembered the day he escorted the strange little red-head girl on this very same route and smiled. Charlotte had been so much easier to find than he could ever have hoped – what with Neva and the hospital, everything had practically fallen into his lap.

'Good morning, Adele my love,' Etienne announced to the chubby blonde-haired woman who sat behind the reception desk.

'Good morning, Mr Aherne, lovely to see you again, you're just in time for some good news too: Edessa is off the ventilators.'

'Now now, I've told you about that, Adele, it's Etienne to my friends; and yes, that is encouraging news.' He plucked a flower from the bunch he held and presented it to her in a flourish. Adele giggled like a school girl; her cheeks flushed.

'Edessa is very lucky to have such a charming uncle,' she cooed. 'We don't need to bother with your ID card, I think we know you well enough by now,' she said, waving Etienne through to the private rooms.

'Always my favourite,' he winked at her before heading down the corridor.

Edessa's room was a good size, with clean white walls and a large window that let in a lot of light. Etienne moved over to the window and adjusted the blinds.

'That's better,' he whispered in the gloom and lay the flowers on the bedside stand.

'Now then, little girl, do you have any answers for me today?'

The only reply was the beeps and whirs of the various machines surrounding the bed. Etienne waited as if he expected Edessa to suddenly sit up in bed, before sighing and turning his attention to the flowers.

'See what I brought you today, Edessa,' he said, arranging them into an empty vase. 'I really do want to be friends.'

More beeping and whirring but Edessa just lay there.

'I've met that sister of yours, did I tell you? Oh, I must have done in one of my visits. She's quite a feisty one; I do hope you know what you're doing,' he chuckled. Still he was greeted only with her silence.

'You really would be the better choice but I guess the decision is made now, the game begun, no point dwelling on it now. Let's hope she can make it to the end. Of course she might just get her hands on a useful little book, if she knows how to ask nicely. What she really needs though is a key.'

The machines continued their steady sounds and movements.

'Well, if you won't talk to me by your own volition, there are always other ways,' he sighed and pulled up a chair to the bed.

Once he found a comfortable position, he placed his hands on Edessa's temples and closed his eyes. Inside his head, he heard her scream.

⁓

In the still of the night only the soft clicking and whirring of machines could be heard in room 11 yet the room was a hive of activity. A young security guard was sitting in the lobby playing Candy Crush on his mobile so it completely escaped his notice when the lights in the corridor dimmed slightly for a moment before returning to normal.

In the glow of the bedside lamp, Edessa could see her body lying in the bed and it felt so strange to see it so still. It was disturbing to be so detached from her body, something she had only been able to do since Etienne's visits. Edessa shuddered at that thought.

She took a deep breath to steady herself and focused on the task in hand. She knew her sister was in Syluria but how to know where? As if in answer to her question, a vortex opened in the air before her, widening more and more by the second, and drew her in.

'The Dreamtime,' she whispered to herself. She had no idea how she knew, but this must be what Etienne had been trying to access through her mind as he plundered her thoughts. Her ethereal body squirmed as she relived the discomfort; no amount of flowers and soothing words made it bearable.

As the Dreamtime engulfed her, she saw it in more detail. Everywhere, golden mist swirled around her and shadowy figures faded in and out of focus just like when Charlotte had found her. Edessa felt a cold wave of fear radiating through her limbs and it was as much as she could do to keep upright. She didn't want to be trapped in this place again.

She managed to relax as she realised the shadows were oblivious to her presence. Edessa focused instead on the shining silver thread of light that grew in the darkness ahead of her. It pulsed with light and seemed to sense her presence. Snaking around her for a while, it eventually attached itself to the centre of her chest and she felt a sudden surge of energy explode through her body.

*Follow the breadcrumb trail I guess*, she thought with a wry smile and allowed the thread to pull her gently into the darkness.

The thread guided Edessa past broken half images that played fleetingly in the dark pools of the craters, which loomed out of the twilight of the pock-marked landscape. A low drone reverberated through the place, vibrating the ground beneath her feet, filling the air around her and jarring her bones. Etienne had told her the Fey lived in the Dreamtime, but there was no sign of life anywhere.

The landscape hadn't changed in hours; all around was more of the same desolate flatness and grey dust rippling across the ground.

The only things that had changed were the images in the pools. Perhaps these were exit points, though they looked nothing like the vortex she had entered. Edessa stopped by the nearest pool and waited, looking for any clues.

The cord tugged urgently at her chest but she ignored it, absorbed by the strange patterns that swirled through the water. The various shades of grey consolidated into the image of a bedroom where a Chinese girl with long black hair slumbered peacefully. Edessa could make out the floral pattern of the duvet and curtains in the monochrome scene. The curtains undulated in time with the breeze of the Dreamtime and a creeping darkness deepened in the corners of the room. The girl whimpered in her sleep as the shadows crept closer.

'Wake up,' Edessa whispered urgently, feeling powerless to help.

The cord tugged again at her chest but she couldn't turn away from the scene below her. The girl began to moan and arched her back unnaturally as the shadows covered her, seeping into her open mouth which was fixed in a silent scream.

Edessa felt a sadness flow through her, a sense of loss that made her heart feel as if it would burst out of her chest and tears streamed down her cheeks. She thought of her own parents, lost in the desert somewhere, their lifeless bodies slowly being buried in the sands and despair froze her to the spot while the cord tugged at her in vain. Darkness poured into the room and as she began to sink. Edessa realised in horror that it was flowing from the Dreamtime, taking her with it.

Suddenly, brilliant green and blue flashes of light filled the room and the shadow recoiled as if in pain.

'I've got this one, you stem that hole.' A wiry blonde-haired woman in a skin-tight aqua blue jumpsuit nodded vaguely in the direction of the ceiling, already focusing her attentions on the sleeping girl.

The green light obeyed, rushing towards Edessa.

The green flash floated beside her when Edessa came round, verdigris hair wrapped around a tall, thin female frame, tendrils of which drifted in the air as if she were suspended in water. A string of crabs scuttled around her neck like a living necklace and she radiated a rainbow of coloured light.

'Tis not many who can see our true colours… until the end.' The woman eyed her with curiosity.

'Am, am I dying?'

'You were, very nearly… but you are safe now.' The lady spoke with a voice that sounded like quivering seashells. 'An unusual catch indeed, you are. What are you doing in the darkness anyway? This is no place for the likes of you.'

'I don't really know, it just sort of happened… but, I think I'm trying to find my sister.'

'Well, let's hope she is not here. The place is withering around us.' The hair rippled in a gesture of emphasis to the woman's words. 'I hope you find her – somehow.'

The woman turned to leave and Edessa realised this might be her only chance to get some answers.

'My name's Edessa.' She offered her hand to the lady who looked at it with curiosity.

'That's a beautiful name.'

'Please, I need help,' Edessa tried again.

'I don't know what I can do for you, but feel free to ask,' the woman said, but she was clearly oblivious to Edessa's distress.

'Could you tell me how to get to Syluria? Everything here looks the same and I've been walking for hours.'

'Your trouble is, you think you want one thing when actually you want something totally different.'

Edessa thought about this for a while. 'I want to find my family.'

'Focus on one and you will find the other. I can keep you

company if you like, but all you have to do is follow this cord.' The lady gently let the cord drift through her fingers radiating rainbows along its length where she touched it. The rainbows seemed to be rejuvenating and Edessa was filled with hope and confidence.

The lady stayed with her as promised and it wasn't long before the cord had led her to another crater.

'It's alright,' the lady encouraged her, 'you are meant to look into this pool, it's yours.'

Edessa stared into the crater as the familiar greyness swirled into form and Ella and Richard Stone came into view.

'They... they're in trouble!' Edessa gasped as she witnessed her parents staggering across the desert. 'Please, can't you help them?'

'There is nothing to be done. These are images from the past,' the lady said. 'But I have never seen this before.'

'What?' Edessa was transfixed on the strange scene unfolding in front of her.

'Your cord has led you to your family. Your love for them must be very strong indeed.'

'Of course, surely that must be the same for everyone? Where do the cords lead to normally?'

'To one's heart's desire – sometimes.' The lady smiled sadly. 'More often than not though, it leads people to their deepest fears, the shadows that lurk in the soul. It is always the individual's choice. What they focus on, the cord will lead them there.'

'Do... do you think... maybe I could find anyone else?' Edessa asked, her heart in her throat.

'Not at this time I suspect,' the lady replied. 'And it would be best that you do not visit this place any more than you absolutely have to. The Dreamtime changes people... and not for the best. It is too easy to be pulled into the darkness, even for the most brilliant soul. You should have learnt that from your experience tonight.'

'But that wasn't my darkness.'

'Darkness is darkness. It doesn't discriminate,' the lady shrugged.

'But with practice I could…'

'It's not about practice, little spirit, it is about timing,' the lady said, then she was gone.

# Song of the Nymet

The week had gone without incident (unless you included Jude's misadventure with a set of hair straighteners) and Charlotte had even managed to get through five days of school without either getting a detention or bumping into Mr Ransell. All their school classes were now focused on trees and in particular the Brackenheath Oak, which Charlotte suspected The Morrigan had had a hand in. Life was good and even starting to feel normal, plus she had her first karate lesson to look forward to.

The Jade Moon Chinese restaurant was not exactly a conventional location for a martial arts lesson but it appealed to Charlotte for just that reason. Though it was currently closed, the kitchen was in full swing judging by the sweet, spicy aromas in the little courtyard by the back door.

'Welcome, Miss Stone. I have been waiting for you,' Mr Lei beamed from the door, waving her inside.

Mr Lei was an unassuming man who looked much younger than he was. Short and slim, he was dressed in a simple tunic and trousers and a smile that creased his face.

'Thank you, Sensi Lei.' Charlotte made a small bow in respect for her new teacher and Mr Lei nodded in approval. He led her past the bustling kitchen where a number of cooks were already making preparations for the night's service. It was much more exciting than Clarissa's with lots of fire, steam and flying vegetables as the cooks danced round each other – no pickled ash keys or dandelions in sight.

'My apologies but today will be a short session, Miss Stone. I must get to work soon, but your aunt was anxious for your training to begin as soon as possible and I must say, I am interested in seeing how much you know,' Mr Lei said, bringing her back to the reason she was there as he led her into a small room about the size of a double garage.

One of the long walls was lined with mirrors and the floor, with the exception of a small area near the door, was raised and covered in reed mats. A gong and green banner covered in Chinese kanji sat at the far end of the room next to a large Buddha statue festooned with flowers, incense burning at its feet.

'This is our family temple,' Mr Lei explained, indicating she should remove her shoes before stepping on the mats. 'It is not normally a place for combat but we will work here just for today. Your regular lessons, however, will be at Wykenhall High.' He bowed to the statue then turned back to Charlotte.

'Why don't we start with you showing me one of the forms you have learnt.' Charlotte nodded and took a couple of deep breaths before working through the last routine she had been taught, before her old life had come crashing down around her ears. Mr Lei studied her movements like a hawk, correcting her posture every now and again.

'Good, good,' he smiled when she had done. 'And were these the moves you tried on Mr Trull?' Charlotte blushed with embarrassment.

'That is a good sign,' Mr Lei continued, 'it seems you understand that the school yard is not an appropriate place for practising your skills.'

'I was only trying to stand up to the bullies, Sensei,' Charlotte retorted.

'Ah yes, very admirable, Miss Stone, but a true warrior knows that fighting must be the last resort. Finding a diplomatic solution through words is always preferable. If you start with a fight, where is there to go from there?'

The door from the kitchen corridor creaked and a slim Chinese girl peeked round at them. Her sleek black hair was woven into several plaits that were twisted into a bun and adorned with a sprig of white jasmine.

'This is my daughter Sang.' Mr Lei motioned her to come closer. 'She will be your sparring partner for today.'

Charlotte recognised Sang as one of the many faces Isla had introduced her to on her first day at Wykenhall High but couldn't remember having spoken to her during the whistle-stop tour of what Isla considered the 'less popular' kids. 'Nice to meet you properly,' she smiled.

Sang smiled nervously before running her thumb down her face and wiping her hands.

'Sang says hello,' Mr Lei interpreted. 'She chooses not to speak, preferring instead to express herself through movement. Some people find it a little strange at first but you soon get used to it,' he explained.

Charlotte, who had seen far stranger things, wasn't at all fazed.

Sang was stronger and quicker than she looked, beating Charlotte in the first four rounds. Just as Charlotte thought the next round was hers, Sang floored her with an illegal move.

'Hey, that's not fair,' she protested but Mr Lei just smiled.

'The lesson here, Miss Stone, is that you cannot always rely on the rule book. One's opponent will not generally play by the rules – they are only interested in winning.'

'Are you saying I should cheat?'

'Not at all, you must simply trust your inner wisdom. Observe what is going on around you and you can determine what your opponent is planning. Then you can act accordingly, using their intentions against them. But you must have a still mind.'

Charlotte was soon exhausted but she felt more like her old self. Mr Lei certainly promised to be an inspiring teacher and Clarissa was turning out to be the coolest aunt in the world.

'We are out of time, I'm afraid.' Mr Lei smiled. 'You have skill,

Miss Stone, but there is much Sang can teach you. I expect you to be much improved by the time I see you again.' Mr Lei gave a low bow as he let Charlotte out the front door, locking it behind her.

On the coastal road between Brackenheath and Wykenhall, Alexanders shot out of the hedgerows with the full force of spring and warm rain poured through Tar'sel's ethereal body. He may have a free pass through the Dreamtime but that did not make it any easier to journey through the desolate landscape of nightmares and craters. However, here in the soft warmth of the single Albion sun, the disturbing images finally melted like frost in sunlight and he was able to focus on the task in hand. He had to find Charlotte.

He didn't know how he'd ended up so far off course – Mor'seka must have miscalculated the jump – but he could see the cliffs to the north. This side of the Dreamtime Tar'sel's beloved Nellpa Barra looked so alien, so barren. While the ground beneath his feet felt familiar, where were the trees, the wild herbs and grasses, the Nymet?

Tar'sel tried to find his way by closing his eyes and following the contours of the land and the throb of the Mother's heartbeat, faint as it was here, but she was drowned out by every tree, leaf and flower. They were all singing so loud Tar'sel couldn't hear himself think. This was not the harmonious song of Syluria where each voice wove naturally into the one song; here every individual blade of grass was vying with each other, desperate to be heard. Tar'sel couldn't understand how the people of Albion were able to bear it.

That was when he stumbled across Boris.

It was sunny in between the rain showers and Charlotte was glad she had chosen to walk home, ambling along the country lanes and picking bunches of elderflower as she went.

'Do you have permission to pick those?' said the nearest hedgerow.

It took Charlotte a while to notice a rather scruffy-looking man wearing a wrinkled brown shirt and jeans at least two sizes too big for him tied up with rope. His face was covered in white stubble and he had the same swarthy complexion and eagle eyes as Charlie Mitchell, the boy Giles had been picking on. This must be the infamous Lloyd that she had heard so much about.

'I'm sorry, I didn't realise I needed permission.'

'I'm surprised the Fey didn't tell you, they're sticklers for rules. In any case, elderflower won't help you. Besides, these have been weaved,' he wrinkled his nose in disgust.

Charlotte was wondering what Lloyd could possibly know about weaving when he started rummaging around in the meadow behind him. 'Ah, this is what you need,' he exclaimed, gathering handfuls of nettles with his bare hands.

'Er, thanks, but I'm good. Clarissa dosed me up and I'm all better.'

'Well, that's a start I suppose but not nearly good enough,' Lloyd said, gathering more nettles and stuffing them into an old plastic shopping bag he had pulled from his pocket.

'Can't you hear it, child, the Nymet song? It's coming from everything, ever since the old girl was struck.' He thumbed in the general direction of the park. 'There's no silence anymore, it's almost unbearable.'

Most people avoided Lloyd and Lloyd himself did nothing to counter the gossip she had heard – most of it from Clarissa's neighbour, Mrs Bunratty. Clarissa, on the other hand, had always spoken fondly of him and Charlotte had learnt to trust her judgement. Besides, she found him much more fascinating than many of the residents of Brackenheath.

'Can you tell me more?' she asked.

'Not here!' the man gasped. 'The trees have ears – all I will say is this: last time Herself started singing, there was all kinds of trouble. Anyways, I have to get this tincture ready for you. It's a matter of utmost urgency. I'll bring it over later tonight.'

'But what do I need it for?'

'Ask your aunt, she'll know. I want to test some of my theories first before I worry you.'

It was a bit late for that in Charlotte's opinion but she couldn't get him to say another word.

---

'Quit it, I's not a freak show.' Boris swiped Tar'sel's hands away, nursing the bump on his head from where Tar'sel had sent him flying.

'But a real-life Veshengo. It's not possible, especially not in Albion.' Tar'sel ignored the fairy's protests, forgetting for a moment why he was there.

'Well, there's many a Fey that are beings where they shouldn't, thanks to you humans.' Boris had scampered into a nearby holly bush to observe Tar'sel from a safe distance.

'I'm sorry for that but I'm not an Albion human; I just need your help. I'm here to heal the Nymet. Can you take me to her?'

'Is don't know what you bes talking about.' Boris refused to make eye contact and clambered further into the bush.

'Come on, what do you take me for?' Tar'sel was beginning to lose patience. 'If you could just get me to…'

'Is take you for a Sylurian, Tree Weaver.' Boris pointed to the swirling gold patterns that adorned Tar'sel's body.

Tar'sel reached into his pockets and produced a handful of snacks. They were as translucent as he was but the Veshengo salivated all the same.

'I can get you real ledome moss and bokh nuts…'

The Veshengo squealed with delight before darting into the undergrowth.

'Here we go. Time to get lost,' Tar'sel muttered to himself before chasing after him.

Tar'sel was shocked to see the state of the Brackenheath Oak once Boris finally decided to take him there. This explained so much. His own people may have deflected the lightning blast, at the cost of a life, but the Nymet had not been so lucky this side of the Dreamtime. Had they caused this somehow?

'She looks really sick!' Tar'sel flinched at the painful cracks in the bark and curled brown leaves.

'It's not the outsidings yous need to be worrying about, Tree Weaver,' Boris replied. 'You humans is all the same, whichever side of the Dreamtime you comes from. Only seeings what is under your noses.' He rapped his knuckles on the trunk. 'The sap flow has beens babbling nonsense for days... I should know,' he added proudly.

Tar'sel tried to get close enough to properly inspect the damage but whenever he tried flocks of crows flew from the boughs and dive-bombed him, screeching so loudly his ears rang.

'We've got to do something,' Tar'sel gasped. 'I don't understand why they won't let me near.'

'Them's her birds.' Boris' voice was thin with fear. 'Yous be needing the girl as lives on the cliff.'

'How did the training go?' Clarissa called from the kitchen as Charlotte came in the main door.

'I think I made a friend.' Charlotte dumped her school books on the heavy oak table.

'Sang?' Clarissa asked.

'Actually, Lloyd!' Charlotte smirked.

'What has that ruffian been up to now?' Clarissa said, a tone of affection in her voice. 'Has he been scaring the locals again?'

'No. Just me,' Charlotte replied. 'I don't know what you've been telling him but he wants to feed me nettles too. I'm sure there was mention of warts as well.' Charlotte pulled a face at the mere idea of eating warts.

'Mugwort? St John's Wort?' Clarissa stopped what she was doing and stared intently at Charlotte.

'I don't know.' Charlotte reached for one of the freshly made cupcakes on the counter before Clarissa slapped her hand away.

'You really could do with being a little more… *aware*,' Clarissa chided, wiping her hands on her apron and putting a pot of water on the stove.

'Well, he's coming over later if you want to ask him. Anyway, I need to do some more research. Do you have any books on local legends?'

Clarissa was adding sage leaves to the water. Behind her Charlotte wrinkled her nose.

'It's not for you,' Clarissa said over her shoulder before adding, 'Have you tried the library, dear?'

'Library? I didn't know you had a library!' Charlotte was stunned.

'Oh yes, dear, we are a family of book-lovers. It's the door in the centre of the gallery just before the stairs to my room but I warn you, they're in no particular order.'

The library was exactly as Charlotte had expected: musty with the smell of the books piled on the floor, on tables, windowsills and even in the empty fireplace. Romantic it may be, ordered it was not; this was going to take some time. Charlotte started wading through the mountains of books.

Along with the usual classics were ancient first edition tomes on Egyptology and more modern works on cookery, archaeology and eco landscaping mixed with astrophysics, politics and herb craft, but nothing that suited her needs. Quintillian hopped from one pile to another staring intently at her as she worked, meowing at intervals.

'These bookcases are no better, Quin,' Charlotte addressed the cat as she flopped into a recently emptied chair. 'Got any ideas?'

The cat padded in a circle before settling down for a nap on the most precarious of the book towers.

'I'll take that as a "no" then.' Quin just yawned in response.

With her head in another book, Charlotte didn't see Luned's tell-tale shimmering appear on the table beside her.

'And what schemes are you planning now?' Charlotte jumped at the Undine's question.

'Do you have to sneak up like that? And why do you always assume I'm up to no good?'

'Because, generally, you are... and you don't keep the best of company. I saw you and Boris again the other day.' Luned shimmered into view.

'You know, I'm actually trying to save your stupid tree and it would be nice to get a little appreciation for a change.'

'When did we ask for your help, human? I must have missed that memo.'

'You didn't, The Morrigan did – and she's a higher authority.' Charlotte was annoyed that had come out more like a question than a statement.

'She is a law unto herself, which is very different,' Luned scoffed.

'Well, this has been nice, as you will see I am nowhere near any Veshengo or the Nymet and I'm really rather busy...'

'Just doing my job, human. You realise, the cat will help you if you simply ask the right question,' Luned said before melting away.

Charlotte laughed. 'What do you know about the Nymet, eh Quin?'

The cat's ears pricked at the word and he lazily opened an eye and stared at Charlotte. After a deep stretch, Quin hopped from his perch, toppling the books as he went, and landed heavily on a nearby bookcase. Twitching his whiskers as if to say, 'I meant to do that', Quin plodded along till he reached a shelf right in the top corner of the room. Charlotte hadn't managed to get anywhere near it yet due to the sea of books and boxes on the floor.

Quin cocked his head over the top of the bookshelf and meowed at Charlotte. Seeing that she wasn't going to follow him, he chirped as if to say 'silly human' before hanging over the edge and swiping at a folder with his paw. After a few minutes Quin successfully caught the folder with a claw, and deftly sent it flying through the air to land at Charlotte's feet. She felt the tell-tale tingling she always got when she was about to discover something special.

Clearing a space on the main table, Charlotte opened the folder, pulling out yellowing newspaper cuttings and a book – *Local Legends of Brackenheath-on-Sea* by Peter Aherne. The hairs on her arms began to stand on end and she knew instantly the folder was a real find.

'Good kitty.' Charlotte stroked Quin who was now standing on the table beside her, but he just shook her off, making it clear she had had all the help she was going to get, before wandering off to do much more important things elsewhere.

The book creaked with age as it naturally fell open to the entry for the Brackenheath Oak. Charlotte clearly wasn't the first person interested in its story it would seem. She settled down to read.

*The oak tree found in Brackenheath Park has long inspired both awe and dread in local residents. The oak is easily located, elevated on a small hill. Due to this prominent position, it is thought to have been used as a gallows tree and certain residents have sworn they have heard the cries of these unfortunate souls when walking their dogs late at night or on particularly misty mornings.*

*On very rare occasions, people have reported a strange humming coming from the general area of this fascinating tree. It is not known what causes this unusual sound but local experts have not been able to find any scientific explanation.*

*The most interesting legend involving the Brackenheath Oak (otherwise known as the Evergreen Oak) states that there is an ancient evil held fast in the roots of the tree and the felling of it will bring great misfortune to the area. Anyone who has spent time with this special tree will agree there is something magical about it. It certainly has a very spooky atmosphere.*

*See page 98 for 'Evergreen Oak'*

Charlotte rolled her eyes at the last line. She was much more interested in the intriguing 'ancient evil'. It reminded her of the figure on the Egyptian stela in Paris burying the unknown object under a tree.

Charlotte lifted the top corner of the page which had been bent down. In the corner, a handwritten note in pencil read *'The Echo'* under which was a strange-looking symbol: a horizontal line off which were two sets of bars and a tail that looked like… a root. A chill flowed down her spine – it was the symbol she had been seeing in her dreams since finding the stone and here she had proof it was somehow linked to the tree.

Charlotte had no trouble feeling the fear of the person who had put them there but could sense nothing of their meaning. She reached for the plaster mould she had made at the Nymet and rolled it around in her hands to help herself think. Tracing her fingers along the imprint she suddenly realised it mirrored the symbol. More proof.

There was an essay in the folder with an old-fashioned photograph stapled to it, the colours faded. Charlotte recognised the woman in the picture. The slim figure, boyish looks and red hair – it had to be a younger version of her mother. She must be about the same age as Charlotte was now and the date on the back read *'Jan 1993'*.

Ella Stone was wearing a deer stalker hat and duffle coat as well as thick hiking boots against the cold judging by the snow that could be seen on the tree's branches. In spite of this though, the oak was in full leaf, acorns hanging in abundance from its branches.

What were the chances? Olly had told her the legend of the Evergreen Oak that bloomed in winter dated back to the 18th century yet here seemed to be photographic evidence it had happened since. Why not again? Still, there would be nothing unusual about leaves and catkins in May. *Then perhaps we need to engineer something even more unusual*, Charlotte thought. The kernel of an idea formed in her mind.

She read the essay through several times; there was a plethora of information about the age, history and legends of the tree, a bit on Nymets and sacred groves as well as reputed wishing trees and hanging trees in the local area. There was nothing, however, that explained the evil or the symbol. On the bottom it read:

'History of the Brackenheath Oak by Ella Aherne and Irving Batterbee, 1993'

Tucked in the back of the file was another, even older photograph – black and white and faded around the edges. It showed a newly married couple posed under the Brackenheath Oak. They smiled at the camera but Charlotte could also sense tension and anxiety. A thought drifted across her mind. Grandparents, these were her grandparents. The realisation that her family belonged in Brackenheath left her reeling; but it was also oddly comforting.

A shuffling sound at the window made her look up to find Tar'sel climbing through the window.

'What are you doing here?' Charlotte hurriedly tidied the file away.

Boris stepped out from behind Tar'sel and waved apologetically.

'Boris! Aunt Clarissa will have your guts for garters if she finds you here.'

'What are garters?' they asked in unison.

Charlotte rolled her eyes. 'Never mind.'

Charlotte sat and listened patiently as Tar'sel unloaded his horror and guilt about the condition of the Brackenheath Oak. She waved away his suggestions that his people must be to blame and that perhaps they only had themselves to blame for their predicament. She understood how he felt though; she couldn't help having similar worries over her parents' disappearance.

'The Morrigan told me this was destiny so I guess it was

inevitable. Blaming yourself over something you couldn't have changed is a waste of time and effort.' She comforted him in the best way she knew how.

'You're probably right, and it doesn't change anything. Something still needs to be done.'

'Just to play devil's advocate for a moment, what's the worst that can happen if we… I, fail? The world is left with one less tree.' Even Charlotte couldn't buy into her argument, she was becoming very attached to the Nymet.

Tar'sel looked at her in shock. 'That in itself would be unthinkable.'

He couldn't imagine how anyone could be so cold about the death of another living being and he was beginning to think these Albion folk were not right in the head. Had his people really got it so wrong as to think one of them would be able to save the Nymet?

'It's more complicated than that,' he continued, trying to keep his fears in check. 'The Nymet truly is special – it holds the memory of an entire forest and without it that forest will vanish. As for your world, it will become weaker without the Nymet too. Not only does it cleanse the air, it maintains the magic in the very soil, magic which protects you from many unseen dangers. Do you understand?'

'I think so. And you?'

'For the Tree Weavers it's more immediate. Without the trees we die.'

'No pressure then.' The truth hung heavy in the air. 'Well, I guess what we need is some inspiration.' Charlotte rapped her fingers on Quintillian's file.

# Charlotte's New Skills

'Time to see how everyone is getting on with their projects.' Mr Thomlinson beamed at them as he dumped a pile of paperwork and a briefcase on the heavy wooden table at the front of the class.

Sissy was first up.

'The "Evergreen Oak of Brackenheath" is a famous local landmark, depictions of which can be found in various locations in the local area if you know where to look, including the local church and a number of the older houses. Perhaps the most beautiful example can be found in the old Wykenhall Manor (now a private school).

'This is our main source for the local legend that tells of how the local population was saved from starvation during a particularly bleak winter and poor harvest. In spite of the season, the Brackenheath Oak bore acorns throughout the months and months of heavy snows and frost, ensuring their survival.

'There are suggestions that this famous local oak is the same tree that stands to this day on the hill in Brackenheath Park.'

'Very good work, Miss Pike, that was well researched. An excellent addition to our project.'

Sissy blushed, before mumbling something unintelligible and scuttling to her desk.

Sang stood up and signed about how her father learnt English under a tree when he arrived in England, Govinder narrating her story for the benefit of the rest of the class. Charlotte wasn't the only one that didn't need Govinder's narration, but she was impressed how quick and accurate he was. It was easy to forget that she had only been Sang's friend for a short time and she didn't have the monopoly on being good at languages.

Connor McNamara got up next and talked about the Celtic myth of the Hazel and Salmon of Wisdom while his sister Finnula told them of the fairy trees and how, in ancient times, when land was cleared, at least one tree was left standing to become the focal point of any new village. A place to meet and celebrate.

Olly talked about how the Brackenheath Oak had survived the Second World War and had been a place where local soldiers had married their sweethearts, which reminded Charlotte of the picture of her grandparents. Charlie discussed the humming sound that was sometimes heard near the tree, waving a copy of Peter Aherne's book as if for proof that he was not mad.

Mr Thomlinson congratulated them all. 'You're up next, Charlotte,' he whispered as Giles finished his tale about the 'Golden Rider', a notorious highwayman who was hung from the Brackenheath Oak until the earth swallowed him up. Charlotte couldn't understand why she was so nervous, she never usually had any problem with public speaking.

'It's a load of nonsense,' Olly whispered in disgust. 'There's not a shred of historical evidence there was ever a highwayman in this area.'

Charlotte smiled weakly. That may be true but she knew there was often a thread of truth in the wildest folktale and something about Giles' story made her feel decidedly uncomfortable. It reminded her of the 'ancient evil' mentioned in Peter Aherne's book. She didn't have time to worry about it as Mr Thomlinson waved her to the front of the class.

'My grandparents were married under the Brackenheath Oak,' she announced and all eyes were glued to her in expectation.

'Now that is interesting, Miss Stone. How about you tell us a little more?' Mr Thomlinson encouraged her.

'I don't really know much more than that. I only found a picture,' Charlotte lied.

'OK, well, how did it make you feel when you realised you have family ties to this place?'

It had felt weird. In fact, it was something she couldn't put into words and she felt stupid as tears pricked the back of her eyes. Charlotte could feel twenty pairs of eyes boring into her; Giles and Wilbur were sniggering in the back but perhaps worse than that was the look of pity in Isla's eyes. The silence seemed to stretch on forever.

Only, it wasn't… silent. At first she thought it was the sound of her own blood in her ears from the flush she could feel creeping up her neck – but there was something musical in the sound. She began to forget where she was as the melody overtook her and the memories of the Nymet threatened to engulf her. Low, sad notes chimed… before it was gone on the breeze.

'Charlotte, Charlotte…?' Mr Thomlinson was looking at her with concern. 'Perhaps have a little think about that and come back to us with what you discover.' He gestured for her to take a seat.

'Sir?'

Charlotte was grateful when Olly drew attention away from her.

'Yes, Mr Batterbee?' Mr Thomlinson replied, distracted.

'Sir, what if we staged an… "awareness campaign" in the local library… and outside the town hall during the debate. Dad always told me we have a duty to try and protect our local landscape… and it would make a great project for my political studies class.'

'As long as you have everyone's permission I don't see why not. It could be a good learning experience on the processes of local government,' Mr Thomlinson nodded with approval. 'I must stress, however, it would be in your own time, not an official school trip, and I couldn't attend with you – I can't be seen to openly show bias. As such, no uniforms please.'

The student common room was buzzing during the break. Olly

and Govinder were formulating a plan for the campaign, and they had already enrolled half the class when Charlotte came in.

'Your name's already on the list, Charlotte,' Govinder called over to her. 'Olly figured you would be there come hell or high water.'

'No problem. What have you got me down to do?'

'Thought you could tell the story of your grandparents getting married, if you get anywhere with it; reckon my dad could help you there. A nice bit of local history to tug at the heart strings.'

'Olly, do you think that's fair? We don't want to set Charlotte up for embarrassment, she's clearly not a natural public speaker,' said Isla with that look of pity again. Charlotte ignored it; annoying as she was, Isla meant well.

'Maybe you two could put it to music for me to make it more emotional,' she nodded at Olly and Govinder.

'We could do that,' Olly replied, 'if you're willing to sing it.'

'Maybe not then.' Charlotte grinned, collecting her bag from her locker and making for the exit.

'Where are you going?'

'Got plans of my own to make,' she winked before heading out the door.

It was a warm, sunny evening as Charlotte arrived at the Nymet tree and Tar'sel was already floating nearby.

'You want to call off the guard crows?' he called exasperatedly from halfway down the hill, which was as close as the birds would let him. As soon as Charlotte appeared, the crows lifted off together and flew off towards the sea.

'It's like they don't realise I'm a Nymet Draoi,' Tar'sel complained.

'Perhaps it's because you're see-through.' Charlotte tried to placate him but he was still annoyed.

'So what's your inspired idea then?' He changed the subject and Charlotte told him the story of the Evergreen Oak.

Tar'sel was clearly sceptical when she had finished. 'I can't believe such a thing would have become a legend. That's not so strange.'

Charlotte smiled. 'It is strange here, Tar'sel, Albion humans don't weave.'

'But I don't see how it's going to help at this time of year. The tree is full of budding acorns anyway.'

Tar'sel wasn't so sure of himself now; he clearly had much to learn about the ways and environment of Albion, but he was relieved when Charlotte agreed.

'But with you here we could create something unusual. What if the oak started blooming something it shouldn't?' Charlotte's eyes glowed with excitement.

'What did you have in mind?'

Charlotte fell quiet. The idea had come from her mother's essay and Charlotte wished her family could be here to share the moment.

'Roses are Mum's favourite,' Charlotte shrugged, as she wondered about the logistics.

Tar'sel beamed. 'That should be easy, and I'm guessing it would be... unusual?'

Charlotte nodded.

'What good would it do though, I mean... who would see it?' Tar'sel continued more confidently.

'Leave that to me, we have a thing called "media". They would certainly be interested in reporting such a thing.'

'Me... diee... aa.' Tar'sel rolled the word around in his mouth. He had no idea what it meant but it sounded good.

Tar'sel did a circuit of the tree, inspecting every branch and twig, sucking in a breath at the sight of the charred remains of the heartwood.

'She's pretty sick, we'll need to do some healing first, there's still a lot of pain there.'

'How do you know?'

'Can't you feel it?'

Tar'sel still couldn't get used to how backward these Albion people were but he tried to keep his tone neutral. He didn't want to insult Charlotte.

'You have to tune in. Sense it here,' Tar'sel motioned to his stomach.

He showed her how to control her breathing and focus her attention on hearing the Nymet song. Charlotte found it surprisingly easy; the techniques were similar to those Mr Lei taught her in her karate lessons.

'Someone has been doing healing already,' Tar'sel looked confused. 'I can't quite work out the signature but there's definitely been some deliberate work done here.'

'Perhaps it's The Morrigan…' Charlotte's sentence trailed off as Tar'sel shook his head.

'I can't see that, there would be dire consequences if a member of the Shriven intervened – only happens in real emergencies, and when they do… it isn't pretty.'

Tar'sel didn't need to say any more.

Coming to a stop at the place where he started, Tar'sel closed his eyes and stood stock still for what seemed like forever.

'What are you doing now?'

'Sssh, concentrate. You have to break through the silence to get to the song,' Tar'sel chided her.

This was not the awkward young boy unsure of himself and his surroundings; this was an experienced and confident healer – a proper Nymet Draoi, unlike her. She did as she was told, but it was hard. She had so many questions.

She watched as Tar'sel began to chant a neutral, even tone, eventually knitting in other notes. When he started singing a rose song, flowers began to bud all over the lower branches, quickly uncurling their petals into full bloom.

Pleased with his work, Tar'sel stopped chanting and admired

his handiwork but in moments the roses began to die and fall to the ground.

'What's happening, why isn't it working?' Charlotte asked with alarm. The scene was uncomfortably close to her vision.

'I don't know,' Tar'sel replied.

He didn't want to admit he had had difficulty drowning out the cacophony of sound that was plaguing Albion, besides, he was positive that wasn't the problem. The song of the roses had been true.

'It should have worked in theory. Maybe the roses just aren't compatible with the Nymet, or maybe she's still too sick.'

'Perhaps I have to do it,' Charlotte suggested, 'being as I am from this side of the Dreamtime.'

Tar'sel agreed, guiding her through the process. 'Once you start to chant, you have to keep going till the process is complete,' he told her. 'If you don't you'll damage the plant. You can't go too far either though or the new growth won't have energy left to sustain itself.'

After hours of practice they were still no further forward and the sun was setting.

'Maybe I need more practice.'

'It wouldn't hurt, I guess.' Tar'sel felt the tell-tale tug at his chest. He smiled apologetically at Charlotte as he began to fade.

'I can't work on the Nymet alone. When will you be back?' There was an edge of panic in her voice.

'Hard to say. You know all you need though, trust your instincts and go with your gut. You shouldn't overthink weaving if you want it to work – for a beginner you've done well.' He smiled encouragingly. 'Practise if it makes you feel better.'

Charlotte barely said a word to Clarissa as she came in the kitchen door and went up to her room. Her head was still with the Nymet. Sitting at her desk, she absentmindedly played with the picture of her grandparents under the Brackenheath Oak.

She had hoped this time would be different; that she wouldn't feel the sense of pain and loss that emanated from it, a contradiction of the happy smiling faces. She willed it to tell her more but she got nothing.

'It doesn't work so well when it's family.' Clarissa stood behind her with a cup of hot chocolate and a roasted vegetable and hummus roll. 'You need to eat something.'

Charlotte realised then just how hungry she was.

'How's the project coming on?' Clarissa admired all the various books and pieces of paper that covered Charlotte's desk.

'I have a load of information on similar circumstances… I'm trying to find a legal precedent to support our campaign.'

'That all sounds very impressive and informative but people don't generally care for facts and figures, Charlotte. They are more interested in people and stories.'

'Well, I'm out of those.' Charlotte sighed tiredly through a mouthful of food. 'Olly is much better at that sort of thing.'

Clarissa leant over the desk and picked up the picture of Charlotte's grandparents. 'You have one right here.'

'I don't know the story,' Charlotte replied blankly.

'Would you like to?' Clarissa smiled.

Luned found herself summoned to the 'Hanging Gardens of Fargale' once again. She seemed to spend more time underground these days than she did when she lived in Agrimony. Malik and Davlin were deep in discussion in the meeting room of the comms room when she arrived.

'If the worst happened, could you keep the comms room going?' Malik frowned as he scrutinised pages and pages of print-outs.

'I'm downloading as much as I can onto the section of the web that is still undamaged,' Davlin replied, tapping away at a nearby terminal, 'but without somewhere to send it, the information is highly vulnerable.'

'You're telling me there is not a single living tree in the Sylurian forest?'

'There's no trace of a bluprint for the Nymet oak.' Davlin looked apologetic. 'I've searched through every note of the subsonic code across the whole Triverse. Fargale is not a copy.'

An alarm sounded, diverting their attention from the matter in hand and Davlin sprang into action.

'This is not a drill people, we have an unauthorised breach.' He broadcasted a warning on the tannoy before leading Malik and Luned into the Tap Room.

Davlin worked with dexterity and Luned was surprised at such speed in a dwarf. He had soon located the problem.

'Someone is weaving!'

'In Albion?' Malik gasped.

'But that hasn't been possible for nearly a millennia,' Luned added.

'Don't believe it; where do you think the humans got their little legend of the "Evergreen Oak"? That was someone messing where they shouldn't have been messing.' Davlin didn't look up; he was still madly tapping away on a nearby terminal.

'Boris?!' Malik gasped.

Davlin shook his head. 'It's the girl.'

'What!' Malik's face was now purple and his hands in fists. 'Luned, sort out that *dilino* human child once and for all – ASAP!' he roared.

'On it, Sir.'

Luned stepped into the sap flow for a quick getaway.

Charlotte woke early, surprisingly refreshed. Tar'sel had said that could happen. Connecting with the Nymet song was connecting to the song of creation, or something like that. Charlotte, however, put it down to the hot chocolate.

'No time like the present,' she yawned at Cicero as they both stretched out the kinks of a night's sleep.

The sun was just breaching the horizon as Charlotte entered the garden. The air was fresh and salty from the sea, while the dew looked like a handful of jewels scattered over the lawn and vegetable patch. Charlotte stretched as she looked around for a victim. Clarissa would not be happy if she messed with the produce, it was her livelihood.

Walking down the side of the building, she found herself outside the impressive main door. The natural spring bubbled up from the bottom of the little pool and Charlotte wondered if she might see her parents if she stared into it for long enough. All she saw, however, was a reflection of the recently pruned winter jasmine that climbed the wall by the stained glass window.

Perfect.

Chanting a neutral tone as Tar'sel had taught her, she listened for the jasmine's song. She was surprised and thrilled when she heard a high tinkling melody. She was really getting the hang of this.

Charlotte eagerly started weaving in the tones she heard Tar'sel make, the sounds of the rose song. One by one, tiny rosebuds appeared on the stems of the jasmine. She remembered Tar'sel's advice not to stop till the process was complete, so she kept singing till the roses bloomed.

The song of the rose and jasmine tumbled over and over each other and became so quick she didn't know where one started and the other ended so she continued to sing; she didn't know when to stop. As she sang, the jasmine grew to accommodate more roses and before she knew it, the whole side of the house was covered, the main door buried under the mass of rose-covered jasmine. It wasn't till she felt Clarissa's voice joining the song that she dared stop.

Clarissa quickly and skilfully brought the song to an end and the jasmine rose stopped growing.

'Nice try for a first attempt, but next time, could you stick to house plants, it'll give the neighbours less to talk about,' Aunt Clarissa said, making for the back door.

'DARRRLINGS!'

There was no mistaking Jude's voice and even Aunt Clarissa visibly shuddered.

'Oh! Well, I say. What on earth has happened here, Clarissa?' Aunt Jude eyed the new greenery with wide-eyed wonder. 'It looks like someone has set off a miracle-gro bomb on your front doorstep.'

Mrs Bunratty's begonias twitched as Aunt Jude continued to extol the 'wonders of nature' and declared how they were 'truly blessed by the fairy folk'.

'Blessed by fairy folk, my fanny-adams,' Clarissa hissed sternly at Charlotte while trying, but failing, to maintain her steely glare.

'Tea anyone?' Clarissa finally said to distract Jude from her monologue. 'We'll just have to use the backdoor for the time being.'

'Why don't you just trim it?' Charlotte asked.

'This is your doing. Why should I punish the jasmine?'

Charlotte couldn't help grinning; it was a typical Aunt Clarissa response.

Tea in their house meant peppermint, sage, jasmine and the like made from the carefully dried leaves and flowers from Aunt Clarissa's garden, but Charlotte had her usual hot chocolate. It went perfectly with yet another continental breakfast courtesy of Jude.

As they tucked into a breakfast of jam and pastries, a loud pop filled the kitchen and an angry Luned appeared on the kitchen table.

Jude squealed with excitement and Luned looked at her as if she thought the woman must be ill – the suggestion in her expression was that she thought it might be a mental problem.

'A fairy, an actual real-life fairy,' Jude cooed, in awe.

'Madam, I am an Undine; quite different,' Luned barked, her pointy ears twitching in indignation.

The Undine turned and strode purposefully across the kitchen table, her sea-green robes floating around her, before lifting a slender finger at Charlotte.

'Are you Charlotte Seshat Stone?' she demanded.

It was a procedural requirement in accordance with the P.O.D charter. Having the offender state their name of their own freewill added power to the binding spell that would be cast later on.

'Er, you know I am – we've already met, remember?' Charlotte replied, ignorant of the charter requirements.

Luned rolled her eyes and sighed; it was always such hard work dealing with humans.

'Who are you?' Clarissa asked calmly.

'I am Luned, Charlotte's fairylore caseworker and under the authority of sub-section 492 of the P.O.D charter, I hereby summons her to appear before the Seelie and Unseelie Courts for the unauthorised use by an Albion human of Sonic Adjustment Therapy.'

'Sonic what? Do you mean weaving?' Charlotte asked.

'Well, yes… in very basic layman's terms.' Luned was not used to being questioned by an offender.

'Oooh, sounds fabulous. Where can one experience Sonic Adjustment Therapy, is there a training course I could apply for? How long does it…' Jude fell into silence at not just Luned's glare but Clarissa's.

'If we might focus for a moment,' Clarissa addressed the Undine. 'If you are Charlotte's caseworker that means you've had her under surveillance for some time?' She was eager to get to the bottom of this intrusion into her home.

'We have.'

'The reason for this, please.'

'She came to our attention almost the moment she arrived in Brackenheath and has exhibited behaviour that we have found not only disturbing but threatening. Just yesterday, she tried to modify Fargale – the tree also known as the Evergreen Oak or the Nymet.' Luned handed Clarissa a thick file.

It was hard to know what Clarissa was thinking as she read the file but when she had finished, she fixed Charlotte with one of her trademark stares.

'There is nothing I can do for you, Charlotte, you've broken Fey law. You're going to have to attend. The court date is tomorrow.'

# The Seelie Courts

Sang sprang bolt upright, her breathing heavy and sweat dripping down her face. The wind was high outside and rain fell hard against her window. Hunkering down under her bedclothes, she squirmed to get comfortable. She figured the rain must have woken her and everything seemed normal and ordinary but she couldn't shake the feeling of foreboding.

The darkness pouring into her had seemed so real as had the scream from the red-haired girl that looked so much like Charlotte. Even now, wide-awake in the familiar surrounds of her room, Sang could still hear the word repeating in her head. *Echo, echo, echo…*

The dream was rapidly evaporating so Sang hopped out of bed and quickly made notes before it disappeared. She had no idea what it meant but she knew she had to find Charlotte.

'A hearty breakfast, very good.' Jude nodded to Charlotte with approval over the kitchen table. 'You need to be able to concentrate and focus today. Fairies can be rather tricksy and will try to catch you out. It's revealed in all the classic fairytales.'

'Actually, the court will be very fair.' Clarissa poured them both a steaming cup of coffee. 'But the best thing you can do is just stay quiet and… well, not antagonise them.'

Charlotte knew it wasn't worth protesting; Clarissa had got to know her pretty well, so she just smiled mischievously.

Luned soon appeared on the kitchen table in the same official-looking robes she had worn the previous day.

'Are we ready?' she asked.

The usual underground courtroom was far too small to accommodate Charlotte so the hearing was to take place under the boughs of the large weeping willow on the riverbank, Luned explained as she led Charlotte inside. The inner leaves had been curled upwards and sewn together with gossamer to create temporary bowers which hung the full circle of the willow canopy from top to bottom.

Charlotte started to feel nervous as she realised the bowers were already occupied by the scores of Fey that made up the Seelie and Unseelie Courts.

One half of the canopy was awash with the blinding light of the 'Shining Ones' of the Seelie Court. Only when they moved could Charlotte see the features of these perfect creatures as they glided about in an orderly fashion, occasionally turning to look at her and whisper behind their hands. 'The True Fey,' Luned had whispered discretely and Charlotte agreed they certainly looked like the traditional fairies that filled the fairytales Jude had mentioned.

On the other side sat the unruly members of the Unseelie Court who laughed raucously and threw bits of food at the Seelie members while chanting obscenities at them. Their ranks were made up of sinister gargoyles, deformed goblins with gaping mouths and boggled eyes and strange women with purple hair, twigs growing from their limbs and forked tongues that tasted the air around Charlotte. Despite their gruesome appearances and behaviour, Charlotte suspected she would get a much more favourable ear from this group of chaotic Fey.

They were not the ones passing judgment, however. Charlotte was acutely aware of the shrouded elfin warriors, bows at the ready, who stood stock still in a semicircle between her and the courts. A dozen pairs of hidden eyes looked at her from underneath their hoods, like wolves eyeing up an injured lamb. Luned had explained this was the Elfin Jury and it was they that would ultimately decide her fate.

A cough from the court clerk brought her back to the purpose of the gathering.

'All stand for Judge Dijin,' he squeaked.

On this announcement, a stern-looking Fey marched sombrely into the courtroom, reminding Charlotte a little of Mr Ransell. She had to stifle a giggle as Judge Dijin sat at his podium with a flourish of his fiery robes.

'Lords and Ladies of the Seelie Courts and Elfin Jury,' the clerk began, reading from a large scroll. 'The accused stands trial today for the misuse of weaving, which is banned from use in this Verse.'

A ripple of disapproval went round the Seelie half of the court and they all looked very serious. The Elfin Jury, however, didn't move – and the Unseelie Court were too busy comparing navel fluff to even notice the clerk had spoken.

A fairy in chains was led in front of the gathered Fey. Charlotte recognised Boris in a flash. He stood shaking with fear as Dijin, without giving him so much as a glance, waved a hand at the clerk and pondered some paperwork handed to him.

'Intelligence has come to light that it was you, Boris, who brought Miss Stone to our home and assisted her in entering our realm.' Dijin spoke for the first time, his booming voice filling the courtroom.

'Noo, noo, I's not be doing that, she already had the sight.'

'I can vouch for the last,' Luned interjected.

Dijin turned to the Undine in surprise. 'Your evidence.'

Luned shot a glance to her boss, Malik. He was tight-lipped and grey but nodded curtly.

'I was on surveillance at the house on the cliff and Miss Stone saw me amongst the raspberries… though she had no idea what she was seeing at the time,' Luned added on seeing Dijin's look of thunder.

It looked as if Dijin was going to say something, then thought better of it, before turning back to Boris.

'No matter, it does not negate the fact that it was you who led her to us. However, while it has a baring on today, your guilt will need to be determined in a separate trial.'

'I's not guilty, not guiltys. I's only acting on the orders of the Dark Lady.'

'Why would The Morrigan wish to rain down such destruction on us? We have no quarrel with her,' Dijin scoffed, dismissing Boris' claim. 'Miss Stone, however, has proven to bring nothing but chaos in her wake. If I didn't know better, I would say she has Veshengo blood.'

'I object!' Charlotte shouted. Dijin and the courts were so shocked they just stared open-mouthed and Charlotte took her chance.

'Aside from the fact that I am clearly *not* a "man of the woods", and ignoring for a moment your discriminatory comments, Boris is telling the truth. The Morrigan has ordered me to save the Brackenheath Oak and I bear the Mother's Kiss.' Charlotte exposed her arm and the burn marks glowed in the gloom.

The courtroom exploded at her final comment and Dijin simply stared at her with a face of fury. Without turning away he said something to the court clerk.

'The defendant's last comments will be struck from the records,' the clerk squeaked. Clearly satisfied, Dijin turned back to a still-quaking Boris.

'You should be aware that the consequences are severe, Boris. If you are found guilty your root will be severed – and you are already in enough trouble as it is.'

Boris paled at those last words. Charlotte didn't know what it meant but it was clearly very bad indeed.

'Take him down,' barked Dijin at the guards. 'You will be held pending your trial date; the air dungeon would be most appropriate I think.'

The poor Veshengo seemed to shrink into himself and whimpered softly as the Elfin Jury raised their bows and fired. The arrows twisted through the air, spinning it into silvery rope. As they landed, the ropes wound around Boris, burning his skin as they tightened, and he was led from the willow room.

Dijin, no longer distracted, turned his full attention towards Charlotte. Bathed in the full force of his fiery presence, she suddenly realised why he commanded such fearful respect from his peers.

'Now, Miss Stone, what are we going to do with you?'

⁓

Sang had been looking for Charlotte for over an hour. She had expected to find her in the park with the oak but there had been no sign of her. If Sang hadn't bumped into Lloyd and therefore been by the large weeping willow at the exact same time the guards were leading Boris away, she would still be searching.

It was the rustling of the leaves that had caught Sang's attention and the odd heat haze that floated across the meadow before sinking into the river. She could have sworn she could hear whimpering too. Was it possible Charlotte was hiding out and crying over her lost family? Sang didn't like to interrupt such a personal moment but she had the feeling it really couldn't wait.

It was somewhat awkward trying to get under the willow's veil of leaves. The tree curved round from the bank at an angle overhanging the water and a narrow peninsula of earth. If anyone was sat in the curve of the trunk no one would know they were there – it was what Lloyd called a 'betwixt and between place'.

After assessing the peninsula, Sang decided it was strong enough to take her weight. Taking aim, she jumped, landing light as a cat and sweeping aside the willow branches as she leant forward to avoid falling into the water. What followed was pandemonium.

'*Dook Kascht!*' screeched the court clerk as members of the Seelie Court were sent reeling in all directions. The Elfin Jury swiftly loosened a dozen silver arrows in Sang's direction. The arrows arched through the air before merging into one ball of green light.

Charlotte had pre-empted the elfin guard and rushed to the defence of her friend.

Pulling back a branch, Charlotte waited till the green light was on the descent before letting go. The branch collided with the green fireball sending it flying into the line of the Elfin Jury and sending them scattering like bowling pins.

*Strike!* Charlotte signed at Sang, as they stood together, ready for the backlash.

Several of the Elfin Jury were now on the ground, choking and spluttering as their skin cracked and turned brown – like the bark of a tree, the purpose of the green light disturbingly clear.

'Watch out!' Charlotte shouted a warning but the remaining guards had regained their composure and despite Sang's best efforts to duck, a fresh bout of green flame made contact with the tip of one of her plaits. Charlotte watched with alarm as it solidified into wood and crept closer to Sang's head.

'Do something!' Charlotte cried urgently to Luned.

'I can't undo this, it's earth magic,' the Undine replied in horror, 'and it won't end well for your friend.'

Sang's face twisted in pain as the earth magic touched her scalp.

*'Atch Draba.'* Dijin released a bolt of fire magic.

'Ha ha, stickface human. What a hoot!' roared a hobgoblin, delighted at the impromptu entertainments as the Elfin Jury tried to return order to the proceedings. The Seelie Court were trying to regain their dignity while various members of the Unseelies were dancing like devils and acting out the moment the Seelies had been sent flying across the hall by Sang's grand entrance.

'Let's all calm down, shall we.' Everyone fell silent at Dijin's voice. 'We don't want to shatter the human's notion of fluffy cute fairies by turning petrified children into petrified trees… though it might be a fitting punishment for you, Miss Stone. We might need a new home after all this.'

'I don't think her aunt would allow that, Dijin,' the court clerk squeaked.

'No human is going to dictate fairy law to me,' Dijin spat.

'Remember who you are talking about,' King Rosebay-Willowherb, leader of the Seelie Court cautioned him.

'She made her choice, Sire.'

Charlotte was desperate to ask what they were talking about but she didn't want to remind them she was there and she was busy seeing to Sang who was lying on the ground in shock. Luckily the pain seemed to have stopped and the magic wasn't spreading anymore.

'Don't worry, Miss, there's not much damage done,' a frog-legged sprite cooed reassuringly, 'though nothing will grow back again from that area of her scalp,' she added, snapping off the matted hair twig. 'Nothing else to be done.' She waved it apologetically at Sang.

'Explain the meaning of this defilement of our sacred court.' The king was apoplectic with rage as he adjusted his wig and robes. A wave of sniggering broke out among the Unseelies.

'Order, order,' squeaked the court clerk. The Seelie Court had finally found their seats and, adjusting their finery, glared at Sang.

'How do they get anything done with this lot?' Charlotte whispered to Luned.

'Oh, they're not so bad, even come in useful at times. Besides, it's tradition.'

Sang was now on her feet and signing forcefully, trying to get the courts' attention but they were too busy bickering and shouting among themselves to pay her any heed and she gave up in frustration.

'You need to listen, she's trying to tell you something important,' Charlotte barked at the courts, no longer interested in entertaining their silly traditions.

The flash of fire in Dijin's eyes was the only thing that stopped her from saying more but the courts fell silent at her outburst.

'I can translate if needed,' Charlotte added more politely.

'With respect, human child, I hardly think the accused is the right person to be translating,' King Rosebay-Willowherb added with a calm in his voice not reflected in his appearance. 'You could tell us anything you like.'

Charlotte couldn't argue with that. The frog-legged lady raised her hand and the king nodded for her to speak.

'If the courts permit, I have some experience with this strange human language. I offer my services if His Majesty allows?' The king of the Seelie Court nodded again and the frog-legged lady turned to Sang.

'Are you willing to speak to me, human child?'

Sang nodded.

'If it helps, look only at me and pretend there is no one else about. Now, what was it that was important enough to gatecrash these proceedings?'

Sang signed frantically and the frog-legged lady had to stop and calm her down on several occasions. Once she had finished, the frog-legged lady turned to the courts pale-faced.

'The human child has had a vision that appears to foretell disaster for us all... but especially you,' she nodded at Charlotte. 'If the courts insist on opposing The Morrigan and defying the Mother's wishes by imprisoning this one, it could spell the end for us all.'

'Speak clearly, Andarwen.'

'An unstoppable chain of events will unfold, bringing about the release... of the Echo.'

The silence was deafening. Charlotte and Sang exchanged looks; Sang clearly had no idea what Andarwen was talking about. In moments, the courts came to their senses and a wall of voices hit them like a tidal wave.

'That is preposterous. "The Echo" is a silly fairy story designed to scare baby Fey. It's not real,' exclaimed a portly-looking gnome with a bushy beard that fell down to the floor.

'And what would a human child know of the Echo?' shouted a shrill, bird-like woman with silver hair, clothed only in rubies. The woman gave Sang a spiteful look when she finished speaking. She clearly hadn't forgiven her for her unseemly entrance.

'Many things can be revealed to the uninitiated through dreams. What I have provided is an interpretation of her dream.' Andarwen was calm in the face of such outrage.

'I should have known you would put your own spin on things – I'd expect no less from an Unseelie. This is a courtroom, we require solid facts and literal translation, please,' Dijin replied.

'You doubt my skills as a dreamseer, Lord Dijin? What I say are facts – just not necessarily in any format you seem to respect. If I didn't know better, I'd say you were scared.'

Dijin ignored her, instead looking pleadingly at the king who was already consulting with his advisers. The court clerk exchanged whispers with the group before banging his staff for order amongst the crowd.

'The testament will stand,' he squeaked. 'All rise for the king's verdict.'

The Seelie Court members duly stood as ordered, whereas many of the Unseelie Court, who had been standing, very deliberately sat down. Others started flying loop-the-loop around the room and Andarwen hopped over to Luned and Charlotte.

'Do not be put off by the reputation of the Vorla,' she whispered in Charlotte's ear. 'They may be your only hope before this is done. You'll certainly get no help from this lot.'

The commotion finally died down and the king spoke.

'In light of what we have heard today, I decree that the human child known as Charlotte Seshat Stone will be issued with an A.K.O.R.N for her irresponsible actions.'

There were some boos, but mainly cheers, from the Unseelie Court at this announcement.

'The courts impress on the human child the seriousness of what she has done,' the king continued. 'It is felt that she does not fully understand the possible devastation of her actions, and while a custodial sentence is deemed inappropriate at this time, the conditions of the A.K.O.R.N are that she will make no attempt to cultivate any form of vegetation either by standard or sonic means until this decree is lifted. Any breach will have serious consequences.'

King Rosebay-Willowherb looked down at her in a manner he clearly thought was intimidating, but it was obvious he was not as well practised as Dijin.

'Magic is prohibited for humans in this realm – for good reasons,' he scolded her.

'But why? Please, if I just understood…'

'You are not required to understand, only to comply,' Dijin cut her off. 'No further discussion will be entered into.' He turned to the shining Seelie Court. 'As for the one who so recklessly taught Miss Stone the secrets of weaving, I put it to the courts that further enquiries are needed to discover their identity so they too can be brought to justice for this reckless act.'

Various members of the court nodded in approval.

'I will consider your proposal,' the king replied graciously before taking his seat.

Happy with their conclusions, Dijin and the court looked to the Elfin Jury who still hadn't moved. In unison, the hooded figures nodded in agreement with the ruling before filing out of the courtroom.

Charlotte had expected some kind of formal close to the hearing but Dijin simply disappeared with a pop while the rest of the courts scattered chaotically, leaving the court clerk to unpick the willow leaves.

'Is that it?'

'All done,' Luned smiled. 'You got off lightly there. Thank goodness for Andarwen.'

'Here, take this,' Andarwen whispered behind them, pulling a green, almond-shaped object from beneath her shawl.

'Is it a seed?' Luned gasped. 'She can't take this, didn't you just hear the king's decree?'

'I did indeed!' The lady's grin was full of mischief. 'Oh, put away your silly P.O.D charter, Luned, before you put us both to sleep with boredom. She can keep it close, she doesn't have to TOUCH it.'

'What's it for?' Charlotte asked.

Andarwen shrugged. 'It might be useful at some point.'

'OK, when?' Charlotte persisted.

Andarwen shrugged again. 'No idea, but you'll know when to use it when the time comes. You must not remain underground, Charlotte. Dijin may be blind but some of us realise who you are. I'll leave you to fill in the details, Luned.'

Charlotte was about to ask her who they seemed to think she was, and correct the mistake, but Andarwen dived under the willow leaves and, with a splash, was gone.

Charlotte had so many questions she didn't know where to start. What had just happened? Who or what was the Echo? Why was the Seelie Court wary of Clarissa? Before she could formulate any of these thoughts into words though, Luned was already leaving.

'I trust you can find your own way home from here? Good. Try to stay out of trouble if you can,' Luned said before disappearing with a pop.

Suddenly Sang and Charlotte were alone under the willow.

*'I saw your sister,'* Sang signed to a shocked Charlotte, *'and she has a message for you.'*

# The Warriors of the Oak

The 'Save Brackenheath Park by Class 34A' project had been installed at the Wykenhall Public Library for just over a week. It stretched across two large display boards in the main corridor and included all their stories, not only about the Brackenheath Oak, but of trees from around the world.

Sang had done a piece on how the Buddha found enlightenment under the Banyan tree, Govinder's essay was on the Indian tradition of planting a new tree at the birth of a baby and the McNamara twins had produced write-ups on fairy trees and the Ogham tree alphabet.

Charlotte was especially interested in these. It was a language she had never come across before but it looked just like the symbol she had found in the book from Clarissa's library. According to Connor's essay, the double left-handed bar meant 'oak'. It had to be more than just a coincidence. Charlotte had no idea what the relevance of the 'rowan' bars to the right was though. There were no rowan trees in Brackenheath Park.

Charlotte's list of news stories where trees had been saved from the chop – and some where bad things had happened when they weren't – had also made the display. A certain amount of real life was always important, Mr Thomlinson had said.

It seemed Sissy and Charlie were quite the artists, so they had produced some beautiful illustrations to accompany the stories and, of course, Olly's songs and poems were also on display. The 'crowning glory', however, was a number of old photographs of Brackenheath Park and the Evergreen Oak, the centre picture being that of Charlotte's grandparents.

'It's been very popular.' The librarian was clearly very pleased. 'It has brought in so many new customers. Was it your idea? We'll have to prick your brains for future displays, I think.' She beamed as she handed Charlotte her books along with a bag of chocolates. 'A little thank you,' she explained.

Charlotte was not comfortable with her new-found celebrity as poster girl for the 'Save our Park' campaign and it didn't take her long to assess that she was well and truly out of her comfort zone. It wasn't the librarian so much as the posh do she had been invited to at the Hickling residence later that evening.

Isla's house was a grand-looking town house in the suburbs of Wykenhall on the Brackenheath Road. The white stone cladding reminded Charlotte of the Pimlico buildings that housed the Stone family flat, minus the balconies. Sparkly green, helium-filled balloons bobbed from the fence posts that were also festooned with green ribbons. A tap on her shoulder made her turn round.

'Am I pleased to see you,' Charlotte beamed at Sang. 'I could do with some moral support.'

Sang broke into a flurry of hand gestures that Charlotte was now fluent in.

'Not fair,' Charlotte protested. 'How come you get to sneak off early?'

*'I have very important errands to run – besides, I'm not the guest of honour,'* Sang signed with a wry smile, before squeezing Charlotte's hand in support.

'Welcome to my nightmare,' Charlotte grumbled as they made their way up the drive.

A marquee was erected on the large lawn at the rear and tables laden with food and drink were already swarming with guests.

Isla was a picture of sophistication in a pastel pink summer dress and pearl earrings, making Charlotte feel underdressed in her habitual combat trousers, T-shirt and trainers. Isla was a natural hostess, yet she lacked the easy charm of Edessa, Charlotte noticed with a certain satisfaction.

'So glad you could make it,' she beamed as if Charlotte had had a choice.

'Thank you for inviting me,' Charlotte replied automatically in what she hoped was an interested tone.

'Let me introduce you to some of the guests,' Isla simpered, whisking Charlotte through another sea of strange faces.

'So you're the young lady causing such a furore,' said Mr Hickling, as Isla introduced her. He offered her his hand with a practised but genuine smile. Charlotte could see where Isla had learnt it from.

'I just don't see the sense in destroying a perfectly healthy tree and park, especially one with so much history,' she replied.

She could hardly say it was a matter of life and death; they would think she was mad as a box of frogs if she started talking about Syluria, Tree Weavers or the loss of a new race of people from another dimension before anyone even knew they existed. If only The Morrigan would use her skills – surely this could be sorted out with a little magic.

'Quite right, quite right. History is important, and we must hear both sides of the debate, that's the reason for this little soirée. We must however, also ensure we get the right balance of retaining our history and making progress. We don't want to be left behind, now do we?'

Charlotte made a mental note. He talked a good talk but it was clear where Mr Hickling stood on the matter. She wouldn't find an ally there.

'Is this Miss Charlotte of Stone?' a lady asked Mr Hickling. 'Isn't she doing a fine job,' she cooed.

'She is indeed,' Mr Hickling replied, with no idea who the lady was. 'Well, Miss Stone, I must not monopolise you, there will be many people wanting to speak to you, I'm sure.'

'Lady Morrigan.' Charlotte addressed the woman.

'You are doing well,' The Morrigan nodded with approval, 'but time is running out.'

'Then why don't you do something? I know you could.'

The Morrigan nodded. 'I could, but what would that achieve? The humans would just destroy the Nymet another day. They have to be made to care. If you can't talk them round I will have no choice but to intervene and as I've told you before, you really don't want that.'

'I don't know why you chose me then, why not Oll…'

'I didn't choose you, Charlotte of Stone. The Nymet did,' The Morrigan hissed. 'Rest assured you would have been my last choice… now, maybe that sister of yours…'

'What do you know of Edessa?'

The Morrigan smiled. 'I know about the Sleeping Mother… and how she sometimes changes her mind, but I am only a player in the same game as you.'

The Morrigan faded into the air but before Charlotte had time to respond and she could see Olly's father bounding over to her with a huge grin.

'So pleased to meet you, Charlotte.' He shook her hand vigorously.

'Thank you, Mr Batterbee.'

'Call me Irving,' Mr Batterbee insisted. 'I used to go to school with your mother, you know. I understand you found an old essay we wrote together; I was the one who took that photo of her and the tree in the snow.' He grinned proudly. 'That was one strange winter.'

'Olly has told me all about you,' Charlotte said politely. 'He says you're quite the local historian.'

'Some would be kind enough to say that but I'm afraid I can't help you with the story of your grandparents if that's what you were going to ask.'

'Actually I've got that covered,' Charlotte smiled, 'Clarissa told me all about them. Knowing I have a long line of family from here certainly has boosted my confidence in speaking tonight. I don't feel like such an outsider anymore.'

'There's my girl, I knew that jumped up little turnip Ransell had underestimated you. You are your mother's daughter, eh?'

Charlotte didn't know how to respond, she was concentrating on not welling up.

'We all know those nasty Ransell boys want to sell the land for development; the decision is nothing to do with safety. The destruction of Brackenheath Park in its entirety for restaurants, cinemas, a swimming pool, gym and bowling alley! What do we need with a bowling alley, I ask you?'

Not long ago Charlotte would have been thrilled at such news. She remembered the first time she'd driven through Brackenheath and how her heart had sunk at the lack of such facilities but not anymore. She would much rather have the park, the trees and the Nymet.

As night fell, little solar-powered lights flickered on across the garden and staff began to line the marquee with chairs and run the sound checks. Mr Hickling got up to do the introduction, of course.

'Welcome, friends and esteemed colleagues,' he beamed. 'I have invited you all tonight, for an informal chat about the fate of Brackenheath Park – especially for those of you who will not get to have your say at the council vote tomorrow; it is important to us that your voices are heard. As you know, there are plans for development with some very exciting visions for the future, but in the first instance, we need to discuss the matter of the safety of the Brackenheath Oak that was tragically struck by lightning.'

Mr Hickling gestured for the first speaker to come to the stage. At first Charlotte thought it was Mr Ransell but soon realised this must be his brother. They had the same cold grey eyes and beak-like nose.

'Thank you, Lionel, and may I just say what a wonderful evening, it is a credit to you.' The second Mr Ransell smiled like a shark.

'My name is Marcus Ransell,' the man addressed the crowd. 'Many of you will know I am a long serving member of the local council, tirelessly working behind the scenes, not looking for glory but interested only in what is best for the local community I love.'

Charlotte wanted to vomit.

'You may well hear many impassioned pleas tonight to save the Brackenheath Oak on grounds of spurious sentimentality.' The second Mr Ransell stared directly at Charlotte. 'But rest assured that a full survey has been done and the facts speak for themselves: the tree is dangerous and unstable and as such, it must come down. Heartbreaking as it may be, we must have the courage to do the right thing for the safety of all.' Marcus Ransell left the stage to a ripple of applause.

'Dangerous and unstable? Yes, these words certainly seem to apply, but not to the Brackenheath Oak,' Irving Batterbee announced when it was his turn to take the stage. 'The oak is our most famous landmark; if we destroy it, not only will we be thumbing our noses at the lessons history has to teach us, but we are missing a trick – think of the tourism possibilities.'

'It's already destroyed through no one's fault. That is sad of course, but who wants to come and see a blasted stump?' Julian Ransell challenged.

The fate of the Brackenheath Oak created more debate than the rest of the park with many of the locals getting up to say their piece. While she waited her turn Charlotte thought about the discussion she had had with Clarissa, Jude and Luned earlier that day.

'Couldn't we say there are great crested newts?' Jude had offered as they sat round the kitchen table with steaming cups of tea. 'I'm sure we could introduce one to the area,' she'd added with a wicked smile.

'Won't work,' Luned had replied flatly. 'They've been in such demand in recent years their rates are through the roof. They won't consider even a basic 'sighting' gig for less than 10,000 rose petals. Besides, the impact of having a 'Newt-in-residence' isn't as powerful as it once was.'

Charlotte smiled at the memory; not many families would have such strange conversations, but she knew this was bigger than newts. An entire community and their forest was at stake yet the people around her, debating the Tree Weavers' fate, had no idea they even existed and most would not be open to the truth. She would have to find another way to convince the councillors, she thought as she took to the stage.

Isla was sitting front left so Charlotte deliberately faced slightly right; the last thing she needed was her pitying looks distracting her. Unfortunately, Sang had already left but not before wishing her good luck. Taking a deep breath, Charlotte began.

'There has already been a warning this evening about the possibility of pleas to save the Brackenheath Oak based on sentimentality. You certainly won't get that from me. Until a few short months ago I didn't even know the oak existed and I hadn't heard of Brackenheath or Wykenhall.

'There is nothing to say that just because a tree has been struck by lightning it needs to be cut down. Many lightning-struck trees, most of them oaks, go on to live for decades: fact. The Brackenheath Oak is already showing signs of new growth: fact.

'Thanks to this amazing tree I have discovered new family, made new friends, and found a sense of belonging I have never had before. This tree has witnessed the joys and woes of this community. It has been a reminder of home and loved ones for those who have gone to war, it has been a beacon of hope for the starving – not to mention quietly, unassumingly producing oxygen and maintaining the health of the earth on which we stand. All fact.

'This oak has given this community so much, isn't it time we gave something back? If it was a human, this tree would have been commemorated with a plaque or statue by now: fact. It does not need these things, however. It is its own monument. It should simply be allowed to continue to stand until the day it is ready to fall.'

Charlotte left the podium to huge applause and, with a certain satisfaction, she enjoyed the gormless look on Isla's face.

'Ha, Marcus, how does it feel to be outdone by a thirteen-year-old?' Irving crowed. The second Mr Ransell was calm and measured.

'She is an excellent speaker for sure. But common sense will prevail.' At this, he turned and left.

Charlotte couldn't help thinking Mr Batterbee was right, the Ransell brothers were both 'dangerous and unstable'.

The day of the council vote was bright and sunny, the perfect day to be stood outside. The tables were already set up when Charlotte arrived at the town hall. The green and yellow 'Save our Park' banner, designed by Sissy and Charlie, was tied between the lampposts.

'I hear you were quite a hit last night.' Govinder made her jump.

'Does that chair have stealth mode or something?' Charlotte teased; she didn't want to be the centre of attention. Of course, she couldn't change that as Clarissa had pointed out.

Govinder gave her an evil grin and went to help Olly set up his guitar and mic.

'Isn't this exciting?' Sissy chirped as she arranged and rearranged the petition forms and stickers.

Exciting wasn't the word Charlotte would use but then, Sissy didn't have the extra pressure of hundreds of lives in her hands so she just smiled encouragingly.

Things were soon underway with Olly, Govinder and the McNamara twins drawing in the crowds. There was a carnival feel in the air and people actually started dancing when Connor and Olly played a lively duet. Wykenhall was busy this morning and the local press and radio station, Wyked FM, were about too. By ten o'clock they had already collected eleven pages of signatures.

'That's thirty-two in total from what we already have.' Isla handed the sheets to Charlotte. 'That's a really good result, you know.'

'I couldn't have done it without everyone behind me.'

Isla smiled graciously at the compliment.

Sang was in the middle of a dance when PC Taylor turned up.

'Do you have a permit for street entertainment?' PC Taylor asked them.

Charlotte could have kicked herself, why hadn't she thought of that, though she was surprised Olly hadn't.

'Technically you should have. You've got quite a crowd here.'

'So, are you going to arrest us?' Govinder winked cheekily at the officer.

The officer smiled. 'I'm just here to keep the peace. As long as you do, there will be no issue.' Looking around to see there was no one else around, PC Taylor leant in and whispered, 'So how many signatures have you got then?' He nodded with approval when Charlotte told him. 'Keep up the good work.'

Behind PC Taylor, Charlotte could see Julian Ransell making his way across the road like an angry bee. Before she had a chance to warn PC Taylor, he was at the officer's shoulder.

'I demand you remove these children at once, Officer.'

'For what reason?' PC Taylor asked calmly.

'They are causing a scene.'

'Everything is calm and good-natured here, Sir. And people are enjoying it.'

'I pay my taxes which, I should remind you, pay your wages.' Mr Ransell gritted his teeth.

'As do I, Sir, as do I,' the police officer responded wearily. 'The thing is, my job is to enforce the law and, as I see it here, there is no law being broken. I can't simply go about removing people without cause – that would be corrupt.'

PC Taylor seemed to be daring Mr Ransell to say another word judging by his intense stare and the teacher let out an annoyed grunt.

Some of the crowd were now watching Mr Ransell's little outburst with amusement and some even gave a pantomime boo.

'Why do you even care about this, Miss Stone? Do you realise what you are cheating the local people out of? All for the sake of a bloody tree.' Mr Ransell could barely conceal his frustration.

Charlotte shrugged. 'I've been a rootless nomad all my life, Sir. Now, I finally feel like I belong somewhere. My family is from this village and I have as much right to fight this as anyone.'

'Fine. It won't do any good anyway. That tree is still coming down.' Mr Ransell flounced off down the street.

'As you were, kids.' PC Taylor winked before strolling to the back of the crowd as Olly began his rendition of 'The Tale of the Lightning Struck Oak'.

Just before midday, Irving Batterbee arrived at the town hall.

'Well, it's the moment of truth, kids. Have you got the petition?' Charlotte handed him forty sheets of paper. 'Excellent, now we just need a little common sense to prevail and this will all be over.'

⚡

It seemed like hours before the council meeting was over and the wait was agonising. Unfortunately, the look on Mr Batterbee's face did not offer hope.

'I'm sorry, Charlotte, I really am, but there was nothing I could do, the board was stitched up like a kipper,' Irving fumed. 'I wasn't a lone voice, you managed to convince quite a few so you should feel very proud, but that rascal Marcus and his brother, well… it was an inside job! Nothing would trump the health and safety card.' Irving Batterbee looked genuinely disappointed.

'So that's it?'

'I'm afraid so. The tree comes down after the weekend.'

Charlotte was stroking the branches and leaves of the Nymet when Tar'sel arrived and though she had her back to him, he could tell something was wrong.

'I take it "media" didn't work then?' he said with a tone of disappointment.

Charlotte smiled weakly at his faith in 'Albion magic' as he saw it. She turned to face him and shook her head. They sat together under the now full canopy of fresh, though still sickly looking, leaves as Charlotte relayed the events of the past few days, including the Seelie Court proceedings, petitions and speeches.

'It's just not safe for you to be here; if the courts work out it's you who taught me to weave they will come after you,' she concluded.

'Languishing in Fey jail might just make me the last surviving Tree Weaver,' Tar'sel laughed bitterly, 'but it sounds like weaving won't do any good anyway. Now what then?'

Charlotte considered the message Sang had given her. Tar'sel wasn't going to like it but she didn't see what else they could do.

'We go and see the Manush de Bar.'

Tar'sel paled. 'Are you mad, they're just… a children's story… they're not real.'

'Then why are you so scared?' Charlotte challenged him. 'Look, Sang said my sister told her that's where we need to go and I trust her with my life.' Charlotte didn't mention that saving the Nymet was not her only motivation.

'It's not just your life though, is it,' Tar'sel replied flatly. 'I'm sure your sister has the best of intentions but what can she possibly know about the Vorla? They are likely to kill us before we get anywhere near them.'

'Quite impressive for a make-believe creature.' Charlotte

couldn't help the sarcasm, she was as nervous about this plan as Tar'sel was. 'What choice do we have?' she added more gently.

Tar'sel was still unconvinced, but he couldn't argue. 'To the Vorla it is then. I'll make the arrangements.'

# The Detention

Charlotte wasn't looking forward to biology class. Since the incident outside the town hall, she suspected Mr Ransell would still be in a foul mood in spite of his win, and she wasn't wrong. The sight of packets of seeds, plant pots and compost on the desks made her even more anxious.

'In keeping with the theme of the year that seems to have been set by Miss Stone, today's lesson will see us exploring the world of plant growth, starting with the analysis of positive and negative tropisms. In front of you, you have the ingredients to design your first experiment.'

Charlotte could feel cold fear creeping through her torso as she stared at the offending packet of seeds. *This could be over very quickly*, she thought, thinking of the skills Tar'sel had taught her.

'So who can tell me what a tropism is?' Mr Ransell continued, oblivious to Charlotte's discomfort.

'Something that stimulates plant growth, Sir.'

'Very good, Miss Hickling. And can anyone offer some examples?'

Mr Ransell added the answers to the board – light, water, gravity, heat, chemicals.

'Miss Stone? Do you have an example?'

'Sound, Sir?'

'And I half expected you to say lightning.' Mr Ransell nodded with approval. 'Not a conventional answer, well done, and it will make an interesting experiment. I look forward to seeing your results. Right, class, choose a tropism and begin preparing your samples.'

Charlotte pushed the seed packet around the table with the end of her pencil. Perhaps it was just paranoia but she could swear she saw a shimmering by the window. Was she being watched?

'Miss Stone, Earth to Miss Stone. Just as you start to show some promise… the point of an experiment is practical application. The seeds aren't going to grow by you simply staring at them, girl.'

That was not exactly true. Charlotte was relieved she managed to bite her tongue on that sentence. There was nothing for it but to lie.

'I… I have a condition, Sir.'

'That I don't doubt.' Mr Ransell was clearly beginning to lose patience. 'However, unless it involves an allergy to compost you will desist in holding up your classmates' education and get to it.'

Charlotte seized on the idea. 'Actually, Sir, I do. Compost brings me out in hives.'

'And do you have a sick note to excuse you?' Mr Ransell said in a well-practised tone of sarcasm.

Charlotte couldn't help but retaliate. 'I have an A.K.O.R.N from the elves!'

Mr Ransell was turning more beetroot by the minute and his glasses quivered precariously on the tip of his thin, aquiline nose.

'I suppose that is what passes as a joke where you're from, young lady, but here it will earn you detention. Now enough of your so-called wit. Proceed,' he snapped.

Charlotte rearranged the seed trays, slowly filling them with soil and hoping to enlist Sang's help once Mr Ransell turned his back but he was watching her like a hawk.

'Quickly, Miss Stone. We don't have all day.'

The shimmering was now inside the room as Charlotte ripped open the seed packet. Taking a deep breath, Charlotte sprinkled the seeds, 'accidentally' letting them spill on the table. Sang, who had cottoned on to her plan, made to pick up the seed but a glare from Mr Ransell stopped her in her tracks.

'If Miss Stone wishes to pass this class, she must do her own work, Miss Lei.'

Reluctantly, Charlotte scooped up the seed. Light rippled to her left, exploding into a firework display, as Charlotte dropped them into the soil.

'Drop the seeds and step away from the compost.'

Charlotte found herself looking down the barrel of a NETEL stun gun and into the face of an angry-looking Fey, his uniform catsuit bulging in some very unflattering places.

'We were lenient with you last time,' Malik roared, 'but it's instant incarceration for this infraction. Queen Mab to Blue Fairy – Code Sandman, I repeat Code Sandman. Over.'

'Blue Fairy received.'

The voice on the speaker sounded suspiciously like Luned but Charlotte didn't have time to think about that as she, and the rest of her class, fell into a deep, dreamless sleep.

As she came to, something about where she was didn't feel right, then Charlotte realised, with her knees pinned under her chin, it wasn't the place; it was her. The court cells were hard, wood-lined boxes, ringed with iron and suspended from the dripping, dank ceiling of a cave. They were designed to be cold, uncomfortable – and for fairies. She had been given no food or blankets and was just wondering how long they were planning to keep her there when the rusty screech of a key in an iron lock broke her thoughts.

'You will be seen now,' a gloved guard elf barked at her and, with a wave of his hand, the bottom fell out of her cage. She hit the stone floor with a thud, jarring her shoulder in the process.

'You are to be taken to the chambers,' the guard said with a malicious smile, 'and you're not going to like it.'

Luned took regular deep breaths and tried not to think of the vast amounts of rock and soil just yards above her head. She had to consciously stop herself from running through the corridors, which would have drawn attention to the fact she did not belong here, and focus.

Charlotte was in trouble. Dijin had convinced the Seelie Courts to remove her to the chambers where she would be bound by the roots of the Great Tree till he deemed it acceptable to release her; and he would not calculate for a human lifespan. It was a fate reserved only for the worst criminals and if Luned didn't intervene before Charlotte was moved, no one would be able to get to her again.

Luned told herself that she was acting purely out of duty, this was a definite contradiction of the P.O.D charter. She tried to ignore the disturbing realisation that she actually quite liked this human.

Luned was just assessing which way to the cells at one of the numerous crossroads, when a tremor shook the underground.

'Why does this always happen when I'm here,' she grumbled to herself.

A second tremor hit, shaking earth and stones from the walls and ceiling and exposing a minor root system of the Great Tree. In spite of her fear, Luned couldn't help being mesmerised by the glowing root.

It didn't look very healthy and she was pretty sure it shouldn't be such a dull red colour. What had Davlin said? Luned couldn't remember but, red had to be danger – it was always danger.

As if to reinforce her convictions, a cold wind blew out the lights in the corridor and a low rumbling blossomed in the darkness. The hairs on her arms began to prick up and panic threatened to overwhelm her. This was more than her phobia; there was something out there.

Was this what the human girl Sang had been talking about? How had the frog-legged lady interpreted it, 'the Echo'? Luned hadn't fully understood what the girl had meant, but she sensed for herself the peril Charlotte was in. It didn't bear thinking about that the Echo might have been released but if it had, they were in more trouble than they realised.

The rumbling seemed to be getting closer, travelling through the tunnel towards Luned, full of menace. Suddenly, a bolt of red lightning cracked and bounced off the walls before leaping at the Undine. Steam rose from Luned's body as she began to slowly but painfully evaporate. Just as she thought she couldn't stand any more, the lightning grounded and disappeared into the floor. In the dying light, the imprint of a face twisted in rage formed in the dirt before melting away.

Luned's throat was so dry she couldn't have screamed even if she had wanted to. Instead, she desperately searched for water as her body trembled with shock.

'And breathe,' Luned reminded herself as she tried to clear her light-headedness and nausea, grateful for the nearby fountain.


Mercifully, the cells were no more than a couple of twists away. Luned cursed herself for not bringing gloves, she would never be able to touch the toxic iron door handle, but was relieved to see the cell doors wide open. Charlotte was sprawled on the floor; it looked like Luned was just in time.

'Stand down, Guard Noske, I have this,' Luned croaked.

'This is against protocol…' The guard glared, annoyed that his fun had been spoiled.

'This is no ordinary prisoner and I am the expert – appointed by Officer Malik himself to oversee this human. I assure you, everything is above board.'

The elf guard bowed and retreated with a certain reluctance.

Charlotte was rubbing life back into her limbs. She had never been so pleased to see Luned as she was now.

'Am I glad to be out of there. I was beginning to cramp up.'

'What are you talking about, they gave you the most spacious cell there is. Be grateful they are into high ceilings here or we'd never get you through the tunnels.'

'Ah, but then they wouldn't have been able to get me down here in the first place.'

'Don't be so sure. You think you are the first human the Fey have taken underground?'

Luned wrinkled her nose automatically as she recalled the rumours she had heard the last time that had happened.

'Hurry up, we don't have all day,' Luned urged Charlotte to her feet. 'We need to make a move, it won't take them long to realise you've escaped. They'll have all the main entrances covered. The only thing for it is to head to the Tap Room. Davlin will help us, I am sure.'

'I hope you're a little bit more than "sure". Isn't this supposed to be a well planned rescue?'

'When did I say that? It's a spontaneous "I must be out of my mind" rescue, actually,' Luned retorted.

A low rumble filled the room and put a stop to their bickering and the ground shook.

'What about Boris?' Charlotte suddenly remembered the little Veshengo being dragged off by the elfin guard.

'Oh he's long gone, a regular escape artist he is.'

The ground shook again and red lightning formed at the other end of the room, crackling menacingly.

'We have to get out of here.' Luned was now wide-eyed with fear.

'What's that?'

'Charlotte, meet the Echo… I think. Now move.'

'Isn't that what Sang was talking about?' Charlotte asked as she made for the door as quickly as she could.

'Less questions more crawling.'

The lightning crept across the room, bouncing off the walls and the wooden floors of the hanging cages. It seemed to be playing with them and the faster they moved, the faster it followed.

As they threw themselves into the corridor, Charlotte slammed the iron door with her foot.

The lightning hit the metal and the walls trembled with a wicked roar as the metal absorbed the fiery light.

'That will have slowed it down but it'll be back. We need to keep moving.' Luned winced at the memory of her last encounter with the Echo.

Charlotte tried her best to keep up with Luned but the air in the tunnels was thin and her knees ached from the stones that dug through her light school trousers. She didn't dare stop though, the fairy underground was a maze she would never be able to find her way out of on her own. She was relieved when they came to a large chamber where she could stand up.

'We go through that door over there.' Luned pointed to a heavy, elaborately decorated wooden door. 'It leads to the living quarters of the comms room staff. There's another tunnel.' Luned looked at Charlotte apologetically. 'But from there we're not far from the hanging gardens and a way out. Davlin should be waiting for us.'

'Hanging gardens?'

'It's the nick-name for the complex root system of Fargale.'

While they had been talking, they hadn't noticed a ferocious-looking blue dragon staring hungrily at them from the chamber ceiling – not until it growled.

'So how do we get round that?' Charlotte whispered, frozen to the spot and not daring to take her eyes off the creature.

'Just give me a minute, let me talk to it.'

'To a dragon?'

'It's water like me.'

'Are water dragons not just as deadly then?' It was a genuine question with not a single hint of sarcasm.

In answer, the dragon snarled so loudly it made the hall shake, before letting out a huge plume of cool, blue flame that spiralled round the hall before setting the door aflame. The remains of the tapestries and wooden benches that had lined their only escape route were evidence that water fire was every bit as effective as the regular kind.

'It seems to like its food chargrilled. I really don't think talking to it will help.' Fear cracked Charlotte's voice.

'It should recognise me as one of its own,' Luned insisted. Charlotte was not convinced, but she was pleased to see the Undine had forgotten her phobia of being underground.

Suddenly, Charlotte realised she still had the almond-shaped seed Andarwen had given her. 'We could try this?'

'Do you have any idea what that does?' Luned eyed the seed suspiciously.

'None whatsoever, but Andarwen said I would know when to use it and it's looking like a really good idea right now.'

Luned nodded reluctantly. The dragon seemed to know what they had in mind as well. Dissolving into a bubble of water, it flew across the room like a torrent of rain.

Charlotte took careful aim then threw with all her might; their lives depended on this. The seed arched through the air and Luned watched its trajectory. Just as it passed through the form of the re-materialising creature she shot a growth spell, the green-blue sparks like deadly rain. At the exact moment the spell connected with its target the creature solidified, letting out an ear-splitting roar of confusion. Inside it the seed grew at monumental speed, sending out more and more new shoots that twisted and compacted in the creature's belly.

Charlotte was riveted to the spot with horrified fascination as a tendril of the plant sprouted from the creature's left nostril. Unfurling and thickening in seconds, a blood-red flower sprang into bloom at its tip and several thorns matured from green to brown before plunging themselves deep into the creature's flesh. Another roar filled the cavern, this time the vibrations loosening a number of stalactites which thundered to the floor below, shattering with force in all directions.

'That was cooler than weaving.' Charlotte couldn't take her eyes off the vines pouring out of the dragon's mouth.

'That is weaving, now come on, Charlotte, into the corridor.' Luned tugged at her sleeve.

Even in the gloom of the still-warm tunnel, Charlotte could see the fear in the Undine's eyes as the dragon exploded into a tsunami of water, which was headed right for them.

'Up, UP!' the Undine shouted above the roar of water as she turned to face it.

Charlotte didn't argue, and climbed up a service tunnel that led to a grate above. She hoped Luned knew what she was doing. From her elevated position Charlotte caught glimpses of the Undine, and though she couldn't see what she was doing, the expected wave never came.

'Get that hatch open!' Luned shouted as she zoomed up the tunnel to the sound of an angry roar.


'It won't follow us here,' Luned breathed heavily as she slumped against the wall on the other side of the hatch.

'I get over zealous with a jasmine, you explode a dragon and I'm the one who gets the A.K.O.R.N? How is that right?' Charlotte said when she eventually got her breath back.

'Your actions were frivolous and unnecessarily dangerous, mine were required for survival. Besides, it will recover... it'll just have one heck of a headache for a while.'

'You think the Seelie Court are going to buy that? It wouldn't have been a matter of survival if you hadn't been here, breaking the law to get me out. I'll bet roots have been chopped for less.'

'Severed,' Luned corrected her. 'You're probably right, though technically I didn't break any law. One of the advantages of knowing the P.O.D charter back to front.'

In that moment Charlotte realised Aunt Clarissa wasn't the only one she had underestimated since arriving in Brackenheath.

They now found themselves in a gloomy suite of rooms covered in elaborate tapestries of rich colours that seemed to depict some great battle. In the corner was a solid stone bed studded in precious stones and gold.

'Comfy.' Charlotte gestured towards the bed.

'For a dwarf it is. These are Davlin's quarters,' Luned replied.

At that moment the dwarf in question appeared in the far doorway – naked except for a thin coating of liquid silver. Mercifully, his long bread covered what mattered.

'Davlin, I presume,' Charlotte smiled awkwardly, suddenly finding the ceiling exceedingly interesting.

'K'hul! Take a detour, did we? I take it things didn't go to plan.' Davlin hurriedly dressed.

'There were... complications,' Luned agreed, holding up a towel to preserve the dwarf's modesty.

'Through here,' he ordered, now clothed but still dripping molten silver as he moved into the corridor. 'There is not much time, they are about to go into shut down.'

Davlin offered his hand to Charlotte in the way he assumed humans greeted each other. Charlotte high-fived him out of politeness.

Davlin's rooms led directly into the comms room and he guided them around the various coloured nutripools. Charlotte had never seen anything like it; she was astonished that this all existed underneath the unassuming oak tree she knew in the park. She marvelled at the multicoloured fungi and the extensive root bundles tied into intricate knots. A number of other roots caught her eye too, they were little more than lifeless blackened stumps.

'The cycle of life; things wither and regrow anew,' Davlin said but Charlotte knew they were anything but natural.

'We really don't have time for this,' Luned snapped. 'You're a wanted criminal in case you've forgotten.' She glared at Charlotte.

Davlin picked up his pace but continued to reel off the many functions and features of the comms room. Charlotte, however, was drawn to a low droning that filled her ears and the cloud of gold spores forming in the corner of the room.

'That's the Norn Interface,' Davlin followed her gaze, 'and it doesn't normally do that on its own.'

Luned was losing patience. 'I'm serious, Charlotte. We won't get out of here if we don't go now.'

'Give me a second,' Charlotte said; she had a feeling this was important.

As she approached the Norn Interface the spore cloud morphed into strange, unidentifiable shapes until settling into the form of a face she recognised. Madame Cortes.

'It's just the interface calibrating. It takes a moment to read the user then takes the form of someone you trust,' Davlin talked her through the process.

Charlotte was just wondering why it didn't look like Aunt Clarissa when the face spoke.

'Identifying user. GR000639... B. Charlotte Stone, living descendant of the immortals of the Golden Root. Severed. Retrieving file...'

'Past, present, future. Always loads in that order,' Davlin offered by way of explanation.

'The guards are going to find us.' Luned was beside herself now. 'They must be able to trace the signal...'

'Relax,' Davlin said cheerily. 'The Norn Interface is an independent system. The seers insisted on that.'

'The Golden Root was severed in 1902 (human years),' the face of Madame Cortes continued, 'after the incarceration of the main patriarch Peter Aherne, brother of Clarissa Aherne and known in folktales as 'the Echo'. Since then, the immortals of the Golden Root have lived in exile in Albion and have no representation at the Shriven Council.'

The face shuddered before continuing.

'Present files: Assigned to Luned, Undine of Agrimony for ongoing investigation. Clarissa Aherne: DEFECTED. Further actions: Top secret file, access restricted. Ella Stone nee Aherne: UNKNOWN. Further actions: Possible hostage negotiations under search, 'Nivasi'. Edessa Stone: UNRESPONSIVE. Further actions: To be determined. Charlotte Stone: ACTIVE, consider highly dangerous, possibly defective. Further actions: Constant Surveillance.'

'What the heck does that mean "possibly defective"?! I thought I could trust you Luned…'

'Shhhsh,' Davlin interrupted her. 'You don't want to miss this bit.' The image of Madame Cortes disappeared as the spore cloud swirled but her voice remained.

'The flame-haired girl from Albion, a daughter of the severed root, is destined to be the saviour of Syluria, the Great Tree and her own line. Two from the same acorn, one to grow and the other to wither, one a saviour, one a shadow. Scanning Charlotte Stone… UNDETERMINED.'

'You and me need to talk, Luned.' Charlotte scowled at the Undine but before she had time to interrogate her, the comms room was flooded with the high-pitched squeal of alarms.

'Well, we'll have all the time in the world to talk when we end up in the chamber,' Luned retorted as she followed Davlin to the Tap Room.

'We are now in shut down,' Davlin said. 'There is only one way out now. You know what to do, Luned.'

'Syluria it is,' Luned replied as she took Charlotte by the hand and dragged her into the sap flow.

# The Manush de Bar

The sun was setting over Syluria as Charlotte collapsed in an undignified heap at the foot of the Nymet hill. If she hadn't been ethereal, she would have thrown up. It had been a rough ride through the sap flow and even though she had to discard her physical body to enter the Dreamtime, that part of the journey had been just as bad.

Luned had stayed only long enough to ensure Charlotte had made it through the Dreamtime before streaking back into the darkness. She had to move Charlotte's body before the elfin guards found it and if she was gone too long she would end up facing some very awkward questions.

Charlotte's head was still reeling from the revelations of the Norn Interface but she had to focus on the task in hand. Tar'sel appeared at her shoulder.

'Here try this. It should take the edge off.' Tar'sel wafted the smoke from a twist of herbs – the same as were in Anya's potion the night of his first trip into the Dreamtime.

The twin moons of Sorcha and Kyrene were already high in the sky and the purple tinge of dusk was fading into an inky blue-black.

'Have you figured out how we are going to get to the Vorla?' Charlotte whispered as Tar'sel beckoned her under the cover of a large willow tree.

The Nymet glowed warmly on top of the sacred mound as the firelight from inside escaped through the gaps in the wickerwork. This, together with the full moons, provided them with more than enough light as they made their way around the base and away from the village.

'Dad wasn't willing to talk. The Vorla scare him and he couldn't see how they would be able, or willing, to help.' Tar'sel tightened the straps on the packs at his feet. 'He says only the Fey can help us – and the Vorla are definitely not Fey.'

'Well, I think I can safely say we can't rely on the Fey Nation. Remember Dijin and the Seelie Court?' Charlotte was keen to get moving, Luned had made it clear that time was running out. All they had now was Edessa's plan. 'What I actually meant though was, what are we going to use as transport?'

Tar'sel looked confused. 'We walk.'

'You have to be kidding, it'll take us weeks to get there that way, I have a test tomorrow. I'm dead if I don't go and I'm in enough trouble as it is!'

'Relax,' Tar'sel smiled. 'The Verses all have their own song. Syluria's is higher and quicker than Earth's. So long as we don't hang around, I figure we've got time to get you back before you're missed.' Tar'sel looked her up and down. 'We need to get you a physical body though.'

'Why? Does my being all floaty upset the melodies?' Charlotte barked to hide her nerves.

Tar'sel shook his head. 'I'm going to need some help carrying supplies.'

'A physical body, eh?' Charlotte had a feeling she wasn't going to like this. 'So how is that supposed to work?'

There was a rustle of leaves in the thicket. 'Easy, we swap.' Tar'sel's sister stepped out of the shadows. '*Mishto hom me dikava tute*, I'm Anya. You can use my body.'

Charlotte recognised the greeting as the one Jairo had taught her. '*Gestina*,' she responded politely though she was uneasy that they had obviously discussed this already, without her.

'It's quite common. Me and Anya used to do it all the time when we were younger,' Tar'sel continued, seeing her discomfort.

'I used to hate making arrow heads and Anya hated curing skins, so we would swap.'

The idea of taking over someone else's body unnerved Charlotte but Anya insisted, and she talked her through the process, making it sound so simple. They had to sit with their foreheads touching, staring into each other's eyes till they sensed the switch occurring, at which point Anya would transfer to Charlotte's body in Brackenheath while Charlotte's consciousness was absorbed into Anya's body.

'Before we do this, brother, I have something to tell you,' said Anya, but Mor'seka appeared before she could finish.

'I've got this,' he grinned.

'*K'hul!* Does the whole Barra know?' Tar'sel hissed. 'This was supposed to be a secret mission, you know Father would kill me if he knew what we were up to.'

'Relax, and believe me, friend, you want to hear what I have to tell you...' Mor'seka said, before adding '... and I resent the fact that you think I've broadcast this to all and sundry.'

'So, go on then.' The resignation was clear in Tar'sel's voice.

'Like this, it'll take at least a month to get there.' Mor'seka waved his hand to include all of them. 'I don't think you have a full understanding of how far you have to travel.'

'Knock off the attitude, Mor'seka, and get to the point.' Tar'sel scowled. He hated it when Mor'seka tried to belittle his ideas, just because he was ever-so-slightly older he seemed to think he could act like Tar'sel's big brother.

'Whoa there, *chavi*. I think someone's...'

'Did you just call me *chavi*? You're only two months older and you're calling me *chavi*?'

'Boys! For Goddess' sake, you are *both* acting like children.' Anya didn't need to shout to get her point across which was just as well. Even Charlotte could see why she had been chosen to become a Draoi priestess.

'Now get on with it,' Anya hissed at Mor'seka before turning to Charlotte in order to initiate the swap.

Mor'seka was clearly sulking but did as Anya told him. He explained about the various stone rings that where dotted across the land, at least one per Barra, and how they were used for transportation. He then explained how they could tap into the Nymet circle to use this network.

'But the Nymet is wood, it wouldn't be compatible,' Tar'sel argued.

'Not with stone, no. But here's the genius bit,' Mor'seka replied, excited by his own brilliance. 'Do you remember the weavers of the Morsea'a Forests?'

'But that forest fell centuries ago and the Morsea'a weavers converted to stone. Their circle, if they have one, will be just as unusable.'

'They do have one and it's not as incompatible as you think. The markers above ground will be stone but the foundations…'

'… Are still wood,' Tar'sel finished.

'They grow up so fast!' Mor'seka chuckled and Tar'sel gave him an evil look. Neither of them dared to argue again in front of Anya, especially when she was working magic.

Before Tar'sel could take a playful swing at his annoying friend, Anya's body lurched awkwardly to its feet and stumbled forward. Charlotte hadn't known what to expect but this was the strangest sensation and she felt nauseous. Mor'seka looked at her with sympathy.

'It's going to be a tough night for you,' he said. 'We can patch into the wood/stone ring but it will be a rough ride. Still, it will save you weeks of travel.'

'Let's do it,' Charlotte replied before Tar'sel could object.

Charlotte made slow progress up the Nymet hill and was getting frustrated that this body was not responding to her commands. It was like learning to walk as a child and she had to consciously will her new legs to bend at the knee and lift themselves one after the other but she would not let the others help her. She was exhausted by the time they got to the top.

'Don't worry, you'll get used to it soon, the connection takes a little time to bond that's all.' Tar'sel smiled reassuringly.

'Hush, you foghorn,' Mor'seka hissed, 'there are still people in there. We are going to need to act quickly.'

All three of them ducked into the long grass as a train of priestesses, distinctive in their green robes, dreadlocks and tattoos, left the temple grove and began to wind their way down the hill.

'I think perhaps you should go first, Tar'sel,' Mor'seka whispered. 'If there is anyone else in there at least you can give a valid reason for being here.' Mor'seka pointed at Tar'sel's own marks and newly acquired dreadlock.

'You have too much faith friend, I'll still be asked some awkward questions.'

'You've always been lucky, I have my fingers crossed for you.' Mor'seka grinned and gave him a double thumbs-up.

Charlotte's heart was in her mouth as Tar'sel ducked through the willow weave curtain into the Nymet grove. It felt like an age before he reappeared and waved them in. Mor'seka rushed through their instructions, which basically consisted of choose a tree and hang on tight, while constantly looking over his shoulder.

Charlotte watched as he tapped each grove tree, tracing strange symbols on each of them and chanting words she couldn't hear. He worked quickly and as he finished the final one, Charlotte felt a force pulling at her stomach before the world started spinning. An eerie glow started to grow in the ground and grove trees. Charlotte just caught sight of Mor'seka dashing out of the Nymet temple before a flash, so violent she swore she could hear it, blinded her and she felt as if she was falling.

The wood in her hands soon became cold and it was a while before she got her bearings and realised she has clinging for dear life to a stone pillar.

'Time to go,' Tar'sel whispered in her ear and she cautiously opened her eyes. The world was still wobbly and she wasn't sure if it was this body or their unusual transport but she stumbled a few paces before falling to the ground and vomiting.

'Definitely time to go.' Tar'sel winced and helped her to her feet before leading her out of the abandoned circle towards the river a short distance away. Tar'sel reached into his pack and removed a large sheet of what looked like bark and began folding and pinning it in place.

'A balsa bark boat,' he answered her quizzical looks. 'It's stronger than it looks; in you get.' He loaded the packs. After grabbing a fallen branch from one of the few trees on the riverbank, he jumped in himself.

To begin with it was a pleasant journey, the river currents carrying them silently through pine woods then out to open plains. The eerie call of a skylark filled the air.

'We also call it a Vorla eagle,' Tar'sel told Charlotte, 'because it sounds like the Vorla or... what is the word you use...? Ah yes, "banshee".'

Charlotte felt a cold shiver jolt through her. 'And these are the people we are going to for help?'

'Don't blame me, your sister sent us, remember. The Vorla are the keepers of great knowledge though, so I guess if they can't help us no one can. But they are dangerous, they feel no emotion, no compassion, no empathy, no fear and they can drive men mad – so, nothing to worry about.'

No fear. Charlotte was caught up in her own thoughts as another memory stirred that she couldn't quite put her finger on.

Tar'sel went back to steering their little boat of tree bark. In the distance the lights of Amrith, the main city of the Morsea'a weavers, shone and Charlotte noticed Tar'sel drop his head and sigh.

'You have family there, don't you?'

'Not anymore,' he replied without facing her. 'All root connections were untied by the elders once the Morsea'a weavers gave up the old ways. They are no longer considered Manush de Rukh.'

'But the heart doesn't forget,' Charlotte whispered, half to herself.

'Something like that.' Tar'sel busied himself with the boat.

Charlotte didn't know what to say or do. She wondered if a hug would be appropriate, but she was still ignorant of most of their customs, and she didn't want him to think she was prying, so she left him to his thoughts.

The warm night breezes worked in their favour and the boat ploughed along with little effort. Charlotte sat back and enjoyed the scenery as it floated past. It was mostly wide open plains full of russet and blue grasses that shimmied in the wind punctuated by vast bodies of water, but ahead of them Charlotte could already see the Zolt foothills at the base of the Mountain of Mourne. They were tantalisingly close and it sent a thrill of excitement down her back, but Charlotte knew they were further away than they looked and there were still many miles to travel as yet.

Charlotte was distracted from their goal by a strange change in the landscape. The ground in the plains had taken on a sickly grey tinge, and the grasses had become dry and brittle. The greyness even seemed to seep into the water of the river.

'It's the Withering,' Tar'sel said as he slowed the boat and cautiously steered it as far away from the grey as possible.

'It's where the darkness is leaking out of the Dreamtime,' Tar'sel explained. 'A number of adventurous explorers have tried to see what's inside but no one ever comes out again. It is thought they are the points where two worlds have collided and imploded. It's just speculation of course, no one really has any idea. All we really know is, they didn't exist till recently.'

They were close enough now to see the swirling centre, like molten lead, with tiny electrical flashes sparking here and there. They were surprisingly mesmerising and the smell of ozone filled the air.

A thud brought her back to her senses. Tar'sel's puzzled look alarmed her; this clearly wasn't just noises of the river. A second thud shook the little boat and was soon followed by a dozen more. The water ahead of them was thrashing and foamy and a whirlpool was forming.

'Nivasi! Nasty.' Tar'sel sucked in his breath sharply. 'I take it you can swim?'

Charlotte nodded.

'Good, I'd take a deep breath if I were you and dive deep then swim like *K'hul* for the riverbank there, right?' Tar'sel pointed to a stony beach a few hundred yards up river from them. It was the other side of the whirlpool.

'We need to be on the right-hand side of the river,' he said in response to the look of horror on Charlotte's face, 'and we need to avoid the grey, *Shala*?'

'*Hai, Shala*,' Charlotte replied automatically.

To their left, an orange fish tail, covered in tiny barnacles, flipped out of the water and crashed into the side of the boat, ripping the fragile bark and plunging them into the water.

'Go!' Tar'sel cried.

The river was wide and the strong currents pulled the remnants of their boat towards the whirlpool in front of them. Charlotte shuddered. An unnatural keening filled the water as venomous amber eyes peered at them from only metres away. Several more Nivasi hung in the water nearby, dark hair floating wildly around them. They grinned menacingly, gnashing pointed teeth which flashed in the water-dappled moonlight.

*How are we supposed to out swim these?'* Charlotte signed, already shivering uncontrollably in the icy waters.

*We have to try.'* Tar'sel responded, tugging at her arm as he dived. Charlotte followed his lead.

A blood-curdling scream spurred the creatures into a frenzy as they swarmed around them, their vicious intent clear, sharp talons poised to strike. Charlotte cried out, swallowing lungfuls of water, as one of them sliced through her calf, another piercing her shoulder. *Is this how it is going to end?* she thought, before wondering if in fact it was Anya who was dying. Would she wake up warm in bed at Rosemary Heights as soon as she passed out?

Charlotte's wounds were beginning to tighten and stiffen, making it difficult to move and she began to drift away from the tight coil of water in front of her. Was there some sort of poison in those evil-looking talons? The thought drifted through her hazy mind and she no longer knew which way was up. She could feel herself being dragged into the grey.

A faint green glow bloomed in her vision, getting brighter and brighter, until it filled the water around her. Rainbow colours pulsed and swirled through the river and Charlotte could hear soft chanting. Perhaps this was the light that people talk about seeing in death. However, with the glow the water seemed to become lighter and saturated with oxygen. Her limbs were able to move without effort, all tightness gone and she was no longer falling. Charlotte soon felt the stone bed of the shallows under foot and managed to pull herself onto the little beach, shivering as soon as the cold night air hit her skin.

Charlotte could still hear the chanting, but she could also hear the screeching and she shuddered, amazed at how much malice could be poured into one sound.

Tar'sel emerged from the water, spluttering and coughing up water.

'Is there a little something you forgot to tell me?' Charlotte panted.

'Vorla bad, Nivasi badder.' Tar'sel smiled weakly, his lungs on fire.

'Just because I am so grateful we are still alive, I'm going to let you have that,' Charlotte replied, gratefully filling her lungs with the sweet night air.

The eerie chanting still drifted through the air and Charlotte felt brave enough to look into the water. The Nivasi were still there circling, their eyes as full of hate as ever, but somehow they seemed unable to come near. Except one: a beautiful woman sat on the beach with them, one foot in the water and her verdigris hair wrapped round her like a sari. The rainbow colours Charlotte had seen in the water clearly came from this being and they still pulsed through the river from where her foot was submerged.

'I apologise for my kin but you had better go now.'

'You're not like them.' Charlotte knew she was stating the obvious but it was all her water-addled brain could manage right now. The woman laughed and it sounded like a wind chime made of seashells.

'I am Asrai. We are quite distant relations,' the woman offered as explanation. 'When you hear the song of my sisters you will be safe in the water, though I would recommend you stay on land for the time being.'

With this, the woman stood up and walked into the river. As soon as her hair floated around her shoulders she dived, disappearing from view.

Tar'sel had managed to retrieve the travel packs and handed her the smallest. 'Well, I think we should be following her advice. You alright to walk?'

Charlotte nodded.

Swimming had been surprisingly easy but walking was a completely different kettle of fish. Being in someone else's body was harder than Charlotte thought it would be. Anya's body was strong but Charlotte moved like a robot, unable to make the foreign limbs respond to her commands without a lot of effort. She still had to consciously think about every move and now she was getting tired.

'This is no good,' Charlotte spluttered, collapsing to the ground. 'I can't go another step. You should have had Edessa for this, she would have been dancing by now.'

Tar'sel gave her a sympathetic look; he was tired himself and glad of an excuse to stop. He was silently quite impressed; she'd done a lot better than she realised and they were already well over halfway. The twin moons were both full and bathing the land in a silver glow but they were now hanging low in the sky and a cool breeze played through the tall grass of the plains warning of a storm brewing. The vast lakes of Morsea'a gleamed behind them. On the horizon the snow covered tops of the Zolt mountain range reared up over rainforest. At its heart lay the Mountain of Mourne, where they would find the entrance to the city of the Vorla.

'We need to be off the plains before sunrise.'

'Can't we camp here? It's as good a place as any.'

'Not if you want to live, this is Rheadak country.'

Tar'sel noticed the sky was swiftly getting lighter; they had better move fast. Far to their left were a herd of the giant Rheadak asleep on the plain, but Tar'sel knew they wouldn't be for long.

'We have to move now,' he said, gathering their things. 'It's really not that far, then we can rest.'

Charlotte concentrated, and stood up slowly. She seemed to be getting the hang of it which made her feel a lot better, and with renewed energy she followed Tar'sel towards a jagged cliff face.

'We just need to get to the top of that then we can stop. They won't follow us there.'

'Can't we just build a hide?'

'This is my world, Charlotte. Please, trust me.'

An ear-shattering roar made them spin round to see the Rheadak groggily stretch their wings as tendrils of light snaked over the horizon.

'Stand still,' Tar'sel hissed. 'They probably haven't seen us yet. We'll wait to see which direction they go,' Tar'sel reassured Charlotte, but his heart sank as first one, then another of the Rheadak staggered to their feet and swivelled their long necks in their direction. A second roar and they started to trot, then gallop towards them.

'RUN!' Tar'sel screamed, pointing towards the river.

'But the Nivasi…?'

'I'd rather take my chances with them right now,' Tar'sel panted, leading the way towards the river and a sparse covering of trees and scrub. He could feel the vibration of the Rheadaks' heavy footfall and could tell they were gaining ground. He allowed himself to look back to judge their distance, just in time to see Charlotte fall.

*She's not going to make it,* he thought.

Desperately, Tar'sel scrambled around in the dirt for something he could use as ammunition as he circled away from Charlotte and back towards the bottom of the cliff. His hand fell on a Matuse seed pod, jagged, heavy and full of acid; perfect! He took aim with his sling and fired. The seed pod met its mark, shattering on impact right between the eyes of the first Rheadak. The huge creature faltered, swayed, then fell like a stone, sending a tremor through the dry earth causing the others to stop and look towards Tar'sel. The largest let out a deafening roar, he'd got their attention now!

*'K'hul!'*

Tar'sel ran like the wind, doing his best to dodge the lashing, razor-sharp tongues of the angry Rheadak. A blow to his shoulder sent him crashing head over heels to the ground with blood flowing down his arm. Something soft cushioned his fall and he was so grateful he didn't look to see what it was, he could barely move. It wasn't till the wide leaves of the Matuse plant sprang closed around him that he realised he wasn't out of danger yet.

The Rheadak were confused, their prey had disappeared. He could hear them padding around outside. The mature leaves were thick enough to shield him from sight but one swipe of their tongue would cut the plant in two. Tar'sel's heart was in his mouth and beating so hard he was sure they would hear. He closed his eyes and prayed. The acid sap of the flesh-eating plant began to ooze from the pores in the leaves and Tar'sel could feel it burning his skin; if he didn't fight his way out soon he wouldn't have the strength, but he couldn't be sure the Rheadak had gone.

'Tar'sel! Tar'sel?'

Her voice was low but full of fear. Taking his hunting knife he plunged it into the flesh of the plant and cut it open. He didn't have the energy to weave.

'Tar'sel!'

He was in a terrible mess. Charlotte somehow knew what this plant was; she also knew she must act quickly.

The river was close by and Charlotte managed to half carry, half drag him to the water's edge. Bathing his skin in the cold water, she washed away all traces of the acid and dressed his shoulder with the mugwort and dock leaves that grew nearby. Starting a fire, she made a broth of the roots from her pack and fresh mussels, as well as bread from orris grain. She didn't know how she knew to do all this, it must be muscle memory in Anya's body taking over, but she was glad for it.

She couldn't believe he had risked his life to save hers and she hugged him. Tar'sel flinched in his sleep and Charlotte cringed; she had forgotten about his shoulder. When Tar'sel slowly came round, she fed him some of the cooling broth.

'I see you've got used to Anya's body,' Tar'sel croaked with humour in his voice.

'There's nothing like a Rheadak licking at your heels for motivation,' Charlotte laughed. 'But… I don't understand how I knew what to do with you.'

'Information stays in the body and mind; it's only the consciousness that moves,' Tar'sel replied, rather cryptically. Charlotte wasn't sure she understood what he meant, but she nodded in agreement anyway.

The vortex was soon ahead of Edessa, the point where she had entered, and she was grateful. It had been a long night.

To say Asrai was flighty was being generous and it had taken a lot to enlist her help in saving Charlotte but now Edessa could rest easy. Charlotte's safety was secured – until she reached the home of the Vorla at least.

Without warning, Edessa felt as if her guts had been plunged into a bucket of ice. Red-hot pain shot up her arms as fingers touched her skin and nausea began to build in her throat. A shadow slithered across the ground with a life of its own – red electricity crackling at its heart.

Edessa screamed as she fought to break free from what lay before her, but the thing swallowed the sound. She suddenly felt herself falling before a vice-like grip closed around her neck and pulled. Her vision blurred and darkness descended.

Edessa's body twitched violently in the hospital bed and a word rasped in her throat as she exhaled a final breath.

*'Raa…niiiii.'*

In room 11 of the Crankshaw Wing a heart monitor let out a monotone warning as Edessa Stone flat-lined.

# Rani Johari

*T*ar'sel's wounds were beginning to heal but more importantly, the toxins were starting to leave his system. Anya's healing herbs were working, but they were moving far too slowly and having to stop every half hour. This was going to add another precious day to their journey.

'There has to be a better way, Tar'sel, we need to speed up,' Charlotte panted from the exertion of having to support him as they walked.

'Says she in the borrowed body.'

'Exactly my point, even I'm moving faster than you,' Charlotte retorted.

'So what do you suggest? You don't have the strength to carry me.'

'This river, it leads right to the mountains, doesn't it?'

'*Hai*, more or less,' Tar'sel winced in pain as he shifted his weight away from Charlotte.

'We could try a barge? How long would it take to make another boat?' Charlotte asked.

'Not long but we need the right bark and… well, I'm not sure I fancy risking being drowned again.'

'Asrai promised we would be safe so long as we can hear the singing.' They listened carefully; it was still there, quiet but distinct.

'OK let's do it, but Anya's boats are *g'ami*.'

'Fine, if yours are better then you build, I'll pull.'

Charlotte felt better when they were finally underway again. Tar'sel was asleep and all that could be heard was the sound of whooshing water as the little boat ploughed through the gentle current and Charlotte's footsteps as she towed it along from the shore. The bletchan vine straps were strong and comfortable and the load was lighter than she expected. They were making good time and should make the foothills by nightfall, though there were already two ghostly white moons in the sky. Charlotte found she knew exactly which one was which and all the stars as well. Anya's knowledge again.

*Charrrrlooootte*. The voice was so quiet she thought her ears were playing tricks on her.

*Loooottieeeee*. There was no mistaking it this time, Edessa… but how?

*You need to sleep, sister; you'll need your wits about you to deal with the Manush de Bar*. Charlotte had to admit she was flagging.

*Edessa, where are you?* There was no response and Charlotte wondered if she was going crazy.

*Get in the boat, sister, we will carry you.*

*We*, Charlotte thought; her suspicious side was arguing that this was folly but she could feel it in her bones that she should do as the voice said. Trouble was, these were not her bones and she was pretty sure it wasn't Edessa's voice. Anya's knife was instinctively in her hand the moment she heard the rustle in the reeds.

'Hail to Charlotte of Stone.' A Nivasi gleamed in the growing moonlight. 'We are to carry you.'

'Not likely after the stunt your last lot pulled,' Charlotte replied, anxiously pulling the boat onto the nearest gravel beach.

'Please, do not judge us by their foolishness, The Morrigan already punishes them.' Charlotte froze at the name.

'She is here?'

Nivasi laughter tinkled; there were at least three of them. 'She is everywhere and she has ordered that we assist you.'

Charlotte wondered how many times she was going to have to be in the debt of this strange woman she knew so little about – most of which was bad.

'You need only worry if you do not succeed in your mission,' the Nivasi said as if reading her thoughts. 'Nothing is given without a price. The Rani does not give easily, not even to The Morrigan, but she thinks you may have a chance.'

'You pull anything and I'll have no issue using this, you know.' Charlotte flashed the knife at them to reinforce the point as she stepped gingerly into the small boat, still amazed at how much weight it took.

'Interesting that you feel you would have time to use it, Charlotte of Stone, especially while you are asleep, but if that comforts you, so be it.'

Charlotte could not suppress a shudder as she looked into the cold green eyes of the Nivasi; she sensed it had much experience of killing.

'Why is The Morrigan helping me?'

'She loves that tree,' the Nivasi laughed again, 'now sleep.'

Despite her misgivings and the bright sunlight that poured over the land now, Charlotte fell fast asleep as soon as her head touched the make-shift pillow of her carry pack and the boat sped along the Morsea'a River to the gateway of the Mountain of Mourne.

The twin moons were high in the sky and gleaming brightly again by the time Charlotte woke from the cold. The boat was not moving and there was no sign of the Nivasi but the mountains around her told her they had finally reached their destination. Without thinking, she built a fire and had a broth bubbling away as Tar'sel woke.

'Smells good.'

'Nearly ready too. You up to eating?'

'You really don't know me that well, do you,' Tar'sel chuckled, but the innocent comment froze Charlotte to the spot. She didn't know him very well at all and yet here she was, her life in his hands in a strange land. When had she become so impulsively stupid?

'Here, this might help.' Tar'sel handed her a parka and she realised she had been shaking.

'So, what now?' Charlotte asked.

'Well,' Tar'sel spoke through a mouthful of broth, 'I guess we use the door.'

Charlotte turned to see a silver door shimmering in the moonlight where only solid rock had been a moment ago. She stared at the intricate designs carved into the silver; at its centre was the same Ogham symbol penned in Peter's book – the symbol that had been haunting her every move. It seemed to be appearing all over the place at the moment. Brushing her hand over the familiar but meaningless lines, the door bubbled and melted into the rock to reveal a cave with a staircase to its rear, a purple glow lighting the way.

'Seems we are expected,' she whispered.

Charlotte was unsure how high up they had gone but the stairs seemed to go on forever and she had the unnerving feeling the rock was watching their every move. Snow sat in drifts in the open-air hall they now found themselves in and she was glad to be out of the tunnel despite the cold. The stark light of the salt crystal chandelier and lamps provided no heat and the snow covered a highly polished stone floor that was cut to resemble marble tiles. At the back of the hall a small flight of stairs covered in a black woollen carpet led into the heart of the mountain. Before them a group of Vorla sat on cushions and silk throws reading and painting. They seemed to be deep in conversation though their lips did not move. They were completely oblivious to Charlotte and Tar'sel, who were wondering what to do next when one of the Vorla rose to their feet and approached them.

Charlotte gasped; the Vorla had an imposing attitude not least of all because it was over seven feet tall. This figure appeared female with crystal fangs and obsidian eyes – both of which twinkled in the light. Her skin had the look and texture of veined marble; she actually looked as if she was made of stone.

'That is because I am. Liquid stone.' Charlotte jumped and the figure smiled.

'You have the curiosity of a Vorla,' she continued, crossing her arms and giving a deep bow. 'We have been expecting you. My name is Durga. You must excuse my kin.' Durga gestured to the group who still had not acknowledged them. 'We communicate using a method similar to what you call telepathy; most of them have forgotten how to use their physical voices. I, however, am a renegade.'

Durga studied Charlotte's green skin, pointed ears and single dreadlock before turning her attention to Tar'sel. Charlotte could see the conflict in his eyes. Should he run or stand his ground? Durga stared into him for minutes before speaking again.

'Your companion is not of this world even though she looks like kin.'

'My… my sister… she…'

'An inter-dimensional body swap? Interesting.' Durga's eyes widened.

Charlotte jumped in spite of herself as the Vorla moved towards her again. 'Stay calm,' she repeated to herself over and over.

'Reveal your true form, traveller,' Durga commanded.

The Vorla lowered her face to Charlotte's and stared deep into her eyes. Those black, pupilless eyes for some reason filled her with terror but she could not look away. After a moment the smile on Durga's face disappeared and she backed away with a face like thunder.

'Who are you?' she hissed.

'I… I'm Ch… Charlotte… Stone,' she added the surname as an afterthought, though she doubted it would earn her any brownie points. The Vorla's eyes flashed dangerously and Charlotte was all too aware of the sharp fangs protruding over the bottom lip but Durga merely turned on her heel and headed towards the stairs.

'Come,' she barked and Charlotte and Tar'sel followed, having to jog to keep up, which Charlotte was finding a struggle. *It must be the altitude,* she thought. How high were they?

'We do not interfere with the evolution of any individual life form, not even our own. We have only ever observed the Triverse, studied it, made notes,' Durga stated matter-of-factly. 'However, the Rani has agreed to grant you an audience.' She stopped at another silver door set in the rock and turned slowly. 'There is just a matter of payment. What will you give us in return for our help?'

Tar'sel and Charlotte looked sheepish; they had been so focused on getting to the mountains they hadn't thought as far as an exchange.

'How about her?' Durga pointed a long finger towards a large cluster of clear crystal half buried in the side of the mountain. It was lit from within by a greenish glow and Charlotte went ashen. Inside sat a group of Vorla, in some sort of trance, and with them was Edessa.

'Edessa, NO.' Charlotte smashed her hands against the unyielding crystal till they bled. Edessa did not move.

'Hmmm, what a strange reaction.' The Vorla watched on bemused, but made no attempt to stop her. 'Interesting.' Durga studied Charlotte intently. 'We have very little experience of humans. I should make notes of this encounter for the hall of records.'

'You monster, give me back my sister!' Charlotte screamed, attacking the crystal with her knife but she couldn't make a dent and still Edessa didn't acknowledge her.

'I wouldn't bother doing that, you'll just blunt the blade and I'm sure Anya won't thank you for that.' The Vorla spoke in its usual emotionless tone.

'As I understand it she is not really alive in your world.' Durga nodded toward Edessa. 'Here she could be given a new life, be a useful member of society. She has such pretty talents, she would make such a wonderful Vorla,' Durga cooed. 'For that you get to save an entire people from extinction, which seems like a good deal to me.'

Charlotte was speechless but Tar'sel was a picture of fury.

'It is my people who are in need of your help…'

'And yet they send a mere boy?' Durga spat.

'… It's not fair to ask Charlotte to make the sacrifice. Make your bargain with me.'

'You have nothing we want.'

'My life, in exchange for hers.' Tar'sel pointed at Edessa.

In the silence the Vorla seemed to be considering his offer and Charlotte didn't dare look at either of them. A heavy grip on Tar'sel's shoulder pulled him off his feet and the pupilless obsidian eyes were now in front of his own. They were eyes so full of blackness, eyes you couldn't read, but a wry smile formed on the face.

'Don't be so eager to give away something so precious, boy.' She placed him back on the floor. 'We do not take the freedom of another being; if we did, her sister would already be ours.' The figure gestured at Charlotte. A shiver ran through her at the thought of Edessa becoming one of these creatures.

Durga gave a faint nod to the group and the crystal filled with green smoke, obscuring the scene.

'What have you done with my sister?' Charlotte's voice was low and deadly.

Durga smiled. 'I admire your spirit but you should know, our reputation for driving men insane is not without substance; you would be dead before you got anywhere near me if you chose to attack.'

'I just want to know where my sister is.' Charlotte was close to tears.

'She was dead; we fixed her. We were able to remove some of

the blocks that kept her fixed in a state of coma but not all – however, we calculate that these will dissipate with time. She was worth the investment of time and effort.'

Charlotte wanted to scream at the coldness of these Vorla but she had no reason to believe Durga was lying and she was grateful Edessa was safe.

Durga was watching her with interest as Charlotte worked through these thoughts and emotions and something told her a poker face wouldn't help – not that she would be any good at that. Charlotte felt like a lab rat.

When she was satisfied, Durga turned towards the doorway behind her, shaking her head. 'You humans, always put a price on everything and a value on nothing. I had such hopes for you two, how disappointing. Come.'

Durga stared intently into the darkness of the corridor ahead. Charlotte felt it in her head first but soon the vibrations were pulsing through the rock walls and a familiar purple glow bloomed out of the darkness.

They followed Durga through the maze of twisted passages, and Charlotte couldn't shake the thought that if Durga chose to, she could leave them here and they would never find their way out.

'We are neither good nor evil, we simply are as mirrors,' the Vorla said as if reading her thoughts. 'It is not for us to interfere with the stories of creation – including our own. Look into my eyes, boy; what do you see?' Durga barked as she swivelled towards them.

'Me.' Tar'sel croaked as his reflection stared back at him on the cold blackness of those obsidian eyes.

'Exactly! If you see us as cold, it is the coldness in yourself you see. If we inspire fear, awe, revulsion, respect, if we appear beautiful, regal or ugly it is only these qualities in you that we reflect.'

The air was thin inside the caves of the Vorla, so much so that Charlotte was struggling to stay awake. She couldn't decide if the glow of the walls around her was real or just a hallucination and the smell of hot rocks and minerals swirled in the heat currents that flowed through the narrow corridors like lava. It all felt strangely familiar though Charlotte couldn't imagine why and she hoped she would manage to get back into the fresh mountain air before she passed out.

After what seemed like hours, Charlotte had lost track of what direction they were going but it felt like they were heading into the bowels of the earth. The ceiling above them started to vault upwards and the air was cooling; there seemed less fumes too, for which Charlotte was grateful.

Ahead, the corridor opened into a large vaulted cavern with pillars carved into the walls. Alcoves housed busts of what Charlotte assumed were infamous Vorla leaders and the floor was carved into a pattern of hexagonal tiles. A single empty throne stood at the far end to each side of which were circles of opaque stone. These stones housed a cold fire of blue flame.

The most incredible item was the stone table on the bank of a bubbling silver lake. The table, had it been wooden, would have been in danger of collapse under the weight of all the glittering jewels. Hammered silver plates overflowed with bunches of amethyst grapes, ruby and jasper cherries and polished emerald apples. Danburite plums and peridot pears were piled high in tarnished golden bowls, and various kinds of rough gems filled the gaps between the dishes. As far as it was possible to read the face of a Vorla, Durga was delighted.

'The Banquet Hall,' she announced, hands hovering over slices of calcite watermelon and garnet strawberries.

'I remember the days when we used to dance,' she whispered wistfully. 'The banquets, the tributes. We were respected once. Such glorious days.' Sighing, Durga daintily ate a sliver of calcite while deciding between a sparkling pear or a deep red strawberry.

'It's rather dusty,' Tar'sel said, dragging his finger over one of the huge quartz points.

'It's been here a very long time.'

'I guess it's not likely to go off,' Tar'sel laughed.

'Quite, and we eat very little; this will last me over a year.' Durga indicated to the garnet strawberry.

Charlotte was still running through the dizzying array of jewels. She had become quite familiar with so many of them over the last six months as Clarissa used many of these stones in her healings. A memory of a warm Andalusian night and Madame Cortes stirred, something about diamonds. 'I don't see any diamonds.' she murmured absentmindedly.

Anger flashed in Durga's eyes.

'We don't eat diamonds,' she replied coolly. 'Time is pressing on, come.'

Durga guided them up a wide flight of stairs that led off the upper side of the grand hall. A long corridor and more twists and turns brought them to the mouth of another room.

'The audience is only for one young Tree Weaver and the Rani would speak with her.' Durga waved at Charlotte. Tar'sel smiled weakly.

'I guess I've got you as far as I can. Doesn't seem right though, you being the one fighting for my world.'

'I kind of guessed it would come to this… I had a tip off,' she said with a humourless laugh. 'I'll fight as if it were my own, I promise.' Charlotte hugged him for her own comfort as much as his.

'Be sure to present yourself well, human, the Rani does not react well to… outbursts.' Charlotte blushed as she remembered her behaviour in the main hall but looked at Durga defiantly.

'I should be more like a Vorla,' Charlotte said.

'It wouldn't hurt.'

Sweet-smelling fumes like incense wafted through the thin air and a soft cream glow mingled with the gloom.

'I must leave you here.' Durga squeezed Charlotte's shoulder. 'But before I do, I give you this parting gift, Charlotte of Stone; your sister's story is not yet over in your world of Albion. Now, off you go, and probably best not to mention Morrigan. Good luck,' she whispered before she led Tar'sel back down the passage. Charlotte was reeling with questions.

Charlotte took a deep breath to calm herself, then immediately wished she hadn't as sulphur filled her lungs. Coughing violently, she stepped into the sanctum of the Rani Johari.

# The Blood of Diamonds

The cave was vast, the walls studded with points of light which, Charlotte guessed, were more of the glowing stones that had lined the walls of the mountain corridors. It took her eyes some time to become accustomed to the light after the dimness of the passages, but it was at least cooler here and her head felt less woolly.

Ahead of her, Charlotte could see a figure seated on a plain, roughly hewn basalt throne carved straight out of the cave floor. The figure was as still as a statue, dressed in flowing ivory stone robes embellished with delicate designs in gold and silver, similar to the patterns on Tar'sel's arms, its white hands folded in its lap. The face was hidden under a veil of glittering clear jewels that hung from an ornate silver diadem. Charlotte straightened her clothing and was wondering how best to announce her presence when the figure suddenly spoke.

'Well, well, an Earth creature in a Sylurian body? And to what do we owe the pleasure of such an unusual occurrence?' The voice was feminine and barely a whisper that bounced off the crystal walls.

'I am Charlotte Stone and I seek an audience with the Rani Johari to request assistance for the peoples of the Nellpa Barra.' Charlotte was hoping to project an air of authority but her voice cracked and she practically squeaked out the last part of the sentence. Not a good first impression; she had to pull herself together, she couldn't afford to fluff this.

'It should be obvious an audience has been granted otherwise you would still be trekking across the Morsea'a plains, no doubt a breakfast for that herd of Rheadak by now,' the Rani spoke again, still completely motionless.

As the Rani finished speaking, three pedestals rose out of the stone floor, each one baring a single stone goblet.

'A test. Choose one only… and drink.' The Rani's voice was as deadly as a snake.

'Then you will help me?' Charlotte asked, moving closer to the goblets.

'I make no promises yet, child of Albion.'

'And if I choose the wrong one… will I die?' Strangely, she did not feel afraid, just curious.

'Drink,' came the reply.

Charlotte examined each goblet in turn searching for clues. One was filled with a noxious dark brew, the second contained a grey smoky concoction and the final goblet was full of a sweet-smelling pink liquid.

Each goblet was identical and they were old but, like the stone from the cave, she sensed nothing – until the third one nearly slipped from her hands.

A wave of emotions rushed over her without warning. She felt the guilt that she had been the cause of her parents' fate, the fear that they were dead, doubt in her ability to live up to The Morrigan's expectations, the emptiness of not having her sister by her side. Emotions that had been bottled up for so long washed over her relentlessly and she couldn't control it. This was Edessa's skill not hers.

'You've got the wrong girl,' Charlotte's voice faltered again as she slammed the goblet down. She had to fight the urge to run.

'Pity.' The voice was empty of any feeling. 'But the test is begun, you must still drink.'

*You must overcome your innermost fears… trust the diamond heart.*

Madame Cortes' words came to her from nowhere but in that moment they gave her courage. Taking a deep breath, Charlotte brought the cup to her lips. *I still don't do pink,* she thought as she drank.

The intensity of the emotions, her emotions, coursed through her body like fire and she thought her heart would break. The pain was almost too much to bear. Anger replaced hopelessness, which in turn gave way to betrayal and Charlotte sobbed till her whole body convulsed. After what seemed like an eternity, the torrent subsided leaving her drained and weak.

'If you have finished having fun with me, let's get down to business,' Charlotte said once she had recovered, her voice as cold as a Vorla. She could sense the Rani smile.

'What do you want of the Manush de Bar?'

Charlotte took a deep breath to steady her nerves. 'The Nymet tree of the Manush de Rukh is dying and in danger of being destroyed, I have come to appeal for your help to save it.' She decided it was safest to keep a formal tone.

'And why do you think a tree means anything to me and my kin of stone?'

'But without it, an entire forest dies,' Charlotte protested.

'The Verses are in constant flux and life ebbs and flows through them all. Do you imagine it would be the first forest I have seen disappear?'

'But all those people, the Manush de Rukh, they are tied to their land, to their trees. At best they will be homeless, and all the Nymet guardians and Fey will die.'

'Then as one of the order of the Nymet Draoi, you plead for your own life too, Earth creature. Since my sister anointed you with the Mother's Kiss, if the Nymet dies, so do you.'

The silence was deafening as Charlotte absorbed the full understanding of the Rani's words. She hadn't thought for a moment that her own life might be in danger.

Rani Johari spoke again. 'They are not my people and if they expire, this is not necessarily a bad thing.'

'How can you say that?' Charlotte couldn't keep the indignation out of her voice.

'Because I know more than a mere human, a mere human of

only thirteen years at that. You dare to question me?'

The voice was thunderous now and shook the walls of the small cave. Charlotte had to cover her ears, afraid she might be buried in an avalanche of rock.

'I made a promise and you are preventing me from keeping that promise,' Charlotte persevered once the tremors had subsided.

'Then I suggest you do not make promises you cannot keep,' came the terse, but thankfully less forceful reply.

Clearly logic was not working but Charlotte had an idea.

'You're made of stone and you're old, right? What you don't know about me is I can read artefacts. I could read all your secrets right now, I could just take what I need.' Charlotte advanced slowly towards the statue.

Despite the Rani's lack of movement, Charlotte could feel her recoil and the air was heavy with anger.

'Knowledge is not always enough – and what I know would drive you mad, human.'

This told Charlotte what she needed to know. Her theory was sound, but the Rani's warning stopped her in her tracks. She had a potential ace to play but only as a very last resort. For the time being it was a stalemate.

'Please. Tell me what it will take to win your help, I know there must be something I can do for you. Why else would you have granted me passage to your kingdom?'

The Rani clearly did not hurry in anything she did or said but the long silences were driving Charlotte mad and this one was proving to be the longest. *Stay calm and be patient*, she chided herself; she knew she had found a way to get through to the Rani.

'There is… one thing. Information. You have, no doubt, heard tales that the Vorla love to gather knowledge. Tell me something I do not know, something useful… and you shall have whatever help we can give.'

'The Nivasi tried to stop us from reaching you and it turns out they work for your sister.' It was the first thing that came into her head but she knew as soon as the words left her mouth it was a mistake.

'You insult me, human. You think I don't know who are the puppets of that Lady of Death?' The Rani still sat there motionless but Charlotte could sense she spat the words out in disgust. 'I have a mind to dismiss you here and now…'

'There is an unreadable stone…' Charlotte blurted out. She was greeted with yet more silence but she could feel a sense of anticipation. 'We found it in the mountains of a place called Spain, in my world…'

'Go on…' It was barely audible but enough to tell Charlotte she had gained the Rani's attention.

'This stone has no history. It's like it has appeared from nowhere.'

'And what, pray tell, is your own theory on this stone without a voice?'

Charlotte hoped the Rani couldn't read minds and so know her personal opinion of Neva's theory. The Benu was a myth, pure and simple, and Neva had yet to convince her otherwise. Still, here she was in another dimension, almost drowned by mermaids and talking to a statue. Perhaps she ought to reserve judgement.

'Some say it is the egg of the legendary Benu. The bird of creation.'

The figure remained motionless and silent. Charlotte wondered if she had actually blown her chance when the Rani eventually spoke again.

'That is indeed interesting news… I would see if it is true. You will bring it to me then you will receive our help.' This last comment left Charlotte reeling.

'I… I can't… I, don't have it. Even if I could get it, I could never bring it to you in time to save the Tree Weavers,' Charlotte stammered. 'Besides, you said information only.'

'Quite right… no matter…' the voice whispered. 'Very well.'

It was only a slight movement, and inhumanly slow, but it made

Charlotte start all the same. The Rani took a sparkling jewel from the end of one of the threads of her veil between her thumb and forefinger and plucked it free. She reached under her veil and a piercing sound rent the air while her whole body glowed so brightly it hurt Charlotte's eyes and she had to turn away. After what seemed like forever, the sound ceased and the glow faded. The Rani was frozen once more, but her hand was held out towards Charlotte, a silver vial in her upturned palm.

'Take this. Give it to the Undine of Fargale, and only to her. Instruct her to give this to Davlin; he alone will know what to do with it. *Hai Shala?*'

'I understand.'

'I also have a message just for you, Charlotte of Stone, a message from the Sleeping Mother herself. She sees the unsung question in your heart. To find them, you must heal the Golden Root. This alone will lead you to your destiny… and those who have been lost.'

'They're alive?'

Rani Johari remained still and silent. Charlotte knew this was the last she would get from her and there was no point pushing for more. She would literally be banging her head against stone.

'*Gestina.* Thank you.'

Charlotte bowed respectfully to the Rani before passing out on the crystal floor.

Charlotte woke to a banging headache and Clarissa sitting by her bedside while Luned was impatiently striding up and down her windowsill. As soon as the Undine saw Charlotte was awake she jumped onto the bed and marched up to Charlotte's face.

'Well?' she said sharply.

'How exactly did you get me back?'

Luned looked sheepish and avoided Charlotte's stare. 'We had to disguise you as a neagale. You might find yourself craving pond weed and raw stickleback for a week or so… it's all perfectly normal.'

Charlotte groaned. *Maybe for a fairy*, she thought.

'Do you have it? Time is running out.' Luned was back to her officious self.

'I got it… though I'm not sure what "it" is exactly,' Charlotte replied groggily. Luned was clearly in no mood for pleasantries. She showed Luned the vial and noticed for the first time, the silvery, shimmering contents that floated inside. The little Undine's face was awestruck.

'I wouldn't have believed it if I hadn't seen it with my own two eyes,' Luned whispered. She reverently took the bottle from Charlotte's open hand and folded it into gossamer as if it were the most fragile thing in the world, before putting it in her wing bag.

'What is that stuff?' Charlotte asked, as she passed on the Rani's instructions that the vial be given to Davlin.

'A rare and precious liquid indeed,' said the Undine, eyes welling up with emotion, 'and a sacrifice that shouldn't have to be asked of any living thing.' She marched back to the windowsill and stepped outside.

'Let's just hope it wasn't given in vain,' she barked.

'A "thank you" wouldn't go amiss,' Charlotte grumbled. 'And don't think I've forgotten about our little talk.'

Luned didn't respond and simply stepped into the rain, disappearing in a streak of water.

'Luned told me about the Norn Interface.' Clarissa finally spoke.

'She gave you the heads up, you mean.'

'I understand you must have so many questions,' Clarissa persisted. 'I didn't keep you in the dark to hurt you, believe it or not, it was for your protection. The less you knew the safer you'd be. Syluria is a dangerous place, especially for the likes of us.'

*Just as Madame Cortes had foretold*, Charlotte thought to herself. 'Did my mum know about… all this?'

'She did,' Clarissa replied. 'And she wanted nothing to do with it, didn't want you girls to know either. She wanted a normal life for you.'

'Yet here we are.'

Clarissa just nodded.

'What exactly is the Golden Root?' Charlotte eventually asked.

'It is us, Charlotte. Our family,' Clarissa began. 'Every family everywhere has their own root in the Great Tree.'

Charlotte's head was spinning and all she wanted to do was sleep, but there were a few things she desperately needed to know.

'Who is Uncle Peter?'

'My brother,' Clarissa replied flatly. 'Over a century ago he did something very bad and sealed the fate of all of us.' She rubbed her eyes wearily. 'He was punished severely by the Fey. Like them or not, they are the law keepers for all of the Triverse. Peter was sent to the Chambers to be bound by the roots of the Great Tree and that's where he is to this day.'

'That's where they were going to take me till Luned broke me out.'

Charlotte recalled the cramped iron cage and dank walls dripping with foul goo and shuddered. What could be worse than those cells? She had one more question that she was afraid to ask.

'Am... I... an Echo?' she exhaled the words, hardly daring to say them aloud.

'It's true that an Echo can only be created from twins,' Clarissa replied. 'But they must also be full of darkness. Peter was full of fear... I hardly think that applies to you, my dear.'

'What about guilt?' Charlotte murmured as her heavy eyes closed and she fell into an unusually dreamless sleep.

Clarissa smiled a melancholy smile. Try as she had to shield Charlotte it seemed all her potions and silence had been to no avail. The Nymet had ensnared her anyway. It was just as well Charlotte enjoyed adventure; she would be seeing much more of it.

As Clarissa softly stroked Charlotte's hair she sensed her lack of dreams.

'Probably just as well, my dear. Luned will be very busy indeed this night,' she said as she closed the bedroom door.

All too soon the alarm clock by her bed was screeching its customary wake-up call and Charlotte groggily stirred from the covers before stumbling down the stairs to the kitchen. Her head was still spinning from the revelations of the previous night but she had to witness the execution of the Nymet tree. Clarissa, as always, was up and about, the table laden with bowls of porridge and honey, water whistling in the kettle for tea.

'Feeling better?' she asked as she made the tea.

'I think so,' Charlotte said, tucking into her porridge. The warmth of it made her feel more human and eased the cold from her bones.

'Body swapping will do that to you. I wouldn't recommend it too often if I were you.'

'We are going to have to compare notes,' Charlotte said through mouthfuls of porridge.

'There's no time for that now.' Clarissa jumped off her chair and marched purposefully to the back door. 'You need to eat, wash and dress then get yourself down to that tree. I suspect the Fey are going to be very nervous and will need a little moral support.'

'You mean they want to pinch and punch me and moan about how this is all my fault again,' Charlotte grumbled. 'Why can't The Morrigan just tell them the truth?'

The smile disappeared from Clarissa's face. 'The Morrigan doesn't help anyone unless it suits her,' she said. 'Now go.' She waved Charlotte back up the stairs.

'The Rani... she said... I would die too if the tree fell.' Charlotte's voice wavered.

'Stuff and nonsense,' Clarissa scoffed. 'I won't allow it; you still belong to this world whatever they think. Now, up those stairs.'

'And Tar'sel?'

Clarissa pretended not to hear her.

'I can't do it,' Charlotte said flatly, her feet like lead. She wouldn't have blamed Clarissa and Jude for thinking her heartless but the truth was, she was heartbroken. She couldn't bear the thought of having to watch the Nymet fall because of her failure – Luned had made it clear it was touch and go.

*It's only a blooming tree,* she told herself but she knew that wasn't true. Even aside from the fact that her new friend and all of his kin were doomed, the tree had become important in her own world. Charlotte had never imagined when she had started all this, just how her own family history was entwined with the oak or that the cause would have brought so many people together.

Clarissa, as always, seemed to know just what she was thinking and gave her a tight bear hug.

'What ever happens today, you can be proud of yourself. You tried to make a difference and that's all anyone can ask. Now go.'

There was already quite a crowd at the park, some chanting, others holding placards, but the council and their workmen were also there and had the tree cordoned off already. Sissy was handing out leaflets but ran over as soon as she saw Charlotte arriving.

'Can you believe how many people are here?' She was both excited and angry. 'How on earth can they ignore us when there is this much support?'

'Elfin Safety!' chorused Govinder and Olly behind her. Charlotte smiled in spite of herself.

'I guess when they get something in their head, there's really no changing their minds,' Charlotte replied.

Something felt wrong. There was no sign of the Fey or The Morrigan and there was an eerie silence underneath the noise of the crowd. She had to get closer to the tree.

'You can't come any closer, love,' the workman pointed to the yellow tape surrounding the tree, 'we are going to be starting soon.'

'Please, I just need a minute, to say goodbye.'

'Absolutely out of the question, Miss Stone.' The clipped tones of Marcus Ransell came from behind her. 'Can you imagine the headlines in the local rag if a branch fell on you?' A slimy smile perched on his lips. 'Your health and welfare are my number one priority.'

'It'll be good to see it go, it's a real eyesore,' said a voice behind her and Julian greeted his brother.

'It's nice to see reason and logic prevail,' he went on and Charlotte's presence was forgotten.

She thought about sneaking past but a burly tree surgeon gave her a warning stare and shook his head. Charlotte had no choice but to move back to the rest of the crowd.

'Do you have any idea what you had there?' Luned hopped onto Charlotte's shoulder, watching the proceedings intently and nervously rubbing her hands over and over.

Charlotte noticed her eyes were puffy from crying and the tone in her voice was still accusatory, but Charlotte had never been so pleased to see her. At least not everyone had abandoned the Nymet tree to its fate.

'No idea,' Charlotte whispered, hoping no one was watching. 'More to the point, did it work?'

'We'll see soon enough, human.' Luned pointed to the workman who was now pulling something out of the council truck. 'We've evacuated just in case.'

The chainsaw fired up with a metallic, hacking cough and the workman lifted it out in front of him. It slid through the large side branch like a knife through butter and the branch fell to the ground – the doorway to Syluria destroyed in seconds.

'I... I don't... understand?' the Undine cried. 'By my calculations it should have had time to take effect.'

Someone in the crowd shouted angrily as the chainsaw fired up again and bit through a second branch.

'Where is The Morrigan?' Charlotte murmured. 'Surely she can do something?'

'You don't expect me to answer that do you?'

'She has done as much as she can.' Malik's nasal tones sounded in Charlotte's other ear. 'You do expect a lot from the Shriven, young human, remember they have much more than one little tree to look after.'

'I can't watch,' Luned sobbed.

The second branch lay on the ground as the tree surgeon decided on his next move, making for the main trunk.

'Well, that's the Lower Branch District gone so it's not all bad,' Malik tried to cheer them up. 'I guess we can live without Pookas and Drakes.' Malik held Luned as the Undine's shoulders shook. 'Think of the reduction in paperwork.'

'This is it then, I failed,' Charlotte whispered to herself, wiping away her own tears. 'Goodbye, Tar'sel. I am so, so sorry.'

Suddenly, a strange grating noise came from the chainsaw and bright orange sparks began to fly before smoke and… silence. The workmen looked at each other with puzzled expressions. After exchanging a few muffled words, they pulled another chainsaw from the truck. Charlotte's heart was in her mouth as the two Fey exchanged meaningful looks.

'Would either of you two like to tell me what is going on? I mean, it's only like I trekked halfway across Syluria to help you out.'

The Fey looked at each other again before Malik finally spoke.

'The Vorla are an ancient race that are not born and do not die, they are not made the same way as creatures of flesh,' he sighed. 'They have the capacity for immortality if they so wish.' He paused to make sure Charlotte fully understood.

'The Rani Johari is their mother and leader – their life and death. All Vorla business must go through her, and only with her permission can a Vorla cease to be.'

'You mean… die? Why would anyone choose that if they can live forever?'

'Only a human could say such a thing,' Malik replied without humour. 'You are such fleeting creatures but eternity is a long time and can drive one mad... even those that are built for it.'

'OK, but enough of the Sylurian history lesson, what does the death of a Vorla have to do with the Nymet tree?'

Charlotte was vaguely aware that the chainsaws had stopped again and there were murmurs sweeping through the crowd, which had grown to quite a size now. She could see Aunt Clarissa and Jude had joined the throng and even Lloyd had put in an appearance. Charlotte hadn't realised that so many people would care about the cause. Was it down to Olly and Govinder's entertaining town centre storytelling sessions?

'The Rani doesn't just control death. More importantly, for creatures of immortality, she controls life,' Malik continued. 'She holds in her veil all the life of the Vorla, a finite number of jewels, one for each and all Vorla souls that can ever be.'

Charlotte recalled the many strings of sparkling gems that hung from the Rani's diadem, falling over her chest and almost into her lap. She tried to work out how many there where and wondered what would happen when they ran out.

'Have you worked out what they are yet?' Malik roused her from her thoughts.

'The hearts of the Vorla!' Charlotte gasped as the realisation started to form in her mind, and she recoiled at the revelation, not yet able to put into thoughts why it repelled her so much.

'Clever girl,' Malik nodded. 'Each one a diamond; each one the seed for a timeless life.'

Charlotte felt physically sick; no wonder Durga had been so angry over her comments at the banquet table. 'But the Rani gave me a vial of liquid.'

Out of the corner of her eye, Charlotte could see her classmates heading in her direction, chattering excitedly. A cheer rose from the crowd as the workmen downed tools in defeat.

'Seems it's not as much of a danger as thought, Guv,' one of them said to the confused health and safety officer as they packed the chainsaws into the truck.

'Have you any idea what is going on?' Govinder asked Charlotte.

'I've never seen anything like it,' Olly exclaimed. 'The bark is as hard as a diamond!'

'What was in that vial, Luned?' Charlotte stammered, half knowing the answer.

'The blood of a diamond,' Luned sobbed.

⁓

The TV and radio reporters present were all talking excitedly about this latest development. They wanted to interview Charlotte but she declined. They would never believe the truth anyway. Mr Ransell was, of course, enthusiastically having his say, reporting to be very disappointed with the situation but that it didn't change anything, the tree would still come down and the new build would go ahead.

'When is he going to realise no one wants his stupid bowling alley,' Olly said bitterly. 'Seems we've a lot more work to do, Charlotte.'

As Charlotte was about to reply, she caught the soft notes of a melody she had first heard in her history lesson, the melody she now knew to be the song of the Nymet. At first it was so faint that she thought it was just her imagination but as the volume built, others started noticing it too.

'What is that?' Sissy asked.

*The song of the Nymet,'* Sang signed before anyone else could reply. She seemed just as surprised as the others were that she knew this.

'Do you know what this means?' Olly was like a kid in a sweet shop. 'This proves the truth in all the legends. We are first-hand witnesses to history. People will write stories and sing songs about this day, and we were here.'

Charlotte left him to it. Contagious though his excitement was, she needed to just listen. The main melody was more vibrant than before but there was a second underlying tune, something totally separate, a tune of deep sadness that she had to close her eyes in order to concentrate on.

'What is that?' she whispered as she felt Luned landing lightly on her shoulder again.

'A dirge,' the Undine replied simply.

A gasp from the crowd and the buzz of chatter made her open her eyes. On the branches of the Nymet, roses had begun to bloom – shining white crystal roses that gleamed in the sunlight.

The reporters were the first to recover, filming the phenomenon and recording as many reactions from the locals as possible.

'Impossible.'

'Stunning.'

'I've never known anything like it.'

'Nothing short of a miracle.'

'Try cutting it down now,' laughed Irving Batterbee to the camera.

It was Mr Ransell's turn to refuse to comment.

Only Charlotte seemed to understand the roses' significance and tears rolled down her face. If the song was a dirge, this was the wreath; all in honour of the lives that would never be.

'Mortal creatures mourn those who die. Immortal creatures, like the Vorla, mourn those who are never born.' Clarissa appeared at her shoulder. 'It's quite a sacrifice, let's hope it was worth it.'

# Procession of Gold

*I*t had been weeks since the tree surgeons had come to Brackenheath Park and life was beginning to get a little more normal. Boris had escaped and was on the loose and Belleswater Hospital had called the day after Charlotte's return from Syluria to inform her of her sister's improvement. The nurse on the end of the phone sounded so excited and, while Charlotte already knew what she was going to tell her, it was nice to have it confirmed as more than just a Sylurian dream.

The newspapers had been full of their victory for a few days now – then the strange smog came. The smog that swept across England was especially bad in East Anglia according to the news and Charlotte could well believe it. The treetops were hazy and you could taste the dust in the air. Then the reporter said something that made Charlotte's ears prick up. The smog was made of Saharan sand.

Charlotte sneaked out the kitchen door into the garden. Aunt Clarissa's VW Beetle was parked by the spring at the side of the house and… covered with yellow sand. She scooped up a handful, willing this to work. Charlotte was beginning to cough already as the smog irritated her throat and she would have to go back inside soon but she was determined to get something.

The heat of the sun and a passing camel were all it revealed at first, but then another memory bubbled through. Shifting sands – her parents… somewhere in the Sahara… alive.

The smog had cleared in time for the new Brackenheath Summer Festival, which fell on Charlotte's birthday. Sitting in the glorious sunshine, amongst a crowd of picnic blankets, Charlotte still couldn't quite believe that the Nymet tree had survived.

'It's not for long,' Luned warned her and Charlotte was surprised to find her guts felt like squirming ice cubes.

'Surely they are not going to remove it now? It's never been so popular, the parish council arranged this fayre in its honour. No one is going to talk about cutting it down now.'

'Charlotte dear, a fairy's idea of "not long" is different to a human's,' Clarissa chuckled. 'We will get to enjoy this beautiful oak for many years yet.'

'Ha! They'd have to dig it out by the root to get rid of it now.' Jude was grinning like a Cheshire cat.

Charlotte hadn't missed Clarissa's deliberate choice of words. 'But it won't be the Nymet, will it?'

Clarissa couldn't quite hide her look of disappointment. 'Not as we know it, probably not.'

'You've bought it time but it's still sick and the withering hasn't stopped,' Luned mumbled through one of Clarissa's rosepetal sandwiches before going on to explain the complex process and countless forms involved in the decommissioning of an interworld gateway.

Charlotte stopped listening at this point. Fey politics was a dry old subject and besides, she couldn't stop staring at the Nymet. Was it her imagination, or was it surrounded by the same soft, golden glow as when she had first seen it? Without it she would never be able to enter Syluria again, never see Tar'sel again. It seemed this was a year for losing so many special people in her life and she would be happy when it was over.

'I'm going over to say goodbye,' she mumbled, more for her own benefit, not expecting or waiting for an answer.

A sea breeze meandered over the park cooling the heat of the sun; it was the perfect day to be outside.

The boating lake had been cleaned and new plants added which had attracted a family of swans, while the bandstand had been transformed with bright paints, the inside decorated with a mural by the local primary school.

In the bandstand a local band played while people with picnics were dotted across the now lush green lawns and the Nymet tree still stood proudly, on its little hill above the scattering of birches, presiding over it all.

The sounds of the crowd were instantly dulled as she entered the tree line and made her way up the small hill. For a moment it felt like hers again but a group coming down the path ahead of her shattered that illusion and she realised the place would never be quite the same again. She smiled politely and was grateful they didn't want to talk.

The Nymet looked different these days. Olly's songs of the wishing trees seemed to have captured the imagination because the tree was festooned with colourful ribbons, hanging crystals and corn dolls. This was the first time she had been alone with the Nymet for weeks so she hadn't noticed it before but, despite the positive buzz in the air, Charlotte could sense a tinge of sadness underneath; and it wasn't hers.

'I oooowe you a debt of thaanks, Chaaarlottte.' The wind sylphs danced through the branches, lending a voice to the Nymet. 'Yoou haaaave done sooo much moooore than you reealise.'

Charlotte gently stroked the rough bark of the oak. Since Tar'sel had shown her how to weave plants, she could feel the subtle flow of their sap and even hear their song if she was still enough. She had learned patience too living in Brackenheath; and trees always spoke slowly.

'I have ssomething for yoooou, little one.' The voice was so low the sudden rustling of leaves made Charlotte start. A catkin unfurled from a branch in front of her and a small flower behind it matured into an acorn before her eyes, before developing a golden sheen.

Charlotte gasped.

'A gooolden aaaacorn. For you, and you alone, consider it a thank you and a birthday gift. Plant it soooomewhere discrete aaaand prooootect it; thaaaat is important. This gift haaaas the condition thaaaaat you tell no one.'

'But Tar'sel, Aunt Clar…'

'Noooooo one.'

'And Syluria? Will I be able to return?'

'Thaaat is down to yooooou, little one. Yoooouu haaaave always beeeen the link, I am sssssure you caaan find a waaaaay.'

Charlotte pocketed the acorn. She wanted to stay and speak with the Nymet some more but she could tell it had already retreated. She was about to return to the park when the sound of drums stopped her in her tracks. It seemed to be coming from the other side of the hill, getting louder the closer she got to the wilds of the heathland.

'There you are, we were wondering when you were going to show your face.'

Tar'sel gave her a reassuring smile as she emerged from the woodland on the opposite side of the hill. His ethereal body shimmered in the midsummer sunshine and he was dressed in his usual simple woven tunic and trousers except they were now coloured gold and his green skin was covered in gold paint.

'I could say the same about you,' Charlotte smiled. 'I've been worried sick.'

'It took Anya and me a week to walk back to the Nellpa Barra.' Tar'sel pulled a face at the memory. 'She was interrogating me the whole way.'

'Sounds like I might have had it easier for a change,' Charlotte laughed.

Though she hadn't known Anya very long, she already knew she was a force to be reckoned with.

'I didn't think I'd be able to get back,' she added, her mouth dry and her heart racing at the idea.

'You're not back yet,' Tar'sel said, 'but this is midsummer, the solstice day. Even the most *dilino* human could stumble through the veil at this time of year.'

'Even Giles or Mr Ransell?' Charlotte shivered at the thought.

'Afraid so, but they would have to know what they were looking for, so I think we're safe… besides, things have changed since the withering. The Morrigan herself is performing the incantations to keep the worlds joined for now… not for our benefit of course. Once the Fey have done their thing, the pathway will fade forever.'

Charlotte hung her head; this might be her last chance to speak to him but she didn't want to be saying goodbye just yet.

'The Nymet is fading in my world, Tar'sel.'

He seemed to realise what she was telling him and they walked in silence for sometime. Only the sound of the drums kept them moving. They were well and truly in Syluria before they spoke again.

'It's the festival of Son'kai, our festival of thanksgiving and we have a lot to be grateful for right now.' Tar'sel beamed at her and Charlotte could feel herself flush.

'Look there goes the Procession of Gold.' Tar'sel gestured towards the train of people making their way across the valley towards the river delta.

Each one of them was covered head to foot in gold just like Tar'sel – gold jewellery, gold clothing, gold skin and hair. Even the drums were painted gold. In fact, the only thing that wasn't, was a statue of a beautiful woman with pale skin and long verdigris hair that was wrapped around her body.

'It's Mother River, we are taking her to bathe in the Nellpa to let her know we remember her and are grateful for her gift of life.'

'Don't you think she looks familiar?' Charlotte smiled.

'Mother River has many sisters,' Tar'sel replied cryptically. 'Come and join us, I know the elders would love to meet you, you are the guest of honour after all and the feast is to…' Tar'sel paused as Charlotte waved at her opaque body. 'Oh; well, just come for the dancing.' He smiled, charging down the bank as Charlotte floated after him.

Unnoticed, in a small field of lotus grain, a grey vortex opened up and red lightning flickered through its centre. At the edge of the field a hedgerow filled with wild roses withered and died.

Charlotte was famished on returning to Brackenheath Park. Tar'sel had made sure she hadn't missed too much of the fayre, in fact she was just in time for the show.

Govinder's family were already on the bandstand dancing a traditional Indian stick dance as Charlotte made her way back to the picnic. Edessa would have been in heaven right now, trying to find a way to join in. Charlotte giggled to herself at the thought. The sting of remembering her sister was less painful these days and she felt closer somehow since their adventures in Syluria.

Aunt Clarissa had prepared a delicious spread for them all from her garden and Charlotte and Luned had helped her. There was a salad of lettuce, tiny tomatoes and cucumber cubes with a creamy cheese made from Obadiah's milk, all topped with summer flowers.

Charlotte remembered with a smile her indignation the first time Clarissa had fed her flowers; how much she had changed since then. She was particularly impressed by the homemade potato and rosemary rolls she'd helped Aunt Clarissa to make, with their basil-flavoured olive oil oozing out of the centres.

No one seemed to register the extra, empty place Aunt Clarissa had laid out, and certainly didn't see the cheerful little Undine, happily munching away and enjoying the strange human spectacle. Sang and her father had now taken to the stage to perform a fan dance, while Olly, who was on next, practised his latest song at the side of the stage. Isla and her family were there too of course, simply relaxing and watching the show complete with camping table and a wicker basket of goodies. They were not ones for roughing it.

'You're back then?' Clarissa quizzed her. 'They will be celebrating Son'kai I suppose; it will be a particularly special one this year with the excitement of recent months.'

'Do you think I'll ever be able to go back?'

'Already planning your next adventure, eh?' Clarissa fixed her with an intense stare, much like the one at the train station when they first met. 'Why don't you enjoy the moment, Charlotte, and let the future take care of itself for a while.'

Charlotte knew there was no point asking any more questions; Clarissa had said all she was going to say on the matter. For now, Charlotte poured herself a glass of elderflower cordial, which was fast becoming her favourite drink. It reminded her of the first day she'd arrived at Brackenheath.

Sang, Olly and Govinder joined Charlotte's birthday feast as their head teacher made his way onto the stage flanked by a girl Charlotte hadn't seen before.

'And now ladies and gentlemen, we have a special treat,' Mr Thomlinson announced. 'This is a last minute addition to the programme from a very talented young lady who will be joining Wykenhall High in the autumn. Please put your hands together and give a warm welcome to Bonnie Fonteyn performing a sequence from the Russian ballet, "The Firebird".'

Charlotte's skin prickled with goosebumps. She had forgotten all about the Benu egg in the race to save the Nymet but now she recalled the Rani's interest. She wondered how the egg of a firebird was linked to Syluria and the Vorla.

Even Charlotte was mesmerised as Bonnie pirouetted across the stage at lightning speed in her sparkling red tutu, her curly blonde hair trailing behind her like a comet's tail. Her performance gained a standing ovation. She bounded across the grass, beaming and chatting to her new fans before heading towards a blanket next to Charlotte.

'That was awesome, I reckon you could give my sister a run for her money; she loves ballet too,' Charlotte said, introducing herself.

'Bonnie Fonteyn.' Bonnie shook Charlotte's hand enthusiastically.

'Why don't you join us for dessert?' Clarissa offered, throwing Charlotte a knowing smile. 'We've got strawberries with vanilla cream and a Victoria sponge birthday cake!'

Charlotte finally followed her aunt's advice, enjoying the moment as she chatted and laughed with her new friends while the sun went down over Brackenheath-on-Sea.

# The Shriven

A fire burned on the banks of the silver lake that flowed through the vaulted banquet hall. Heavy tapestries hung from the walls, their metal threads twinkling in the flickering light, but they did nothing to insulate the place from the cold of the mountains.

'Next time we meet in Agrimony,' Dijin grumbled as he shivered, despite being sat on a pile of hot coals.

Luned and Malik nodded in agreement, their fingers blue in spite of the mittens they wore.

'Why have you called us here, sister?' Morrigan demanded, pacing the room swaddled in furs and a number of woollen tunics as Rani Johari sat deathly still as always, Durga at her side.

'There are urgent matters we need to discuss,' Durga replied to Morrigan's question. 'Certain information has come to light, so to speak.'

'The tree has been saved and is to be removed from the hands of the destructive humans. The gateway can be closed. What more is there to discuss?'

'Do you really think it is a good idea to withdraw Albion's last defence?' Durga laughed. 'Always so short sighted, sister.'

'I could easily rip out that diamond heart of yours, you know,' Morrigan growled. 'It would make a lovely addition to my mantle.'

'I think not,' Durga said, totally unfazed by The Morrigan's outburst. 'In any case, I am only speaking the words of my mistress.'

'How do you know I'm not talking to her?'

'It's all in the eyes.' Durga's fangs glinted in the harsh blue light of the crystal fires as her mouth curled into a smile. 'Would you like me to look further into your soul, dear Morrigan?'

'In the name of the creation, be civil. We need to be united.' Satvari, Queen of the Slyphs, floated between them. 'Trouble is brewing, the zephyrs whisper stories of the covenant breaking and the Nivasi are growing restless. There are even disturbing rumours of a plot to kidnap a member of the Golden Root.'

'You do not scare me, Durga,' Morrigan roared, ignoring the sylph. 'I am the mistress of death and I govern ALL life... including you...'

'You steal life; there is a difference... besides, we are immortal, you have no sway over us.'

A loud clicking echoed around the hall, interrupting their sparring. The human male, who had till now sat silently outside the glow of the fires, walked towards the Shriven Council. Shadows fell menacingly across Etienne's face.

'Enough with the small talk. Don't you think it's time we talked about the girl?...'

# Charlotte Stone and the Albion Gate

*Some say Syluria rose from the sea… and the Nivasi didn't like it*

The seas are restless as Charlotte Stone returns to Syluria. There have been disturbing rumors surfacing that the House of Mer intends to destroy all Dry territories throughout the Triverse unless the 'Vorla Lamp' is returned to their keeping.

Ancient bloodlines reveal hidden alliances and reluctant loyalties threaten to rip apart the tight-knit community of Brackenheath-on-sea as friend is forced to betray friend.

Meanwhile, the destruction that lurks in the Dreamtime continues to silently ripple through the Nymet.

**_Charlotte Stone and the Albion Gate_ is book two of the Nymet Chronicles.**

**Due for release 2016**

For more information on pre-ordering, special giveaways and competitions, as well as to learn more about Charlotte and the world of the Nymet, sign up to the official Nymet newsletter at www.NymetChronicles.com

Tasha O'Neill was born July 1975 in the city of Cambridge and grew up in Suffolk. Over the years she has lived in various parts of the UK but always ends up being drawn back to her East Anglian roots. Currently she lives near Woodbridge with two black cats.